He helped her change a tire...she helped him change his world.

He turned to walk back to his truck when she stopped him.

"Hey, Jake! We didn't properly introduce ourselves. I'm Lily. Lily Burns."

"Nice to meet you, Lily Burns," he said as he reached over to shake her outstretched hand.

"Nice to meet you, too, Jake. And thanks again for changing my tire."

"Anytime. You have a nice trip to wherever you are going."

"I will, thanks."

Hands in his pockets, Jake walked back to his truck and watched as she climbed into hers. She started it up, pulled into the road, and drove off. It wasn't until she was quite a ways down the road that he started up own truck, U-turned in the other direction, and headed to work.

The momentary distraction wasn't unwelcome. The brief encounter was actually quite amusing.

Lily seemed like such a breath of fresh air that Jake had made sure he filled his lungs, in case the past came back later to drown him.

He was only slightly aware of the tingle he still felt in the palm of the hand she had shaken.

Just when he thought his life was turning around...

Things haven't been easy for Jacob Morgan. Persecuted by the ghosts of his past, Jake lives each day just going through the motions, barely getting by. Then Lily Burns comes to town and befriends him. As Jake starts to heal, he begins to hope that he has finally overcome the mistakes and tragedies that have tormented him for so long. But just when he thinks his problems are solved, his past comes back to haunt him, and once again, Jake is confronted by situations he is ill-equipped to handle. Can Jake hold on to the progress he has made, or will the lies, guilt, and secrets he's tried to ignore shove him back into an abyss from which there is no escape?

KUDOS for *Three Days of Rain*

Hope. Fear. Love. All three take center stage in Christine Hughes second novel, Three Days of Rain. The well-crafted story centers on Jake, a man who has walled himself away from the emotional world. As we join Jake on his journey, Hughes weaves a narrative that slowly begins to remove that wall brick by brick. Hope and love brighten Jake's dark world of heartbreak and loss as he befriends an out-of-town visitor. For the first time in years, Jake is ready to hope again, to love again. But just when all seems so promising, Jake must grapple with the very demons from which he walled himself away. Three Days of Rain will actually have you leaning forward with each turn of the page. Hughes commands a stunning ability to bring her characters to life in ways that make them feel like members of your own family. You will laugh with them, cry with them, dance with them and sing with them. Three Days of Rain does not disappoint until the moment when you realize there are no pages left to turn. – *Jack Klett, Dean of Graduate Studies, Philadelphia University*

There is something about Jake that makes her want to stay and she falls in love. But in life and in love there are always twists and turns and the book takes an interesting course to an unexpected ending. – *Taylor, Reviewer*

I really liked Hughes' characterization. She didn't give us the usual alpha male, sexy hero type so common in novels today, but instead Jake was a realistic, flawed, and fallible man, trying to put his life back together after a tragedy of monumental proportions. The book was well-written, thought-provoking, and has an authentic ring of truth. – *Regan, reviewer*

ACKNOWLEDGEMENTS

First, I'd like to thank my family for their support. There is no way I could have realized my dream of becoming a writer without them. To my Beta Readers, Jack Klett and Christa Lewis, a huge thank you for your thoughts and ideas. I'd also like to thank Black Opal Books for giving this book the shot I know it deserves – Lauri, Faith, and Reyana – thank you for your superb editorial direction. I would also like to thank Jay Sabo for his cover design and Simone Becchetti for working with me on taking a fabulous cover photo. I am so happy we were able to work together on this. And lastly, I need to thank Jay Liberatore for writing the song Three Days of Rain. Your words inspired this story and I am so grateful you decided to pick up a guitar and share your music with the world.

THREE DAYS OF RAIN

Christine Hughes

A BLACK OPAL BOOKS PUBLICATION

GENRE: WOMEN'S FICTION/MAINSTREAM/ROMANTIC ELEMENTS

This is a work of fiction. Names, places, characters and incidents are either the product of the author's imagination or are used fictitiously, and any resemblance to any actual persons, living or dead, businesses, organizations, events or locales is entirely coincidental. All trademarks, service marks, registered trademarks, and registered service marks are the property of their respective owners and are used herein for identification purposes only. The publisher does not have any control over or assume any responsibility for author or third-party websites or their contents.

THREE DAYS OF RAIN
Copyright © 2012 by Christine Hughes
Cover Design by Jay Sabo
All cover art copyright © 2012
The song, "Three Days of Rain" written by Jason Liberatore, 2008 from The Wood Music (BMI)
All Rights Reserved
Print ISBN: 978-1-937329-82-2

First Publication: JANUARY 2013

All rights reserved under the International and Pan-American Copyright Conventions. No part of this book may be reproduced or transmitted in any form or by any means, electronic or mechanical, including photocopying, recording, or by any information storage and retrieval system, without permission in writing from the publisher.

WARNING: The unauthorized reproduction or distribution of this copyrighted work is illegal. Criminal copyright infringement, including infringement without monetary gain, is investigated by the FBI and is punishable by up to 5 years in federal prison and a fine of $250,000.

ABOUT THE PRINT VERSION: If you purchased a print version of this book without a cover, you should be aware that the book is stolen property. It was reported as "unsold and destroyed" to the publisher, and neither the author nor the publisher has received any payment for this "stripped book."

IF YOU FIND AN EBOOK OR PRINT VERSION OF THIS BOOK BEING SOLD OR SHARED ILLEGALLY, PLEASE REPORT IT TO: lpn@blackopalbooks.com

Published by Black Opal Books **http://www.blackopalbooks.com**

DEDICATION

For my boys – Jim, Jimmy and Jack. I love you.

PROLOGUE

Jake had just finished playing a set at Billy's and was taking a five-minute break. He caught Billy's eye from across the room, raised his hand, and nodded. *Man*, he thought, *I need a beer*. Regardless of the fact that he'd already put back half a dozen and some shots with his brother, celebrating the fact that Megan just popped out kid number two, Jake needed another drink. These days it was all about having a good time, playing his guitar, working for his dad, and taking home some random girl he'd never call back. The pickings were slim, he noticed. Most were locals, though there were a few married chicks from the next town over just visiting to say they checked out the local scene. No one caught his attention tonight. He'd probably be going home alone.

He saw Maddie's blonde hair weaving through the crowd, with a tray of pints in her hands, and appreciated the way her T-shirt clung to her curves. *She's been quiet since she came back from college*, he mused. Maybe she decided drama wasn't her thing anymore. Some said people grew up in college, not that he'd know from experience.

When his mom died, he'd decided to stay in town and work for his dad and brother over at the docks. Madison's father, Mr. Olsen gave him a job the day after he graduated high school and Jake was grateful at the time. He needed to keep busy. Mom's death hit him harder than it had anyone else.

Jake had done everything he could to block out her death. A long drawn out bout with cancer wasn't the easiest thing to remember. Drinking helped with that, as did fighting anyone and everyone that pissed him off. As that thought passed through his mind, he noticed a small ruckus starting in the middle of the bar. Marty Donaldson and Nick Jones were mouthing off to a few out-of-towners. One thing led to another and the stranger clocked Jonesy good. He hit the floor cold.

Insanity erupted instantly. Although Jake was glad he was out of the way of the flying chairs, elbows, and drinks, he thought it might be fun to join the fracas. But it wasn't until he saw some idiot elbow Maddie to the ground that he jumped into action.

Leaping from the makeshift stage, he grabbed the guy who'd hit her. Jake's six foot two stature easily bested the other guy by almost half a foot. It didn't matter if it was an accident or if she was just at the wrong place at the wrong time, Jake fisted the guy's collar, clocked him with a head-butt, and threw him into the wall. The crash was loud. The guy hit the photographs on Billy's wall. *That guy's gonna get it*, Jake thought. Billy was so proud of those photographs. Apparently his niece, the one who lived in Connecticut, took them. Billy hung up every one she sent. When he heard Billy yell, he turned to scan the room for Maddie. Fighting was going on everywhere and she was sure to get trampled.

He looked all over, shoving people out of the way, punching his way through. Finally, he found her cowering under a table with a towel wrapped around her arm.

"Maddie, you okay?"

"Yeah. Son of a bitch. Those guys piss me off. What the hell?" She flinched at the sound of breaking bottles.

"You're bleeding."

"So are you."

Absently, he lifted a hand to his eyebrow. "I'm fine. Are you alright?"

"I'm okay. Just a small piece of glass. I pulled it out. I'll live."

They both looked over to the entrance. The sheriff had shown up.

Jake grabbed her arm. "Time to go, Maddie."

"What? Why? I didn't do anything."

"Yeah, but I did and you're bleeding. Let's go."

Jake pulled her up and led her by the hand through the bar to the stage Billy had set up. He grabbed his guitar and guided her out the back entrance.

Pulling his keys out of his pocket he yelled, "Get in!"

Maddie jumped into the passenger side of his new pickup and held on as Jake peeled out of the parking lot.

CHAPTER 1

Five years later.

Jake pulled into the parking lot at Billy's, turned off the ignition, and dropped his head to the steering wheel. He wasn't sure how much more remembering he could take. When Madison left two years ago, she'd taken every dream, every hope, every future Jake had planned.

He knew it had been too long for him to still be too broken to mend. Waiting two years for her to come back, just so he could confront her, was tragic and sad. But still, there he sat, trying to convince himself she'd come back, just as he had every day for the past two years. When he was finally able to shake the past from his head, he threw his worn baseball hat on the seat and climbed out of his pickup. The graveled lot was wet with early summer rain. As he walked into the bar, Jake's eyes couldn't help but search the tables with tired eyes for Maddie's familiar face. The same face that had haunted his dreams the past two years—a face that burned in his memory with a mix of emotions. She wasn't there and despite the promises, she probably would never come back. He knew it, but that didn't stop him from looking anyway.

Danny watched his brother walk in. There wasn't much he could do for him but buy him a drink. Every day, Jake would come to the bar after his shift and sit for a while. All Danny could do was show up and take part in the charade. If anyone ever asked Jake what he was looking for, he'd respond, "Nothing. Just having a drink." But Danny knew better. Jake was looking for her and though he didn't show it on the outside, there were small clues that let Danny know his brother was broken.

"Hey Jake! When ya gonna play us a song?" Billy, the owner of the bar would ask just about every day even though he knew the answer.

"What's up Billy? You know I don't really play anymore."

"Well, let me know when you do. The place is a tomb since you dropped the guitar."

"Yeah, yeah. I'll let you know."

The conversation rarely varied. Sometimes there was a "yo" where the "hey" should be but other than that, it was more of a greeting than anything else.

Billy had been there when Jake began to crumble. He knew the how's, why's, and who's. They all did. It was a small town, after all. Mostly, they all just watched and waited for Jake to wake up.

As Jake caught his brother's eye and walked over to him, Danny noticed his little brother's normally jet-black hair was littered with sprinkles of gray and his pale blue eyes were bloodshot. *When did that happen?* Not that Danny could really judge. He'd let himself go a bit over the past couple of years and carried twenty extra pounds around his middle that he couldn't seem to get rid of. Still, he hated the fact that Jake looked so serious and dejected all the time. So much had happened over the past five years, it was hard to see all the little things.

"What's up, Danny?" Jake's voice pulled Danny out of his reverie as he slid into the booth across from him.

Danny passed Jake the beer he'd ordered for him. "Nothin' much, Brother. Lookin' a little tired around the eyes, Jakey."

"I'm fine. They got me workin' hard lately. How's Megan? The boys?"

"They're good. Been wondering when you're gonna come around. She's been playing around in the kitchen and she's dying to test out her newly developed kitchen skills on someone other than us. You should come by for dinner one night."

Megan was Danny's high school sweetheart. They fell in love the minute they laid eyes on each other in the eleventh grade. Married right out of high school, they started a family right away and had two beautiful boys to show for it. It was a life Jake had wished for with the fervor of a preacher promising his flock a heaven bound exit.

"I know. Just been busy."

Busy. Jake was always busy, Danny thought. Busy letting life pass him by. Busy working. Busy drinking. Busy remembering a girl that wasn't good for him, and busy practicing a needless apology for when and if she ever returned.

"You can't avoid us forever."

"Who's avoiding? I told you, I've been busy." Jake avoided eye contact as he took a long drink of his beer.

"Busy, right. Didn't you have a date with that girl from the island? What was her name? Charlene?"

Looking down at his beer, Jake prepared himself for where he knew this was eventually going. "Charlotte. And that was a month ago."

"How'd that turn out?"

Jake's knees began to shake as he drummed his fingers on the table. "It didn't."

Danny took a deep breath. He knew it would be no good trying for eye contact but he began anyway. "Look, Jakey, when are you gonna let this go? She's gone. She isn't coming back and if you ask me, good riddance. She wasn't good for you then and, God forbid she comes back, she won't be good for you now. And after all this time, you've got to know none of it was your fault. I know I can't relate. Lord knows I wouldn't want to. But, Jake, it's been two years. You have to let her go. You have to let both of them go."

A dark cloud passed through Jake's eyes as he white-knuckled the grip on his beer bottle. The muscles in his jaw tightened and Danny waited for the explosion.

Jake spoke through clenched teeth without looking his brother directly in the eye. "No one asked you. She is none of your business. I am none of your business. I'll come around when I have time. But for now, like I said, I'm busy."

Jake downed the last of his beer, stood up, grabbed his keys, and took one last look around the bar. "You of all people should know when to let things lie. I'm sick of the pity, I'm sick of the whispers, and I am sick to death of you and dad and everyone else treating me like I'm some sort of fragile *thing*. I am, in case you hadn't noticed, a grown man. I can take care of myself. Just leave it, Danny. Just leave it, her, me—leave everything alone."

"Jake…" Danny called out as his brother turned and walked out of the bar but it was no use. Jake tuned him out. Jake always tuned him out. And now all he could do was slip back into the charade and play by his brother's rules.

Billy walked over and sat down across from Danny. It took a few moments and a few pulls from his beer before he spoke.

"What happened?"

"Nothing, Billy."

"Did you mention her?"

Danny played with his pint glass. "Maybe."

"Good for you. Someone had to. And with Jake's temper, I'm sure glad it was you and not me. You're lucky he didn't clock you."

"Yeah, I know. I just can't stand the way he can't get past her. It's been two damn years, Billy. She's trouble, she's always been trouble and I hope to God, for all our sake, she never comes back. Especially after what happened. She wasn't there when she needed to be. Damn it." His fist hit the table a little harder than he wanted, garnering glances from a few patrons of the bar.

Danny dropped his head and rubbed his hands over his face. "He just can't wrap his head around the fact that it wasn't his fault. No matter how tragic, he isn't to blame. And he forgets that he isn't the only one hurting over all of it. He's lost in his own little world."

Billy leaned in to catch Danny's eye. "I hear ya. Jake's just gotta figure this out for himself. Though, to be honest, in all my years, I've never seen a boy fall apart like he has, especially over a girl."

"It's not just her that broke him."

"I know. He's just not the same Jake he was before."

"Some might say that's a good thing, Billy."

"True enough. All that fighting he done before, all that anger. At least one good thing came out of this."

"Oh yeah? What's that?"

Billy laughed his big laugh, the one that made him sound like Santa Claus. "At least she took the fight out of him!"

Danny's eyes crinkled when he smiled. Billy noticed he was looking more and more like his father every day. "You're right there, Billy. I just wish he had something to fight for."

"She messed him up, that she did. How's Megan dealing with it?"

"Megan's fine. She just wishes she could do something. Jake won't even look at her. He won't come over. He won't answer the phone if she calls. He won't see her when she stops by. When he looks at her, all he sees is Maddie.

"We all want to move on, but for some reason we're glued to Jake and his memories. I'm beginning to think none of us will move on if he doesn't and I am sick of walking on eggshells over ghosts."

"I never understood how two sisters could be so completely different." Billy said. "Your Megan is an amazing woman. Her sister, however, was quite the manipulator. And after how she left, it's a wonder he hasn't gone completely nuts."

Danny knew, all too well, that Billy was right. Both he and Megan had tried to convince Jake not to get involved with Maddie. Jake just wouldn't listen and Madison just did what she always did. What no one understood was how Jake couldn't see it. He'd known her for years. He knew what she was capable of and he knew she was no good.

Maddie and Megan moved to town when Megan and Danny were in eleventh grade. Maddie was in eighth and Jake was a freshman. She rebelled right away, unhappy that Mr. and Mrs. Olsen decided to move their brood from Philly to this podunk town on the coast of South Carolina. Mr. Olsen accepted a job running the docks. He was a hard worker and everyone in town respected him right away. Mrs. Olsen ran the PTA, organized town picnics, and helped bring life back to this sleepy shore town. But Maddie wasn't having any of it.

She started smoking, cutting classes, hanging out with the wrong type of kids. She did everything she could to break her poor mom's heart. Maddie was beautiful—movie star beautiful—and she knew it. By the time she hit high school, she'd developed a reputation for getting what she wanted. She dated a lot, slept around, and ran away twice before graduation. At one time, even though her sister was dating him, Maddie tried to seduce Danny. It all backfired, however, and after she graduated, she set her sights on Jake. He wasn't interested, though. At least not then. And it made Maddie crazy. She went off to school and Jake went to work with his father and brother for Mr. Olsen at the docks. They all thought they were rid of her. She, of course, came back every summer, raised hell then left for school again, leaving everyone to clean up her mess. Then one night, a few years later, Jake looked twice and that was all the invitation Maddie needed to strike.

She was working at Billy's bar as a waitress and, for a time, the guys who hung out there didn't come for the food or the drink. They came to see Maddie. Billy knew she was no good but who could argue when she was filling the bar every night she worked? The night Jake noticed her, he was playing guitar on a Friday night like he had been since he was seventeen. No one really knows how it happened but Jake woke up beside her the next morning and sealed his fate for the following five years of shit.

"She's a bitch," Danny grumbled. "And she fucked up my brother. He's a damned mess and there ain't nothin' I can do about it."

"Sure there is. You just have to be there for him. Wait it out. He'll eventually come to know what we've all known for years. And if she ever walks into this town again, kick her ass back to whatever hell she calls home now. She's not welcome here. Not in this bar, not in this town."

With that Billy downed the rest of his beer and walked back behind the bar. He was right. Maddie would be back and whether or not she decided Jake was worth her time, she would crush whatever remained of his heart and not think twice about it. That was her way.

Resigned to "wait it out" for now, he dropped a ten spot on the table, grabbed his keys, and drove home to the family that needed him and the normalcy that he needed.

CHAPTER 2

As Jake was driving home, he cursed his brother and the memory of Madison Olsen. Two years and no word from her. The day she left, he knew she was the devil everyone thought she was. He thought he knew her like no one else did. They spent three years together. Not all of it good, but not everyone can have a perfect life like Danny and Megan. When was Danny going to realize he didn't need to take care of him anymore? When would he figure out not everyone needed perfection in their lives?

Jake pulled into his driveway, took the keys out of the ignition, and leaned back in the leather seats of his new truck. With his eyes closed he allowed the memory of that first night with Maddie to flood his brain...

ఇఇఇ

Maddie laughed as he peeled out of the parking lot. "Jacob Morgan, you are crazy!"

Her laugh was nice and she seemed to have calmed down a bit since the last time she'd rolled into town. He'd have to ask her about it one day. For now, he just wanted to get the hell out of there before Sheriff Finley showed up and decided Jake was the cause of the fight. The assumption wouldn't be unfounded, of course. He had been a bit of a renegade lately. His temper was becoming legendary.

Jake glanced at her sideways. "How's the arm?"

"Fine. Stopped bleeding already."

"Regardless, when we get back to my place, you should clean it out."

"Look at you, Dr. Morgan! Awfully presumptuous, aren't we? Going back to *your* place? I'm not that kind of girl."

He rolled his eyes and shook his head. "Sure, Maddie. I forgot you're a good girl."

She took his assumption as a challenge. She'd spent years trying to get Jake's attention and she wasn't going to let this opportunity slip. "For your information, I have changed."

"So you keep trying to tell everyone. Look, if you want me to drop you off at your parent's, then I will. Just say the word."

Maddie kept silent and Jake drove back to his place. When they pulled up he turned off the car, grabbed his guitar, and jumped out. He was halfway up the walkway when he realized Maddie was still sitting in the car.

"What are you doing? Are you coming in or not?"

With a playful huff, she hopped out of the truck. "You know Jake, I am a lady and as such, I expect a man to open the door for me."

"You do, huh? I'll remember that next time." He turned away and reached for the lock with his key.

"Next time?"

"Figure of speech."

"Right."

They walked into the house—a small bungalow Jake bought a few years back. It wasn't much but the mortgage was cheap and it served his purpose. He turned on the lights and dropped his keys on the table before walking back to his bedroom and placing his guitar on its stand. When he returned, Maddie was standing in the living room looking around.

"Nice place, Jake."

"Thanks. I bought it from your dad. Let me get something for that cut."

"It's fine, really."

"Then it will be even more fine when it's cleaned up."

He walked into the bathroom, grabbed the peroxide, antibiotic cream, and a bandage.

He motioned for her to sit at the kitchen table. "Have a seat."

Maddie did as she was told and watched as Jake poured peroxide on a cotton ball. She flinched and he laughed.

"Peroxide doesn't hurt you know. It just bubbles a bit."

"I know. Just get it over with."

She turned her head as he went to work on her arm. The peroxide was cool and not at all painful but she still refused to look. It wasn't until he patted her arm and told her he was finished that she looked at his handy work.

"Not so bad, huh?" he said. "You should be fine in a few days."

"Thanks. It feels better already. You have anything to drink?"

"Sure. What do you want? I have beer, whiskey, water..." He opened the refrigerator door and scanned its contents.

"Whiskey would be fine."

"Whiskey, huh? You don't strike me as a girl who drinks whiskey."

"There's a lot you don't know. Pour me a double and I'll introduce you to the new me."

He noticed the glint in her chocolate-brown eyes as he grabbed two glasses and a bottle from the cabinet then moved them to the couch. He poured the drinks and flipped on *Sports Center*. Pulling his cell out of his pocket he noticed a couple of text messages from his brother. *I'll get back to him tomorrow*, Jake thought as he dropped the phone on the side table.

When he finally sat down, he made sure to leave room between him and Maddie. He still wasn't sure what was going to happen, but he had a feeling it was going to be a late night.

"So Jake, nice to see you're still playing at Bill's. You're good. Have you ever thought of playing someplace bigger? Even the next town over? Tons of tourists and vacationers there."

"Nope. I like playing here. If they want to hear me, they'll come and listen. Hold on."

Maddie was quiet as Jake turned up the television and listened to the baseball scores from the day. The Mets beat the Phils, the Yanks beat the Sox, and Peterson was now on the DL.

She remembered how much Jake loved baseball. Scouts were interested back in high school when he pitched. Then his mom died his senior year and he lost interest in playing. Everyone was shocked he walked away from it so easily. And instead of going to college after graduation, he signed up for a job at the docks.

"You ever think about playing again? You were good in high school. Everyone thought so."

He looked at her sideways. "Play what? Baseball?"

"Yeah."

His attention went back to the scores. "That was years ago, Maddie. I don't play anymore. No big deal."

"But you were good enough to go pro. You had a scholarship."

"And? There are more important things in life than baseball. I'm happy now. Life treats me good. And not everyone needs to escape."

He could tell his tone irritated her a bit. Maddie's main goal in life was escaping this little town and doing something with her life. Like so many others, she was back with nothing to show for her time away but a piece of paper stating that she graduated from some random college. No job, no prospects, no found dreams. The grass was always greener and all that.

"Sorry. That was uncalled for."

"No, no. It's fine. You're right. I escaped. Then I realized I needed to come back and make things right."

"Make what right?"

"Jakey, you know what a terror I was. I needed to make it up to my family, my friends. Too bad no one believes me. They keep waiting for my head to spin around and vomit lies all over them. It's fine, though. They'll see."

Her words gave him pause and he looked at her with new eyes. Maybe she really *was* trying to change. He noticed the sincerity and determination in her voice and thought twice about his motives behind bringing her back here.

"Look, Maddie. If you want to go home, I'll drive you."

"Who said anything about going home?"

"You aren't stupid. You've got to know why I brought you back to my place."

"You mean you didn't just want to play doctor?"

The play on words was almost too much and he got a funny feeling in his stomach as she inched closer to him on the couch.

"Well, maybe a little bit," he said as he took the empty glass out of her hand and placed it next to his on the coffee table. Then he switched off the television.

"I wouldn't be here if I didn't want to be."

"But I thought you were trying to change?"

He was playing with her hair, looking at her mouth.

"Change, yes. And part of that is getting you to finally notice me."

"I always noticed you, Maddie. I also noticed everyone else was noticing you."

She stood and walked over to look at some photos hanging on the wall. "Well, what if you're the only one I want to pay attention now?"

"Well, you've succeeded. I'm paying attention. I'm noticing a whole lot."

Walking across the room, he grabbed her elbow and turned her to face him. His hands slipped around her hips and settled behind her and as she reached up to playfully bite his ear. He squeezed her breast, causing a quiet moan to escape her lips. Her breath on his neck sent shivers down his spine. With her firmly in his hands and his eyes locked with hers, he stepped forward guiding her backward toward the wall. He interlocked his fingers with hers and slowly slid her arms up the wall holding them in place firmly with his left hand. With his right, he ran his fingers down the side of her body and across her stomach.

Tucking two fingers behind the button of her jeans, he tugged her to him, pushed his knee between her legs, and forced them apart. As his tongue ran softly across her lips, his thumb flicked open the button and pulled the zipper slowly down. Her head fell back against the wall as his fingers teased the top of her panties. He buried his head into the crook of her neck as his two of his fingers found a home. Letting go of her hands, he grabbed her chin, forcing her to look him in the eye as his fingers explored her.

Her arms fell to her sides and her fists clenched as the knot in her belly tightened. In a rush of adrenaline, she cried out, grabbed the belt loops of his pants, and pulled him against her.

His fingers frantic, his eyes closed, and his body moist with sweat, he kissed her hard. When he pulled back, she looked at him and whispered, "Now."

She leaned in to kiss him and that was all it took for her to seal his fate. As much as he had tried to be distant, she closed the gap with that kiss. When he woke up next to her the following morning, she had changed his mind about her completely.

※※※

Pulling himself out of his memories, Jake got out of the truck and walked into his house. Grabbing the nearly empty bottle of Jack from the counter, he walked toward the back of the house. He finally turned on the lights when he reached his bedroom. Unscrewing the cap, he took a long pull. His eyes were drawn to his old guitar sitting on the stand, covered in an inch of dust. Stepping over the piles of laundry that littered his bedroom floor, he picked it up and stood in front of the mirror. He lifted the strap over his head and let the Gibson fall in front of him. It still fit as it had two years ago. The last time he played was the night before his life went to hell. His eyes burned with the memory. His throat burned as he poured the rest of the alcohol. He removed the strap and held the guitar by the neck. His eyes shifted to the stand in the corner, but as pain and heartache overtook him, he lifted the guitar above his head and smashed it into his reflection.

CHAPTER 3

Sun streaming through his bedroom window stirred Jake from his restless sleep. He shaded his eyes from the unwelcome intrusion and rolled his neck, trying to stop the throbbing that had begun creeping up from his shoulders. Tangled in his sheets, he pulled a pillow over his head and closed his eyes, not quite ready to face the day. He had almost forgotten what he'd done the night before. It wasn't until he finally decided to pull himself out of his bed and walk over to the dresser that he stepped on a piece of glass and remembered.

"Son of a bitch." He yanked a piece of mirror from his heel. Realization dawned as he looked around—he had, once again, let memories control him. For once he'd just like to be able to think about the past without feeling like he was going mad.

He surveyed the damage. The shattered mirror could be replaced, but the destroyed guitar kicked him in the gut. He fought the pain that threatened to overtake him again and refused to allow it to weaken him as it had last night.

Instead, he carefully walked across his bedroom to the bathroom and took a shower. He needed habit to dictate his days or he knew he would lose it. It was important to keep busy and, regardless of his inner demons, he had to get to work. He was already running late.

Stepping outside, he felt the sun wash over him with teasing irony. He'd long since given up trying to understand why, if the day was so bright and the sun was so warm, he felt dark and cold inside.

As he backed out of his driveway, he thumbed his cell and it blinked to life. Chirps from missed calls and text messages filled the cab. *Danny*. His brother was probably calling to apologize or explain—or whatever. Danny was good at all that. He was the politician in the family. He could get out of anything with a few smooth words. Jake? Not so much. He was more of a fist guy. Or at least he used to be. Now, he just didn't care. Again memories haunted him...

ଏଓଏଓ

"Jakey, you want a drink?"

"Sure. A Jack and Coke would be great."

He watched Maddie walk back towards the bar. They'd only been dating a few months but he was sure she was the one. His brother had given him a few not-so-subtle "be careful" talks. Apparently, Jake was the only one convinced that she had changed. Why couldn't anyone else see it? Even her parents and sister were skeptical. Billy was skeptical but he'd kept her on her because she was one hell of a waitress. And Billy wasn't known for giving second chances. At least that was something.

As Jake watched her make her way through the labyrinth of the normal Friday night crowd, he noticed a few guys walk in that he didn't recognize. They couldn't be more than twenty-one, twenty-two, and by their rowdy entrance, they'd been partying awhile.

Maddie appeared in front of him with his drink and gave him a quick peck on the cheek before walking over to the table where the new guys sat. As she was taking their order, one of them looked at her with a bit more than fleeting interest before leaning over to whisper to his friend. After a big laugh from the two of them, the man who had whispered caught Maddie's attention. As he talked to her, a red flush crept to her cheeks and her lips pulled tight. Before Jake could decide what to do she walked away from the table. Shaking his head, he convinced himself it was probably nothing and started his second set.

In the middle of his second song, Maddie dropped off the order at the table and flinched when one of the guys grabbed her wrist as she began to walk away. He pulled her into his lap. She struggled to stand back up. The look on her face was indecipherable, but it was all the prodding Jake needed. He stopped playing, mid-song, carefully placed his guitar down on the stage, and strode over to Maddie and the group of guys. A dangerous calm kept him focused.

Flexing his hands, he struggled to hold his anger in. "Is there a problem here?"

His sudden exit from the stage had caught the attention of the bar patrons and it was deathly quiet as he spoke.

The man who had grabbed Maddie laughed. "Nope. No problem, dude. Why don't you go play your guitar? I've got it covered here."

Looking at the man through narrowed eyes, Jake smirked. "I think there is a problem, *dude*. I think you need to let her go."

"She's fine. Aren't you Maddie? At least you were the last time we hung out."

He knows her name? Do they know each other? No, Jake thought, she probably just introduced herself when she first went to the table. But the innuendo was as pointed as a knife.

Resting his hands on the table, Jake leaned in and did what he could to control himself. "I told you. Let her go. Now."

"I don't think so, man. We were just catching up. Isn't that right, Maddie?"

Jake grabbed her and pulled her away from the guy. "Go, Maddie. Back to the bar. I'll take care of this."

"No, Jakey. Really. It's all right. I went to college with these guys. Mark was just saying hello."

Jake never broke eye contact with Mark. "It's not all right. Go. Now," he said, through clenched teeth.

Maddie protested a bit but what she saw in Jake's face must have convinced her it would do no good. He was angry and, more than likely, he was about to zone everything out but the man and his friends. There was no reasoning with him when he got like this.

"You guys need to leave," he snarled.

The rest of people in the bar were staring, knowing what would happen if these guys decided to stay. Billy was already on the phone to the sheriff.

"Nah. I think we're going to stay, *Jakey*." Mark said as he turned to give Maddie a head to toe once over. "We like the view in here."

That was all Jake needed to hear. He grabbed Mark, lifted him out of the chair, and tossed him to the ground. Mark's three buddies sprang up, and, quickly processing his odds, Jake went for the biggest one first. He knocked him into the next table with two hits to the face. Another swung at Jake but wasn't quick enough with his punch to do any damage. Jake hit him square in the jaw with an empty beer mug he'd grabbed from the table. The last guy was helping Mark up off the floor. Jake stepped over, grabbed Mark, and started punching him in the face. The splatter of blood did nothing to detract from his focus. He didn't hear Maddie screaming or the sheriff pull up. He barely felt anything as Billy pulled him off and the deputy slapped cuffs on his wrists. When he looked down, he saw Mark was unconscious and bloodied, his friends backing away.

Sheriff Finlay said, "Time to go, Jake."

The last thing Jake saw as he was walking out was the glare Maddie threw at him. The last thing he heard was the ambulance pulling up as he ducked into the police car.

☙❧

Jake shook the memories from his head and looked back at his phone.

"Not ready to deal with you today, Danny. Let's just keep the personal out of it," he spoke to himself as he threw the phone on the passenger seat without checking any of the messages.

Despite his inner demons, Jake was happy the sun was starting to peek through the clouds this morning. It was going to be hot, according to the weatherman, but Jake loved the heat. It made him just tired enough to crash when he got home. He didn't think when he slept and, for that, he was grateful. He was tired of being held prisoner by his memories.

Halfway to work, he passed a girl on the side of the road kicking the tires of a Jeep. Through his rearview he noticed one of the rear tires was flat. Checking his watch, he pulled a U-turn and parked behind her. The first thing he noticed was her hair. It was wild and curly and the color of chocolate. Amused by the fact that she was yelling at the jeep while trying to find a signal on her cell phone, Jake chuckled to himself as he turned off his truck and stepped onto the road. "You know, kicking the tire won't fix it."

She gave him the once over with her honey-colored eyes and her annoyance was quickly replaced by wariness. "I'll be okay. Just have to make a call."

"Well, since I'm here, I could take a look at it. You know, see if I can fix it."

With one hand on her hip, she used the other to push stray curls behind her ear. "Do you actually know how to change a flat?"

Jake laughed out loud. "I think I can manage. You have a full size attached to the back. I'll just replace it. All you'll have to do is buy a new replacement tire."

He had a nice laugh but she still wasn't sure if she could trust him. "Sure. Go ahead. If you try anything, I'll kick your ass."

Jake's eyebrows shot up. She was so tiny; she barely came up to his shoulders. And he wasn't sure she could do much damage in a blue sundress and flip-flops. "I'll do my best to control myself. You have a jack?"

She softened a bit. "I'm sorry. I've just been driving forever. This is the last thing I needed right now. And I have no idea if I have a jack."

"That's okay. I'll grab one from my truck. Where're you coming from?"

"Connecticut."

Jake paused. "Connecticut is a far cry from South Carolina. You sure you're in the right place?"

Her laugh was warm. "Of course, I'm sure. Are you gonna help me or not?"

"Yes, ma'am."

After retrieving the jack from his truck, Jake went to work on changing the tire. It took all of fifteen minutes. When he was done, he walked around to the front and waited while she finished her phone call. He noticed a couple of suitcases in the back and a camera on the front seat.

"I'll be there soon. Don't worry about me. Some nice guy just changed it for me...Yeah...No. I don't think he's a psycho murderer. Hold on." Covering the mouthpiece with her hand she asked Jake, "Are you a psycho murderer?"

He shook his head and she went back to her conversation. "He's not...Yeah, I know. See you soon...Love you, too."

She punched off the call and looked at him. His eyes were so sad, tired. "Done?"

"Done. I just fastened the other tire to the back. There's an auto shop about fifteen minutes down the road. Chase Peterson owns the place. You can tell him Jake sent you."

"Well, Jake, thanks but my uncle told me he'd take care of it."

"All right. Well, have a nice trip and be careful. Get that spare replaced."

He turned to walk back to his truck when she stopped him.

"Hey, Jake! We didn't properly introduce ourselves. I'm Lily. Lily Burns."

"Nice to meet you, Lily Burns," Jake said as he reached over to shake her outstretched hand.

"Nice to meet you, too, Jake. And thanks again for changing my tire."

"Anytime. You have a nice trip to wherever you are going."

"I will, thanks."

Hands in his pockets, Jake walked back to his truck and watched as she climbed into hers. She started it up, pulled into the road, and drove off. It wasn't until she was quite a ways down the road that he started up own truck, U-turned in the other direction, and headed to work.

The momentary distraction wasn't unwelcome. The brief encounter was actually quite amusing. Lily seemed like such a breath of fresh air that Jake had made sure he filled his lungs, in case the past came back later to drown him.

He was only slightly aware of the tingle he still felt in the palm of the hand she had shaken.

At the speed he was going, he pulled into the parking lot in five minutes. Danny was outside smoking a cigarette, waiting for him. Danny threw his hands in the air as he flicked the butt to the ground. "Jesus, Jake! Where have you been?"

"I had to change a tire."

"All night? I've been calling you, texting you."

"My phone was off."

"Right, and I'm the Dalai Lama. You don't make it easy for someone to apologize."

"You don't need to apologize," Jake said as he reached into the bed of his truck to grab his bag. He slung it over his shoulder and began walking towards the docks.

"I do. Look, I'm sorry I mentioned her. It wasn't my place. Jesus, Jake! Would you stop and look at me?"

Jake stopped and turned to face his brother. He was quiet for a minute, reminding himself that Danny wasn't the enemy. "Look. I'm really trying here. What do you want from me, Danny? I told you to leave it alone. You're sorry for mentioning her and yet, here you are again, mentioning her. When the hell are you just gonna leave it alone? Look, she's gone, all right? I know that.

"I'll get over it when I'm ready. None of this happened to you. One minute my life was making sense and the next it was shattered into oblivion. I know you keep trying but you'll never understand. Not completely. You're just a bystander, an audience. You get to watch my life crumble, feel sorry for me, then go back home to your wife and kids—your perfect life. I don't need your pity, your apologies, or your thoughts on the matter. Look, I'm late for work. Just let it go, Danny. Please."

Danny was left standing alone in the parking lot as he watched his brother disappear through the building. *Aw, Jake,* he thought, *when are you gonna wake up?* He lit another cigarette and called his wife.

"Hey, Meg. I tried to apologize to Jake. He won't have it. I don't know what to do anymore."

"Sweetie, just let it be," she said. "Jake's a big boy. He'll snap out of it."

"It's been two years! Two years! What the hell is he waiting for?"

"I don't know. I just don't know what to tell you."

CHAPTER 4

Lily pulled into the parking lot of her uncle's place, got out, stretched, stared, and took in her surroundings. Taking a deep breath, she closed her eyes and rolled her shoulders before she walked through the door.

There were only a few customers and the bar was exactly how she'd pictured it. The well-worn booths and aged hardwood flooring welcomed her like an old friend. The walls, a pale shade of blue, were sprinkled with photographs she'd taken over the years and sent to her uncle. She walked across the room, taking it all in, pulling her hands slowly across each table she passed.

"This is my home for the next few months," she whispered.

Billy came in from the back, grabbed a menu, and hurried over to the young girl in the dining room. "What can I get you?" It wasn't until she turned around that he recognized her. "Lily! You made it! How was the drive? Your tire's okay? Let me look at you!" He spun her around, noticing just how much she looked like her mother. Even her laugh was the same.

"Uncle Bill! I'm fine. I'm fine. I'm just happy to have finished the drive."

"I told your mom you shouldn't have driven all by yourself. I would have paid for you to fly."

"And leave my Jeep behind? No way! And besides, I'm a college graduate now. I can handle anything."

"I can't believe you graduated from college, Lily. The last time I saw you, you were what? Like ten?"

"Yeah, ten sounds about right. Thanksgiving, if I remember correctly."

"Right, Thanksgiving. I wasn't sure I'd see you again after that argument your father and I had over the money I lent your mother."

"Well, I'm here now and regardless of what Dad says, I'm staying. You've got me for the whole summer!"

"I've looked forward to it. You'll be staying at my house. I've made up the basement room for you. It has its own entrance and bathroom. You can come and go as you please. And as far as money, you can work here, if you'd like. A few shifts a week should keep you in some spending money."

"And rent. I'd like to pay my way. I don't want to put you out."

"Put me out? Never. And I wouldn't take a dime from you, anyway, young lady. You're family and family sticks together. Let me get your bags. I'll call Chase in a little bit and we'll see if we can't get that tire replaced."

She watched her uncle walk out to grab her things then she looked around again. *Just the summer*, she thought. And then she thought of the guy with the tired, sad eyes who'd changed her tire earlier. *Yeah. Just the summer.*

CHAPTER 5

Jake finished his shift a half hour late. Mr. Olsen hadn't said anything to him but he wanted to make up for the time he was late this morning, and he knew the boss appreciated the extra time he put in.

Muscles sore and stinking like fish, he headed for the locker rooms. All the guys were happy Mr. Olsen decided to put in showers when he took over the docks. It made for happier relationships now that they didn't have to go home smelling like fish guts, chum, and bait.

He took his time cleansing the day away. Clearing his head of all the excess weight, he allowed himself a few moments of peace. Instead of the usual blankness he so enjoyed, his mind offered a vision of the girl from this morning.

Jake rubbed his hands over his face. He certainly didn't need her intruding on his thoughts. He had enough on his plate without thoughts of some random girl he'd never see again. Annoyed, he shut off the water, stepped out of the shower into the locker room, and got dressed.

On his way out he saw Danny, sitting on the end of the dock, smoking a cigarette. Walking over, Jake dropped his bag and sat down, legs dangling over the edge. He picked up the box of Marlboro's, took one out and lit it, inhaling deeply. "When are you gonna quit smoking?"

Danny laughed. "One day, I guess."

Jake took two more drags and threw the lit butt into the water. He mentally thanked God smoking wasn't a vice he'd ever held on to. He looked out over the water and watched as rays of sunset sparkled over the waves. "We okay?"

Inhaling one last time before throwing the filter into the water, Danny replied, "Yeah, Jakey. We're okay."

"You sure?"

Clasping his hand on Jake's shoulder, Danny said, "Yeah. I'm sure."

"Good. Now get up. I'm starving. Billy's got those crab cakes on special tonight and I could eat about ten."

"Oh, yeah. It's Wednesday. Crab Cake Wednesdays also mean dollar pitchers."

"Call Meg and tell her you're having dinner with me. I'm buying."

"But she made meatloaf."

Jake stared at his brother like he had two heads. "Really?"

"All right. You don't have to tell me twice."

Jake walked back towards his truck and threw his bag in the bed.

Danny knew buying dinner was Jake's way of apologizing. He flipped open his cell. "Hey, Meg. How're the boys?"

"They're fine. How was work?"

"Good. Good. Listen, I'm goin' over to Billy's with Jake for dinner. I'll be home in time to read the boys a story."

"Have fun. Tell Jake I said hi. Love you."

"Love you, too, sweetie."

Twenty minutes later, Danny parked his beat up minivan next to Jake's pickup. He noticed his brother staring at something in the parking lot.

"Whatcha lookin' at?"

"Oh nothing. Just thought I saw something familiar." Jake shrugged it off and walked into Billy's bar like he did every night.

"Jake! Danny! Comin' in for a drink?"

Danny patted his stomach. "Sure enough, Billy. We're starving, too."

"Have a seat over and I'll send someone to take your order."

"Crabcakes, Billy," Jake informed him. "Just crab cakes for both of us and a pitcher."

"Make it light beer, Billy," Danny interjected. "Meg's on me to lose a few pounds."

"Will do," Billy said as Jake and Danny settled into the same booth they'd sat in for as long as they'd been coming here.

"Meg's on you to lose a few pounds?" Jake teased.

"Aw, come on. I've put on about ten pounds in the past year and ten the year before that. And it ain't coming off like it used to."

"Jesus, Danny. You're thirty, not fifty. And you're in pretty decent shape. What's she talking about?"

"Listen, sometimes you have to pick your battles. If she wants me to eat green salad instead of potato salad, then that's what I'll do. Light beer instead of regular? Fine. No use arguing over it. Besides, I don't have time to run an hour a day like you do."

"Yeah, I guess. Maybe if you told her you wanted to run with me, she'd help you make time."

"Thanks, but I don't think I could keep up with you. You're just as fast as you were in high school, man. I don't know how you do it."

"Running clears my head. I like it."

"Hey, fellas. Billy said you wanted a pitcher of light. I'll get your crab cakes as soon as they're up."

Jake looked up at the interruption and was taken aback for a minute. The white tank Lily wore set off her tanned shoulders and toned arms. Her hair was still a bit wild, but she'd pulled it back into some sort of girly-ponytail-bun thing.

"Hey! It's you," she said as her eyes lit up with recognition.

He leaned back, confused by why she was at the bar. "Yeah. And it's you."

The two stared at each other for a few seconds before Danny cleared his throat.

"Oh, I'm sorry. Danny, this is Lily. Lily, Danny, my brother."

"Nice to meet you." She held out a dainty hand and Danny took it, still looking back and forth between the two of them.

"I thought you were visiting an uncle or something."

"I am. My Uncle Billy. I'm staying with him for the summer. Why? Do you know him? Oh right, you probably do. This is such a small town."

"Billy's your uncle?" Danny asked.

"Yeah. My mom's brother. I haven't seen him in years and I've never been down here. He always used to come up to visit us."

"Yeah, we know Billy," Jake said in a bit of a daze.

"Okay, well, you boys enjoy your beer. I'm gonna go check on your order."

Lily walked away but Jake couldn't stop looking at her. Danny's snapping fingers pulled him back.

"Dude. What?" he demanded.

"Geez, Jakey. You'd think she'd hypnotized you or something. Who was that?"

"Get out of here. She's just some girl I helped out this morning."

"The flat tire girl?"

"Yeah. No big deal. She's probably working for Billy till she goes home. Hey, I bet she's the one who took all those pictures on the wall. She had a camera in her jeep. And she did say she was from Connecticut."

"I don't know. He did say his niece took them. Why don't you ask her?"

Jake looked at the loopy grin on his brother's face. He knew Danny was challenging him to talk to her again. *What's the big deal?* Besides, he wasn't interested in talking to her, anyway. Looking at her, definitely. Talking to her? What was the point?

Billy walked over to their table and sat down next to Danny.

"What's up guys? How's my fish menu gonna look this week?"

Billy bought all his fish from Mr. Olsen. His menu primarily depended on what the fishermen hauled in. Jake used to go out on the boats but was relegated to the docks about four years ago. Mr. Olsen could have fired him, Jake knew, but instead he seemed to take pity on him. Jake wasn't sure he'd ever be allowed back on the boats after what he did.

He knew Danny and Billy were discussing the day's catch, but Jake couldn't hear them. He was filled, once again, with memories of Maddie Olsen...

✧✧✧

It was just like any other morning. Jake was on the boat organizing the supplies the guys were hauling on board. He and Maddie had fought the night before which wasn't that out of the ordinary. They fought a lot. And that morning, he had a black eye to prove it.

She'd gone nuts when he decided to stay out a bit longer than he told her he would. She accused him of cheating on her with every girl she could think of. He denied it, of course. Maddie was the only girl he'd been with for a year already. Sure, he had, at one point, slept with most of the names she was screaming at him but none of them since he'd started dating her.

The trouble was that fight, like all the others, was out of the blue. Sure, he'd started a few of the arguments but she was master of the sneak attack. She'd find some loose thread and pull on it, obsess over it until she riled herself up to near craziness. And last night was no different.

He'd walked into the house and immediately she was in his face screaming and accusing. Jake had had too much to drink, as usual, and wasn't in the mood for her insane outbursts.

"What the hell are you blabbering about?" he demanded.

"Blabbering? You go out, sleep with some cheap slut, and I'm the one blabbering?"

"I didn't sleep with anyone, Maddie. Relax."

"Then where were you? And don't tell me the bar. I called and Billy said you'd left hours ago."

"I was with Danny and some of the other guys down at the docks. We were having a few drinks. Celebrating the haul we brought in yesterday."

She slapped him hard across the face, leaving a print of her small hand on his cheek. Jake looked at her and his eyes turned hard.

"What the hell, Maddie? Don't hit me."

She raised her hand again but this time he grabbed her wrist right before she could smack him again.

"Stop, Maddie."

She fought against him but he held her wrist and walked her up against the wall.

"Look at me. Look at me! I didn't sleep with anyone else. I haven't slept with anyone else in over a year. Here." He pulled out his cell and punched in his brother's number. "Call Danny and ask him yourself."

He let go of her and stepped back as she took the phone. With her eyes on his she ended the call before anyone answered and threw the phone at Jake, hitting him hard, in the eye.

"Son of a bitch, Maddie! What are you doing? Jesus!"

"Oh my God! I'm so sorry, Jake. I'm so sorry. I didn't mean to do that. Oh please forgive me. I didn't mean to hurt you."

"Well you did. God! What the hell were you thinking?"

"I wasn't thinking, baby. Please don't be mad. It was an accident. Here, let me get you some ice."

Jake walked over to the hall mirror and looked at his face. It was already starting to bruise. He'd definitely have a black eye tomorrow. He shook his head, par for the course, unfortunately.

"Here, sweetie. Come sit down and put some ice on your eye. I'm so sorry."

"I know. Just stop talking a minute. My head fucking hurts."

"You know, I'm just trying to help. You could say thank you."

She was unbelievable.

"Thank you? *Thank you?* You just slapped me and threw a cell phone in my face. You want me to thank you for giving me a black eye?"

"You don't have to be so snotty, Jacob Morgan. Gosh, I said I was sorry. Whatever. You go ahead and pout. I'm going to bed."

"That's it? I come home, you accuse me of sleeping around, and attack me. Is that enough excitement for the day? *You've* had enough, now you're going to bed?"

He knew the tone of his voice would bait her, piss her off. *Good,* he thought, *I'm in the mood for a fight.*

"You think all I do all day is pine over you and think of ways to fight with you?"

He crossed his arms over his chest and stared at her, giving away nothing. "Yeah, as a matter of fact, I do."

"You self-righteous asshole. What the fuck is your problem? You're the one who stayed out late, didn't call, didn't tell me where you'd be. What else am I supposed to think?"

"You're supposed to think I'd be back late. I always come home to you, to this crap. Jesus Christ, Maddie! I'm sick of it. You're a jealous little girl who does nothing but dream of ways to piss me off."

That did it. She looked madder than hell. Jake stood up to confront her fury.

She threw a lamp at him and he ducked just in time. Her temper rivaled his. He knew no one else would put up with her crap, just as no one else would put up with his. Ironically, they were made for each other, no matter how far into a pit they fell.

"Good. Break stuff. That's the third lamp I'm gonna have to replace because of your idiocy. You know what, Maddie? Go have another drink."

She walked right up and clocked him in the eye that was already bruising from the cell phone. His hands flew up to her shoulders and he shook her, hard.

"What the fuck is the matter with you?" he growled before he threw her to the couch. He leaned over her, blocking her kicks and punches as he tried to get her to stop. "Madison, look at me. I didn't cheat on you tonight. I have never cheated on you. I swear to God. Just stop and look at me!"

When she looked at him he could see the tears in her eyes and he softened.

"I'm sorry, baby. Maddie, I'm so sorry. I'll call next time. Just don't cry."

She reached up and pulled him down to her. Her mouth found his, and his hands were already unbuttoning her shirt. They always made up with more intensity than they fought.

The next morning while Maddie slept, Jake went to work, black eye and all, and waited for ribbing from the guys to start. It wasn't so bad. They all assumed he was so hammered the night before that he walked into a door or something. It wasn't until he was setting up the boat, getting ready for the day, that his mood went from bad to worse.

Danny walked on board with Mike, the new kid.

"Jake, this is Mike. Show him around a bit. He'll be on board with you today."

They shook hands and Jake invited Mike over to help him unload some of the gear.

"So, Mike, you ever been fishing before?"

"Sure have. My dad's got a boat and used to take us out all the time. I love it. He wanted me to go to college but I figured I could do that anytime. I wanted to see what I could make of myself on a boat. My friends and I went out this past weekend to celebrate my first day as a fisherman. Lame, I know. But I usually do what my dad wants and they were all psyched I stood up to him."

This guy could talk. If he kept chattering like that, someone was gonna throw him overboard. Jake figured it was his job to let the kid get it all out before they cast off and his gabbing pissed off the captain.

"You went out, huh? Where'd you go?"

"Well, I'm from the next town over so we just went to the local bar and partied a bit. Met a hot chick, too. Gorgeous blonde hair, awesome body—just hot, you know? I think she was older. She certainly knew what she was doing, if you know what I mean?"

The glint in Mike's eyes was familiar to Jake. He knew all about going out, hooking up, giving out fake numbers, and all that. *Good for you*, he thought. Someone had to keep the party scene going now that Jake was attached to a ball and chain.

"Yeah. I know what you mean. You get her name and number?" He flipped through his mental Rolodex and tried to picture all the blondes he knew who hung out at the bar the next town over. None came to mind. He was usually partial to brunettes and red heads, anyway. Maddie was the only blonde he every really noticed enough to remember.

"Yeah," Mike crowed. "Maddie something. She was a spitfire, too. She could drink us all under the table. Her friend left without her so she came back home with me, if you know what I mean."

Jake was too stunned to process much of what the kid said. He heard two things: Maddie and a second "if you know what I mean." *Why do people say that? Of course, everyone knows what you mean.*

"Maddie was her name?" Jake asked, incredulously. "It couldn't be. It had to be a coincidence. Jake had to mentally count to ten before he went nuts. But she did stay with her girlfriend over the weekend. He was painting the bathroom.

She said she couldn't stand the fumes and was going to stay at her friend's house. He had to know if it was *his* Maddie. Trying to keep his anger under control, he asked, "Mike, this girl have any tats? Any that you noticed?"

"Yeah, as a matter of fact. She had a guitar tatted on her lower back. Why, you know her?"

"And you screwed this girl?"

"Hell, yeah!"

As Mike threw up his hand for a high five, Jake punched him in the face, threw him overboard into the bay, and stormed off the boat.

Danny ran after him. As Jake hopped into the truck, threw it in gear, and drove home, he got into his minivan and tried to keep up.

Jake barely put the car in park before he was out and running up the walk. He threw the door open and yelled, "Madison! Madison! Answer me."

She came out drying her hair with a towel. "What? I thought you were at work."

"I was. What did you do this weekend?"

Eyes wide, she took a step back when she saw the look on Jake's face. "What do you mean? Calm down, Jake. You're scaring me. I stayed at Angie's."

"Saturday night? Did you stay at her house Saturday night?"

Jake caught the flash of recognition in her eyes before she yanked it back. He grabbed a picture frame from the table and shattered it against the wall.

She ducked for cover. "I'm so sorry, Jake!"

"Sorry you did it or sorry you got caught?"

He was inches from her, eyes wild and vibrating with anger, and she just cowered on the floor.

"I'm just sorry. So sorry. It was a mistake. Please forgive me."

"Are you fucking kidding me? Forgive you? Why? Why would you do that to me? I take care of you. I put up with your shit and this is how you repay me? Get your fucking shit out of my house before I get back here or I swear to God, Maddie, I will throw your ass out on the street myself."

"Jake!" Danny yelled.

He burst through the door as Jake threw another frame against the wall, directly over Maddie's head. Danny pulled his brother away. Maddie leaned against the wall, holding her leg where some glass from the frame had imbedded itself.

Danny shook Jake back to reality and when Jake saw what he'd done, tears streamed from his eyes.

He crouched in front of her. "Oh my God! Maddie! Are you okay?"

"Jake, leave her alone. I'll handle it. Go cool off." Danny tried to remain level-headed but all he wanted to do was beat them both silly. He'd lost count of the number of times he had to handle their fights.

Jake pleaded for forgiveness as Danny shoved him outside. "Maddie, I am so sorry. I'm so sorry."

She'd stayed with Danny and Megan for the next week before she decided to come back home to Jake. Within that week, he'd taken all the blame for what happened, almost forgetting her betrayal. He'd felt so bad at how he reacted.

He hadn't even given her time to explain, to defend herself. He swore he'd never get angry enough to hurt her again.

Instead, he just found reasons to fight with everyone else. He spiraled and no one could stop him.

∽∽∽

Lily interrupted Jake's traipse down memory lane. "Here you go boys."

Grateful, he started on his dinner.

"Thanks," Danny said as he grabbed his plate from her, too.

"Hey," Billy said. "You've met my niece? Lily, this is Jake and his brother Danny."

"We've met, Uncle Billy. I didn't tell you? Jake's the one who helped change my tire this morning."

Billy's eyes snapped to Jake. "Did he now? Well thanks, Jakey. You done a good thing helping Lily. Hey, sweetie, a new table just popped in. Could you go help them out?"

"Sure thing. See ya, Jake. Nice meeting you, Danny."

As Lily walked away, Billy leaned in towards Jake, picked up a French fry and pointed it at him. "I love you, Jakey. You know I do, right?"

Mouth full of crab cake, Jake responded, "Right, Billy."

"Then you won't be surprised or offended when I tell you to stay away from Lily."

Danny stopped mid-gulp, looked at Jake and waited for his temper to flash.

Carefully placing his fork on the table, Jake leaned back and lifted his beer. "What would make you think I'd want anything to do with her, Bill?"

"Nothing. Just saying."

"Well, thanks for the advice, but I think I'll be okay if I don't fawn all over your niece."

"Good, then. We understand each other. Eat up boys. Enjoy your dinner."

Jake watched him walk away.

"What the hell was that all about, Jake?"

"How the hell should I know? I just changed her fucking tire." Jake stood and dropped money on the table. "Whatever. Listen, I'm not hungry anymore. I'm gonna go."

"Aw, man! Don't leave. I backed out of Meg's meatloaf for this. Just stay. We'll eat. Everything's fine."

"Nah. I'm good. Take my food home to Meg. She'll like it. Talk to you tomorrow."

Danny dropped his head onto the table as Jake walked out of the bar. Everything wasn't fine.

Lily watched Jake make a beeline for the door and moved to head him off. "Hey."

He stepped back when he realized he almost ran right into her. "Hey."

"Where're you going?"

"Home."

"But you didn't finish your dinner."

"Not hungry anymore."

She looked over her shoulder at her uncle and squinted her eyes. "Did my uncle say anything to you?"

"Who? Billy? What would make you say that?"

"'Cause he told me to stay away from you. Said you're really nice but messed up right now. Something about some girl who broke your heart. I told him you looked like you needed a friend."

Jake had to do a double-take. *Talk about blunt.*

"I don't need a friend, Lily. I just need to be left alone."

She put her hand on his arm. "Everyone needs a friend, Jake."

"I don't." Jake shrugged her off and walked out the door.

Lily watched him leave and cursed the foot that apparently was wedged between her teeth. She looked over at Billy, who was looking at her, and noticed him shake his head before pulling another beer for a customer at the bar.

CHAPTER 6

It was early Saturday morning and Jake had yet to return to Billy's since Wednesday's crab cake special. He'd spent the past two days working and sleeping, not leaving the house for anything other than to earn his paycheck and to go running. Billy called to apologize but since no one answered the phone, the apology was left on voicemail. Jake hadn't called him back. He really didn't feel like talking to anyone about anything. He saw Danny at work and, other than a brief conversation with his father last night, he hadn't really spoken to anyone.

He'd finally cleaned up the shattered mirror from his bedroom floor and tossed his broken guitar in the trash. He felt bad, really, for destroying the thing, but it wasn't like he'd ever play it again. It was the broken glass that upset him more than anything. It reminded him of his relationship with Maddie...

After two years of bullshit, he'd finally ended things with Maddie. He'd found out she'd started using and he wasn't having it. What she was using, he didn't know exactly and, at that point, he didn't care. He felt like a huge weight had been lifted off his shoulders. He'd been drama free for a week when she finally called him, sobbing.

"Jakey, I am so sorry for everything."

"We've been over this. Apologies don't matter anymore. We aren't good for each other."

"That's not true. You are good for me. You make me a better person. Please let me show you I can be a better person, that I can be good for you, too. I need to show you I can change."

"How many more times do I have to hear you say that? You haven't changed. You're the same Madison you were before we started dating, and I've become the chump who puts up with you. I'm tired of being a joke."

"No, Jakey. Please. You aren't a joke. I love you."

"No, Madison. You don't. I can't do it anymore."

"Please, Jakey! Please, just let me come over and we'll talk. Just talk."

He was tired and didn't need this right now. And to top it off, she sounded high or drunk or something. As much as his heart was breaking, he needed her out of his life.

"No. No. I'm done. Goodbye, Maddie. You go hang out with that drug dealer boyfriend you've got and leave me out of it."

"He's not my boy—"

He hung up on her protests. He finally saw what everyone else saw. Maddie hadn't changed. He couldn't believe he'd hung on for so long, dealing with her crap, making excuses for her, and believing *her* excuses.

He walked around the house, gathering up anything that was hers, placing it all in a trash bag. He wasn't sure if he'd throw it all out or give the bag to his brother to pass on to her. He sure as hell didn't want anything in his house that reminded him of her. One thing he did know was that he never wanted to see Madison Olsen again. He put the bag on the front steps.

It was hours before he passed out in his bed, filled with exhaustion and disappointment.

In the middle of the night, he awoke to the sound of glass breaking. At first he thought he was still dreaming but when he heard it a second time, he climbed out of bed and reached into the closet.

Baseball bat in hand, he quietly made his way down the hall to the bathroom. The door was closed but light streamed out from underneath.

"What the hell?"

He put one hand on the knob, held the bat at the ready with the other, and gently pushed the door open. What he saw almost brought him to his knees. Madison was on the floor, clothes torn and dirty, with mirrored glass all around her. She looked like hell. He could tell she wasn't in her right mind.

Tentatively, he placed the bat on the floor and took a step into the bathroom. "Madison? What are you doing?"

Her voice was small and shaky and she wouldn't look at him. "Don't come any closer."

Hands up, he quietly responded, "Okay. Okay. What's going on Maddie? Talk to me."

Her eyes darted around the bathroom, not resting on anything in particular. "Now you wanna talk to me? This is all your fault, Jake. You threw me away like garbage. You didn't even bother to try to help me."

Trying not to sound defensive, he asked, "What did I do to you? What's my fault?"

"This. All this. You did this to me." Her hands shook as she looked down at herself. It was then he noticed the shard of glass in her hand and the blood on her wrist.

He froze. "What are you doing?"

Still looking down, she answered, "The only thing I can do. You won't see me or talk to me. This is all I can think of to make you talk to me. You need to see what you did."

As much as Jake knew they shouldn't be together, he knew he didn't want to see her like this. "Don't do this, Maddie. You want to talk? Let's go out into the living room and talk. Just you and me. Let's talk."

"You don't want to talk to me. There's nothing else I can do."

He watched as she turned over her wrist and stared at it like she was contemplating something. The cut didn't look too deep and he took another step into the tiny bathroom, hoping he could get through to her before she did any real damage.

She pointed the glass shard at him. "Don't, Jake."

Hands up, he stopped moving. "C'mon, sweetie. Please."

She started sobbing, shaking her head. "I fucked it all up. You don't want me. No one wants me."

"I want you, Madison." He half believed it.

"Liar!" she screamed, placing the glass against her wrist and closing her eyes.

Vibrating with fear, he said as calmly as he could, "Don't. Come out here. We'll talk. You wanna talk? We'll talk."

"It's too late, Jake. You threw me away. Now I am going to show you what you did to me."

With that she shoved the glass deep into her arm. Her scream ripped through him. He dove on top of her, cutting himself as he wrestled the glass from her hands.

"Maddie! What did you do! No, Maddie!"

With tears streaming down his face, he dragged her out of the bathroom then ran to the kitchen, grabbing a dishtowel and the phone. Wrapping the towel around her wrist that spit blood at him, he called nine-one-one. She was mumbling gibberish, and he couldn't understand a word she said.

"Maddie! Look at me. Look at me. Everything is gonna be okay. I'll help you. The ambulance is coming. Just stay with me till they get here."

"You did this to me, Jake Morgan. This is all your fault."

He'd never felt more alone than when she spoke those words to him before passing out in his arms.

"Emergency. What is your situation?"

"This is Jake Morgan. I need an ambulance. Madison's hurt. She hurt herself."

"Calm down, Jake. Tell me what happened."

"Damn it. I told you she hurt herself. Just get here now."

Jake hung up the phone and threw it across the room.

"Shit, Maddie. What have you done?"

She'd stayed in the hospital a week before they released her to him. He moved her back in to his place and vowed he wouldn't let anything bad happen to her again.

❦

Jake jerked himself back to the present and tied his sneakers. *God, she's like a damn ghost.* He wasn't sure when she was going to stop haunting him. What did he ever do to deserve two years of gut-wrenching memories? He was far past the point of remembering any good times with her. That would have been too easy. All he knew is he must've pissed off God big time if He was allowing Jake to fall into this shit over and over again. Jake wasn't one to cry "Why me" but he needed at least a small break from it. She was paralyzing. Everything about her brought him to his knees.

A small knock on his door caught his attention.

"Jesus, Danny! It's seven in the morning!"

He pulled open the door, fully expecting to see his brother standing on the other side. Instead, he found Lily. She was dressed in hot pink running shorts and a white tank, her curly hair pulled into a loose ponytail. The smile on her face was genuine.

"Morning."

"Lily? What are you doing here?"

He wasn't wearing a shirt and she tried not make her appreciation obvious. "I haven't seen you since Wednesday. I figured I'd come by and see if everything was all right."

"Everything's fine. I don't need you to check on me. Look, I gotta go. I was just about to go running. I'll talk to you later."

Her foot kept the door from closing. She was still smiling when he looked back at her.

"I know. I run, too, but I don't know my way around here yet. I can't figure a good route. I thought I'd go with you and get some ideas."

"This town is small, Lily. You can run anywhere you want. It's not like you'll get lost."

She defiantly put her hands on her hips. "I know. I just need the right pacing. Gotta get the ol' heart rate up, ya know?"

"How'd you know where I live?"

"Like you said, it's a small town."

Jake stared at her, annoyed. "Incredible. Fine. Just keep up. I'm not slowing down for you. Come on in, let me get my shirt."

Lily looked around the space as he disappeared into the back of the house. *Why is there a broken guitar in the garbage?*

"What happened?" She pointed to the garbage as he walked back into the living room.

He looked, shrugged. "Nothing. It just broke."

"But it's *really* broken."

"I know. Like I said, it just broke."

Sure it did. She made a mental note to get more information out of him later. Uncle Billy had told her Jake used to play guitar. She wondered why he didn't play anymore.

He held the front door open and ushered her outside.

"So, where do we go from here?" she asked.

"First we stretch. Usually I stretch in the house but since you're here, there wouldn't be enough room." He needed some excuse to temper the heat he suddenly felt.

They silently stretched out their legs and arms for a few minutes before Jake started to run. He was several steps away before she realized he'd started, and she double-timed a few strides to catch up. "Nice to give a girl a warning."

He didn't hear her. He'd already plugged his ears with his iPod. She decided to bring hers next time as they ran in silence.

For three miles she kept pace with him and, despite himself, Jake was impressed. He'd even kicked up his strides a little bit, hoping to give her a silent clue that he'd rather be alone. But Lily wasn't getting the message. She didn't even look winded, he noticed. He noticed quite a bit about her, actually. The sweat was making her tank cling a little tighter to her body, her hamstrings were perfectly toned, and her focus was unbreakable. He pulled the buds from his ears.

"Good to go another mile?"

"Oh, now you're talking to me?"

"No. Just felt like running down the beach. I like running in the sand."

"I never ran on the beach before. Let's do it."

"It isn't easy."

"Who said it needed to be easy?"

Jake smiled. "No one. Just warning you."

"Well, you can keep your warnings. I'm not gonna melt."

"Okay, then. Don't say I didn't tell you."

He pushed himself on the sand and even though he didn't want to be, he was happy to have some company. She never broke stride, she never once complained. He could tell she was pushing it but she didn't stop. He eventually eased up and they made their way back to his house, walking the last quarter mile.

"Thanks, Jake. I needed that," she said when they reached his front yard.

"No problem. You want a bottle of water or something?"

"Sure. I'll wait out here."

When he came back outside, two bottles in his hand, she was stretching out her legs and he once again noticed how in shape she was. He shook off the thought. "Here you go."

"Thanks."

"Well. I gotta get back in. I told Mr. Olsen I'd put in a couple hours today."

"Sure, no problem. Thanks again for the run and the water. Maybe we could do it again sometime."

"Yeah. Maybe."

"See ya, Jake."

"See ya, Lily."

He watched as she jogged away while a tiny something rolled in his belly. It wasn't until she disappeared around the bend that he turned to go back inside to get ready for work.

CHAPTER 7

"Hey Jake! Thanks for coming in. The haul's been so big this week, we haven't had a chance to get anything properly cleaned or restocked. I appreciate you doing this for me."

"No problem, Mr. Olsen. I didn't have anything planned, anyway. Just had to get my run in this morning."

John Olsen was quiet a minute. He knew Jake was hurting and he knew it was his daughter who had hurt him. He'd tried to take responsibility for it and gave Jake anything he could, be it overtime, small raises when he could afford it, or just alone time on the boat he knew Jake so dearly missed. Jake had changed so much since Maddie left. All of them had.

It was a hard pill to swallow but John knew they were all better off with Maddie gone. No one had seen her in the two years since she left. She called occasionally but, for the most part, his daughter was gone. She never wanted to talk about what happened the night she left and each time he tried to bring it up, she'd hang up on him.

The guilt he felt over the relief of her absence ate at his gut. He prayed for her every day but knew it didn't help. Mostly, he just felt bad for Jake. She was no good for him. John had known there would be trouble the first time he'd heard she was moving in with Jake...

∽∾∽

"Maddie, you sure you want to do this?"

"Jesus, Dad. I'm just moving a mile away. It's not like you won't ever see me."

"That's not what I meant. You barely know him," he said, although he was really thinking, *He barely knows you.*

"I've known him since high school. He's a good guy, Dad."

"But, Maddie—"

"No Dad. Don't, '*But Maddie* me.' I'm a grown woman and if I want to move in with my boyfriend, I will."

"Look, I know his family. They are my employees. Jake *is* a good guy. I just don't want—"

"Don't want what? Don't want me to mess him up? Don't want me to hurt him?"

"That isn't what I said."

"No. But you may as well have. You'll see. I'm not the same girl I was, and if you don't want to support my decisions, then you should just leave us alone."

"I support you. I'm just afraid you don't think things through."

"Sorry if I'm not smart enough for you. Sorry if I can't be more like Megan. Sorry I went away to college instead of settling down in this shit-hole of a town and starting a family."

"Madison Olsen! You listen to me. Stop blaming everyone else for your behavior. You just make sure you remember to treat people like you want to be treated."

Her tone was poisonous. "Jesus. You sound like Mom. You gonna start crying like her now, too?" Grabbing her suitcase, she headed for the door. She stopped and looked at him with hatred. "You ever stop to think that maybe you and Mom made me who I am? That all the crap I've pulled in the past was your fault? Chew on that."

She slammed the door behind her and he stared at the empty space that mirrored the empty hole in his heart. Maybe she was right, after all. Maybe they just didn't do a good enough job of raising her.

∽∂∽

"You okay, Mr. Olsen?"

Jake's question chased away the memories, jerking John back to the present.

"Yeah. Yeah, Jakey. I'm sorry. Just got lost for a minute. You need anything?"

"Nope. I'm good. I'll have the boats restocked, organized, and cleaned in a few hours."

John looked at his watch. It was almost eleven. "Hey, did you eat yet?"

"Yeah, I had breakfast after I ran."

"I'm gonna order lunch from Billy's in about an hour or so. You want anything?"

"Sure. Just a sandwich or something."

"Okay, Jake. I'll let you know. Thanks again."

Jake watched John turn and walk down the dock into the building. He knew the man was torn up over his daughter—like they all were—but Jake was too busy dancing with his own devils to do anything about it. Hard to imagine one person could cause so much damage and destruction.

Two hours later, Jake had completely cleaned, restocked, and organized one boat. He still had another to finish. He saw John walk down the dock with a bag from Billy's. He drained the last of his water bottle and hopped off the boat to meet his boss halfway.

"Here you go, Jake. I got you a grilled chicken sandwich and a soda."

"Thanks, Mr. Olsen. I've got one boat done. I just have to finish the other one. Probably another two or three hours."

"That's fine. Hey, you mind if I eat with you? I know you usually eat by yourself but, truth be told, I'm a bit bored. Too much paperwork makes me feel isolated."

"Sure, Mr. Olsen."

"How many times do I have to tell you to call me John?"

Jake laughed. It was a running joke between them. Mr. Olsen knew he would never call him John. They walked down the dock together to the table that sat under the biggest tree on the property. It would give them both some shade from the intense afternoon sun.

As they ate, they mostly made small talk. They spoke about the boats, the docks, and the large amount of fish that had been coming in these past few weeks. John went on about the weather and his grandkids. He spoke of Jake's dad, Andy, and what a great employee he was. He spoke of Danny and how proud he was to have a man like that in his family. Eventually, he turned his conversation to Jake.

"You're also an asset to the docks, Jake. You're the hardest worker here."

"Thanks, Mr. Olsen. I appreciate that. I love working here."

"You know, I consider you family. If you ever need anything, please let me know."

An uncomfortable shiver sped through Jake. Sweat began to pool at his brow and his legs bounced with nervous energy. He did not like the direction this conversation was taking. "I'll remember that. Well, I should be getting back to finishing the other boat. Thanks again for lunch."

"Wait, Jake. I never really got to apologize for what happened with Maddie."

"It's been two years. You don't need to apologize. You didn't do anything. And I really don't want to talk about her right now, if it's all the same to you."

"I know. I really do. I was just wondering, if, well, if you've heard from her lately."

Jake rubbed his hands over his face to keep her from taking up space in his brain. He was relaxed and focused on finishing up the boats. He didn't need this right now.

"No. I haven't heard from her in two years. Not since she left. Now if you don't mind, I do want to finish what I started. You've been more than generous with me and I'd like to finish the work you're paying me for."

John looked at Jake with the eyes of a man lost. "Sure. Go ahead. I'll throw this stuff out."

With that, Jake turned and walked back to the boat and John sat frozen by memories...

⁂

John grabbed the ringing phone by his bed. "Yeah? Who is it?"

"Mr. Olsen? It's Jake. Something's happened. You need to come to the hospital right away."

John bolted upright and it took him a minute to clear the sleep from his head.

"Jake? What's wrong?"

"It's Maddie."

That was all John needed to hear. He shook his wife from sleep and they were dressed and in the car within five minutes of hanging up the phone.

Abigail Olsen was a slight woman with blonde hair, like Maddie's, and light brown eyes. A bubbly woman, she was well-liked throughout the small community. She did so much to create a feeling of togetherness within the town. She organized picnics, headed the PTA, and felt a sense of accomplishment when she was able to bring about positive change for those around her. Now, however, she was tired and scared. "What did he say happened?"

"Abby, he didn't. He just said 'something happened' to Maddie and we needed to get to the hospital right away."

"Why would Jake call you? I thought they broke up."

"I thought they did, too, sweetie. At least, I hoped they did."

"John Olsen! What a terrible thing to say!"

"I know it is. I know it is."

The nearest hospital was two towns over, about a forty minute drive. John managed to make it in twenty-five, running every red light and pushing the Volvo to its limit. He pulled into the emergency parking lot about the same time as Danny and Andy Morgan.

"Do you know what happened?" he asked Danny.

Danny shook his head. "All I know is Sheriff Finlay called me and told me Maddie was being taken to the hospital by ambulance and we needed to come right away. Didn't he call you too?"

"No. Jake called and said something happened."

Andy Morgan was silent as they walked towards the emergency room doors. John knew he was trying hard not to imagine the worst. He knew that even though Jake had broken it off with that Maddie, they were too intertwined to leave each other alone for long. John, like many others, wondered when Jake was going to wake up and realize she was no good for him. He suspected that Andy felt the same way. Jake was a good kid and Maddie was just...well, not.

It had to be hard raising the two boys after his wife died. Jenny Morgan had been a good woman and John shuddered when he thought about what she'd say about Jake and Maddie's relationship.

John was the first one through the door. He scanned quickly for Jake. Instead he found the sheriff talking to one of the nurses.

"Finlay! What happened?"

Sheriff Finlay turned to look at him with somber eyes and noticed Abby, Danny, and Andy standing beside him. Dropping his head, he walked slowly toward them.

Finlay was tall and skinny. In high school they'd called him "Bean Pole Finlay." He didn't seem to mind too much, though. Back then, he was the fastest kid on the track team, and he still held the county record for cross-country. Now, forty years later, he was sheriff of the small town he grew up in. He'd been able to watch his friends settle down and have kids and watched those kids grow up.

"Why don't we all sit down?"

Abby's voice was weary. "I don't want to sit down. I want to know what happened to my daughter."

Andy spoke up. "And I want to know what Jake has to do with any of this. Is he in trouble?"

"No, no. Jake isn't in any trouble. It's Maddie. You see, it seems she got high on something, we don't know what yet—"

"Oh my God, John! She OD'd!"

Finlay interrupted, "No, Abby. She didn't. It seems she got high and broke into Jake's house. He was woken up by the sound of breaking glass. When he went to investigate, he found Maddie sitting on the floor of the bathroom. She had broken the mirror."

"What? But why? I don't understand."

"Well, John, it seems that she was quite upset about their break-up and she wanted to talk to Jake about it. She'd called earlier and he says he hung up on her. She wasn't happy with the way that call ended, apparently, so she decided to break into Jake's, like I said before." He hesitated. "I'm sorry to say that Maddie tried to kill herself tonight."

Abby sank onto the nearest chair and placed her head between her knees. John sat beside her and rubbed her back. Neither had any words to share.

Danny stepped up to ferret out the information from Finlay.

"When you say 'tried to kill herself' you mean with drugs or pills or something?"

"No, Danny. She told Jake everything was his fault and then proceeded to slit her wrists right in front of him. Jake jumped on top of her to stop her but she'd already done the damage. He got all cut up in the process, too, what with all the glass on the floor.

"She's being admitted now, Jake's with her. I gotta tell you, I ain't never seen Jakey so upset. I think he believed her when she told him she did it because of him. He won't leave her side. I'll go get someone to show you to her room." Finlay stopped and turned back around to look into four shocked faces. "I really am sorry."

∽∾∽

"Mr. Olsen, you okay?"

John looked up to find Jake standing in front of him.

"You okay?" Jake repeated.

"Yeah, yeah. I'm fine. Must've lost track of time."

John had lost track of two hours, Jake noticed. He wasn't terribly concerned though. He knew exactly what and who had taken the minutes from him. Unfortunately, they were all haunted.

"I finished the second boat. If you'd like, I can come back and do the third tomorrow. But right now, I am beat."

Still recovering from his thoughts, John shook his head. "You don't need to do that, Jake. I'll have some of the guys do it on Monday. No need to waste your entire weekend here. You go home and take some time for yourself."

"Okay, but you're sure you're all right?"

"I'm about as okay as you are, Jake."

John walked away from him and disappeared into the building. Jake walked back to his truck, threw his bag in the bed, and headed home.

CHAPTER 8

The next morning, Jake awoke more refreshed than he had in a long time. For the first time in two years, Maddie hadn't haunted his dreams. She was still there, he knew. She just had given him the night off and, for that, he was grateful.

He began his day as usual with a few stretches and push-ups. As he laced up his sneakers, he thought of Lily. A small smile played on his lips. Despite himself, he enjoyed her company, even if she was a pain in the ass. No. That wasn't fair. She wasn't really a pain in the ass. She was just someone he wasn't prepared for. Not that anything would ever develop. From what he'd heard, she was only in town through the end of the summer. Still, it was nice to have a friend who knew nothing of his past, of his pain.

He opened the door of his house only to find Lily stretching in the front yard, this time in a sports bra and bright yellow running shorts. A braid replaced the loose ponytail from yesterday and he couldn't help but look at her appreciatively.

"Hey! Since yesterday wasn't a total disaster, I figured you wouldn't mind a running partner today. Look, I even brought my iPod so we can run in silence!"

She's crazy, he thought as he smiled to himself. "I guess I wouldn't mind if you tagged along."

"Well, thanks for the invitation."

"I thought you invited yourself."

"Same, same. You didn't say no, now did you?"

She had the best smile. Her teeth were just a little bit crooked and her summer skin glowed golden. And her eyes. To Jake, her eyes looked like the deepest warmth he'd ever seen. And as he noticed all of this, the tiny something in his stomach got a little tighter. "No. I guess I didn't. You all stretched?"

"Yup. I got here about fifteen minutes ago. I figured I'd get a head start."

"How'd you know I'd run today?"

"I didn't. I just thought I'd take the chance."

"And what if I didn't?"

"Who knows? Look, you wanna sit here and debate about the what-ifs all day or do you wanna put a hurtin' on those muscles?"

"You're crazy. Let's go."

This time, Jake didn't try to push her. Instead, he settled into a comfortable rhythm right next to her. Their footfalls fell together, their strides matched, and the atmosphere was more relaxed. Whoever this girl was, he was happy to have her around, even if she was just a running partner.

When they finished running on the beach, instead of heading right home, they sat at the edge of the surf and watched as gulls dove for fish and dolphins played in the water. The morning sun hadn't yet hit debilitating temperatures and the early day's breeze offered comfort.

Her shoulder bumped his, playfully. "So, I've been doing a little background checking on you."

Jake was intrigued. "On me?"

"Yup. I got a few tidbits here and there but I'm too much of a stranger to really get anyone to talk to me. Even Uncle Billy tells me to leave it alone."

Jake picked up a shell and threw it into the sea. "Maybe you should take his advice."

"Maybe. Or maybe I should ask you."

"You may not want to know the answers."

"True, but I'm willing to take my chances. You interest me, Jacob Morgan."

"I'm not that interesting."

"Sure you are. For example, I know you gave up a college scholarship when your mom died. I know you work with your dad, and your brother, Danny. I know you live alone and don't have many real friends."

"I have friends."

"Of course, you do, but no one you've let in. No one you'd consider a—oh, I don't know—a best friend."

"A best friend? I'm a guy. I don't need a best friend."

"Maybe not. But I'm willing to bet you haven't talked much to anyone lately. I'd bet no one knows all your demons."

She was getting awfully close. Too close, for Jake's taste, so he figured he'd switch the conversation around to her.

"What about you? What are you doing here? Don't *you* have any friends?"

"Sure, I do. I just finished grad school, and I decided to hang with Uncle Billy this summer on my way to Atlanta. I have a few friends down there, and I'm planning on sharing an apartment with a college roommate. I already have an internship lined up."

"So you're in transition?"

"I guess you could say that."

"And that makes you, what? Twenty-two, twenty-three?"

"Try twenty-five. I took a year between undergrad and grad. That's not much younger than you, you know."

Jake didn't say anything. Instead, he stared at the surf, watching the waves roll in and pull back out. He studied how the water crashed onto itself, over and over again, like it didn't realize it was just repeating itself. Kind of like his relationship with Madison. Sure, things changed, evolved, but in the end all they kept doing was repeating the same behaviors again and again. Nothing had ever changed no matter how much he'd wanted it to.

"Hello? Hello? Lily snapped her fingers in front of his face to grab his attention. Earth to Jake." He looked at her and she noticed his eyes were somewhere else. Sure he was looking directly at her but he was lost for a minute. "So, you wanna tell me who she was?"

That brought him back real quick. Time to deflect. "Who *who* was?"

"I don't know. I figure it must be a girl who keeps you so lost."

"You don't know what you're talking about."

"I don't? I don't know, Jake. You seem awfully defensive."

"And you're awfully nosey." He stood and shook the sand off his clothes. "Look, I gotta go."

"Wait, don't go. We don't have to talk about that."

"Too late. You know, I had a nice time until you went all private eye on me. Thanks for the run."

He jogged off and she sat there, not watching him leave. Instead, she too stared at the waves and noticed the repetitive manner in which the ocean moved. Over and over, the water crashed down on itself and then began again. Looking for a new ending? Or a new beginning?

CHAPTER 9

Lily was counting out her tips at the end of her shift when Billy came and sat down across from her in the booth. She barely looked up as he dropped a bowl of pretzels on the table. "Hey, Billy."

"How you doing, Lil? You have everything you need?"

"Yeah. Of course. Business seems to be going well. At least the tips are good."

She finished counting and put the money in her apron. She reached for the glass of water in front of her, stared at a bowl of pretzels, and debated about getting something to eat.

"Yeah. Yeah. Business has always been steady," Billy agreed. "Mostly townsfolk, some tourists from up the road. How was your run this morning?"

"Good. It's nice to breathe in the sea air. Makes me feel, I don't know, energized."

"How's Jake?"

She looked at him for a minute before answering. She knew he had told her to keep her distance, as he had told

Jake to stay away from her. She couldn't figure out why, but she knew for Billy to become so protective there had to be a good reason, even if she didn't listen to his advice.

Giving in to the rumble in her belly, she reached for a pretzel. "What's the deal with you and Jake? Why can't I talk to him?"

"Jake's a good kid."

"He's twenty-eight. Hardly a kid."

His laugh was forced. "Well, when you've been around as long as me, anyone under thirty is a kid."

"You didn't answer my question."

"Look, like a said, Jake's a good kid. He's just had some issues dealing with his past. I don't think he'd be good for anyone right now, and I don't want you to get hurt."

"Why would I get hurt? It's not like he and I are gonna start dating. I'm leaving at the end of August, anyway. That would give us two months to develop something. Not gonna happen."

"You're a smart girl. Jake's just haunted, for lack of a better word, by the memories of a girl who took his heart and tossed it into the ocean. He walks around like a shell of who he once was. I can see it in his eyes, and until he learns to deal with it, he's not gonna be able to move forward. Like I said, he wouldn't be good for you. He's not even good for himself."

"I don't understand. What did she do that was so horrible?"

"You should ask him that."

She took a large gulp of water. "I did."

Billy lifted an eyebrow at her. "And?"

Lily shrugged her shoulders. "He got a little mad and walked away."

"Well, there you go. He doesn't want to talk about it."

"But if he's hurting that bad, doesn't he need to?"

Billy leaned back in the booth, his eyes clouded over. "Sure he does, Lily. But you can't make someone talk about something they don't want to."

"I just want to be his friend. He looks so sad. No. Not sad. Something else. Like he's empty."

"Lily, if you want to be his friend. Go right ahead. You're old enough and smart enough to make your own decisions. Just be careful. He has a history of snapping."

"Snapping? Like you think he would hurt me, like physically?" Lily didn't think that sounded at all like the Jake she barely knew. But that was the key word—barely.

"Oh goodness, no. At least I don't think so. But I gotta tell you, I am sure Maddie pushed him to the point where he sure as hell wanted to hurt her. She was sneaky. She was a liar and she was no good for anyone. It's a shame, too. She comes from a good family, and she was one of the prettiest things I ever saw. What she did to him, however, was unforgiveable, if you ask me."

Lily's curiosity was peaked. What on earth could someone do that was so awful? She was lucky enough in her life to be surrounded by good people, good friends, and a solid family. Maybe she was naïve in matters of heartbreak and disrespect. "I am sure she had her reasons, whatever she did."

"Lily, listen to me. Madison Olsen did everything she did for selfish reasons. She never once thought of anyone but herself. She never once did anything to better herself or the lives of those around her. She broke a boy I've known since he was in his mama's belly. No one deserves what she did. And *that* is all I have to say on the matter. Tread lightly, Lily. Just tread lightly. That boy's hurtin' a whole lot."

"All right. I'll figure it out. Thanks for talking to me about it."

Billy stood up, adjusted his pants over his soft belly. "Anytime. Listen, you hungry?"

"Sure, I could go for something."

"All right, then. I'll tell Randy to whip you up something. He's on a roll today with the creative crap. That boy fried tomatoes and made a salad out of it. Who would've thought of sticking fried tomatoes with lettuce and that mozzarella cheese? It's good, but what a strange way of cookin', huh?"

"Actually, that sounds kinda good. Have him make one for me."

"No problem, Lil. I'll send Marta over with a beer. You look like you could use one."

"Thanks, Billy."

Billy walked to the kitchen and placed Lily's order before retreating back to his office. He knew his niece wouldn't listen. She was too caring to allow someone to walk around empty. She was just the opposite of Madison, and he walked around with guilt over the fact that he never told anyone what Maddie had done...

೧೨೧

It was a busy Thursday night, busier than usual and Maddie was twenty minutes late. She was always late anymore. Billy toyed with the idea of firing her but, truth be told, she hustled when she was there. She turned tables like no one else. And besides, he liked her family. He figured she was going through something, so he gave her a little time and space. Maybe he'd ask Jake what was going on. He knew she had been in the hospital not too long ago and he knew why. He just hoped she wasn't falling back into that pit.

It had just about hit the hour mark from the time her shift started when she hurried in. Billy's first thought was that she looked like hell. Her normally-shiny blonde hair was disheveled and greasy. Her skin was tinged with gray and her uniform was dirty. Not at all like Maddie. Even when she was going through trouble, she always took pride in her appearance. With her propensity for drama, often her looks were all she had going for her. After all, she wasn't the nicest person you'd ever meet.

Serving up a beer to a customer at the bar, Billy yelled over to her, "You're late."

"I know, Billy. I'm sorry. Just had to take care of something."

"You coulda called. I was about to call the house to see where you were."

"I said I was sorry, Billy. What do you want me to do? Give you my first born?"

Snippy, he thought. At least she usually faked pleasantries.

"We're a little backed up. Those three booths just sat down. Go and take care of them, would ya'?"

"In a minute. I have to use the bathroom first."

"You couldn't have done that before you got here? I'm swamped here."

"How 'bout I piss in a beer mug and serve it up? You want me to do that? Didn't think so. Now, let me pee."

She hurried off to the bathroom. Billy wasn't in the mood to deal with her shit today. Maybe he'd just send her home. Then, he'd take care of the booths. Later, he'd have to talk to her.

Quite a bit of time had passed and Maddie still wasn't back from the bathroom. He dropped his towel on the bar and headed towards the back. He lightly knocked on the women's door. No answer.

"Maddie? You in there?"

No answer. He jiggled the doorknob but it was locked.

"Madison! Open this door!"

When she didn't answer, he grabbed keys out of his pocket and unlocked the door. Madison was sitting on the floor, leaning against the wall. She looked dazed.

"Maddie! Are you alright?"

She rolled her head back and looked at him with glassy eyes. Something was definitely wrong. He kneeled down beside her. An empty syringe lay next to her and her arm was tied with rubber tubing.

"What did you do?"

She didn't respond verbally. Instead, mascara-tinged tears streamed down her face. Billy picked her up and brought her back to his office. He laid her down on the couch he kept there for those busy nights he wasn't able to make it home. After covering her with a blanket, he called her father. No use bothering Jake with this. He was already beat down from the last time she did this.

"John, It's Billy."

"Hey, Billy. What's up?"

"You need to come down here."

"What? Why? What's happened?"

"Maddie's on something."

"On *something*? You mean, on drugs, don't you?"

"Yeah. Yeah. She's in my office right now, sleeping it off."

"Did you call Jake?"

"No. I didn't call Jake."

"Okay. I'll be there as soon as I can. Don't tell anyone."

"I understand. See you soon."

Billy clicked off and looked at the girl with confusion and pity. Grabbing the chair from his desk, he and rolled it over to the couch and sat next to her, stroking her hair and trying to think of ways he could help.

Through the open window of his office, he heard John pull in and park behind the bar near the kitchen entrance. When he walked into the office, the look on the man's face said everything.

John picked up his daughter, gave the Billy his keys, and was grateful he knew to follow and open the car door. John placed Maddie in the back seat, leaving the blanket wrapped around her. The two men didn't say anything to each other. They didn't need to. This was becoming too much of a usual occurrence.

Billy never told anyone about the incident, least of all, Jake. When Jake called that night looking for her, Billy just told him she wasn't feeling well and had gone home with her parents. It wasn't exactly a lie but it wasn't exactly the truth either. And Billy hated that.

❡❡❡

Billy shoved away the bad memories, got up from his desk, and walked back to the kitchen to pick up Lily's order. If anyone could snap Jake out of this, it was her. He just hoped it wasn't too late—that Jake wasn't too far gone.

CHAPTER 10

Jake was in the backyard, working on replacing the flooring of his back deck. He'd ripped it up almost a year ago and all that was left were the concrete footings. For some reason, today he felt like he needed to accomplish something. So he went to the lumberyard and bought the materials he'd need to finish it. What used to be a standard ten by ten space off his kitchen was now going to become something more. He had great ideas for his new deck. Nothing too fancy, just different. Besides, he thought, it was high time he did something that mattered now, instead of reliving what mattered then.

He'd measured everything out, drawn up a rough plan, and now was busy starting on the frame. Since he'd left Lily this morning, he felt antsy, restless. He picked up a pizza and a six-pack on his way home from the store and went to work. For six hours now, he hadn't thought about Maddie. He'd been too busy replaying the conversation he'd had with Lily. He was still no closer to figuring her out than he was before. At least when he thought about *her*, he didn't close himself off and fall into memories. At least with Lily, he really had no memories, good or bad, to trip on.

The sun was still a few hours from going down, so Jake figured he'd keep working until either darkness or exhaustion set in.

He was in the garage he'd turned into a workspace cutting planks for the floor when Lily walked in, six-pack and sandwiches in hand.

She watched him for a few minutes. He was unaware of her presence and she didn't want to scare him. He was working the circular saw like a pro. After a minute or two of watching him, she turned on her heel and walked out.

She went over to the deck he was building. It looked really nice. It wasn't close to being finished, but she could see where he was going and what his plan for it was. She appreciated someone who could create something with their hands. Her parents had always hired contractors and Lily never understood why. Wouldn't it be more satisfying if they'd done the work themselves? She looked at the deck and smiled.

Lily thought her parents were amazing people. Her father was a doctor and her mother stayed at home. Lily had grown up in an upper-middle class neighborhood, had lots of friends, and never wanted for anything. When her parents had wanted to send her to a private school, she balked until they allowed her to attend the public school. It was a decision she appreciated. Her parents trusted her, mostly because she never gave them any real trouble. Sure, she drank at a few parties, brought home the occasional boy, and got into a little mischief now and then. Like all teenagers, she had gone through a short "you'll never understand me" phase. But all in all she'd been a good kid.

There were things in this life she wanted to experience. She'd never consider herself sheltered but she probably was. It wasn't jealousy she felt over the fact that Jake could build his own deck. It was more of an I-want-to-do-that-too.

When Jake walked out of the makeshift workshop, he noticed Lily standing with her back to him. She was running her hands over the wood that he'd framed. She looked different than before. Her hair was down and curly. Strands got caught up in the slight breeze, reminding him of a willow tree. Her jeans were simple but tight enough to highlight her legs and rear. She was wearing a simple pale-purple T-shirt that highlighted the red in her hair. When she turned around, he saw that the neckline plunged just a little and gave a hint of what was just below the opening. She looked freshly scrubbed and beautiful and, for a moment, when the breeze picked up, he smelled lavender. Their eyes met and neither one moved. She just smiled. The ice surrounding Jake's heart melted, just a little.

"Hi."

"Hey."

"The deck looks good so far. How long have you been working on it?"

"About a year."

"Really?"

"Well, I tore it down last year and decided today that I should probably get it done, so I went to the store, bought the stuff, and went to work. Hey, you want a beer? I have some pizza left over from lunch, if you're hungry."

She turned from him and bent down. When she turned back she was carrying a six-pack and a bag.

"I asked Uncle Billy what kind of beer you drank, and I had him make you one of those crab cake sandwiches. I hope you don't mind. They were supposed to be sort of a peace offering."

She looked down when she said this, and the annoyance he'd felt earlier today disappeared. When he didn't say anything, she put the items on a makeshift table.

"Well, I just wanted to say I'm sorry for before. It wasn't really my business. I'll let you get back to work. See ya later, Jake."

"Wait. Aren't you gonna eat with me?"

"I ate earlier. I had to run home and shower so your sandwich is probably cold. I had to get the smell of food out of my hair, ya know?"

"Yeah. Well thanks."

"No problem. And Jake? I really am sorry if I made you mad."

She was halfway down the driveway when he called out, "Lily! At least have a beer with me. I haven't talked to anyone all day. Well, since this morning. I could use a break."

She turned and looked at him. "Sure. I could hang for a beer."

He took the six-pack she'd brought into the house and put it in the fridge. Grabbing two cold ones, he popped the tops off and walked back outside. He had no idea why he asked her to stay. He certainly hadn't planned to. "Here you go. Thanks for the sandwich. I'm getting a little sick of cold pizza, to be honest."

"Anytime. I haven't seen you in the bar lately, so I figured you'd need something. Presumptuous, I know, but that's me."

Jake dug into the brown paper bag. "Aw, you brought me cole slaw, too?"

She laughed. "Yeah, Uncle Billy wouldn't let me leave without it. I think it's a peace offering from him, too. There should be a plastic fork in there."

While he ate, he talked between bites. "So, Lily Burns, you grew up in Connecticut?"

"Yup. Lived there my whole life. Well, except for when I went to college. Spent four years of undergrad in Pennsylvania and lived in New York for graduate school. But I've never really been out of the Northeast."

"Not even to come down here?"

"Nope. My dad and Uncle Billy don't get along. Something about money. It kills my mom."

"Money and family is always a bad combination, I guess."

"I guess so. My dad's proud and when Billy loaned my mom some money, he flipped. Made her give it back. I don't even know why she needed it. I got scholarships to Penn State and we had enough money, minus a small student loan, to pay for graduate school. Grown-up problems, I call them."

Jake laughed and pointed his fork at her. "I hate to be the one to tell you, but you're a grown up now, too."

Taking a long pull from her beer, she thought about how grown-up she actually was. "Huh. Never really thought of myself as a grown-up but then again, I never really had to fend for myself until now."

She told him about where she grew up, about her parents, about college. He asked a lot of questions.

"Do you have any brothers or sisters?"

"Nope. Just me. My parents tried and tried but they couldn't get pregnant. Then, when my mom was forty, I surprised them. Is Danny your only sibling?"

"Yeah. He's two years older. He's married with kids. He was my best friend growing up."

"Was?"

"Still is, I guess. He's a good guy."

"He seems like it. I saw him today. We didn't talk much, I just took his order, but he seemed nice."

"Was he with the wife and kids?"

"Not unless the wife and kids are an older man that looks just like him. Your father, I presume?"

"Yeah. Probably Dad. They were probably hatching up another plan to fix me."

"Why would they need to fix you?"

When he looked up, she saw the sadness seep back into his eyes.

"Oh, I'm sorry. I'm always sticking my foot in my mouth. You don't have to answer that."

"It's okay. I opened that one up. They just think it's about time I moved on."

"Well," she said as he finished up his meal. "It looks like the deck is a good place to start. Could I help? I've never built anything before."

She saw relief pass through him as he relaxed.

"Sure. Let me grab another beer. You want one?"

"Absolutely."

For the next few hours, Jake showed Lily how to work the circular saw, how to hammer a nail, and how to use the power drill. She caught on quick and the deck was moving along double time. By the time the sun began to fall, the floor was done.

They'd talked about nothing, laughed at everything, and Jake, who'd considered himself a relative of the Tin Man for the past few years, began to soften. Lily took his mind off of everything that plagued him. He felt good, he felt loose, and he felt like his old self again.

Lily took in everything Jake told her. She learned fast and felt excited that she was a part of creating something. If she'd had a Bucket List, she'd have had to remind herself to cross this off the list. Jake was fun. They got along easily, and she felt like she did more than help him build a deck.

Standing back with a hammer in his hand, Jake took in what they'd just accomplished. "I can't believe the floor is done."

"I can't either. This was so much fun, Jake. Thanks. I was gonna go home and watch the latest Lifetime movie. You rescued me from sad stories of unrequited love and tragedy. How can I ever repay you?"

His laugh was sincere. "Oh, man. Good thing we had a deck to build then. And I think we'll call this even."

"Good thing. I have no money. Thanks, Jake. I had a great time."

"Me, too."

Stretching her arms over her head, Lily felt the pull of a hard day's work. "Well, bud, my muscles ache in places I've never known. I think I'm gonna go home, shower again, and pass out."

"Yeah. Me, too. Thanks again, Lily."

"You're welcome."

"No. Not just for the deck."

"I know. See ya around."

She grabbed her keys and Jake walked her back to her Jeep. She waved as she backed out of the driveway. He'd thought about kissing her but the idea was fleeting. It wasn't a path he wanted to explore yet. For now, he was just happy she'd blown a tire. Were it not for that, he wasn't sure she'd have shown up in his life like this. For now, for today, he decided he'd be happy.

He cleaned up his tools, closed the garage doors, and walked into the house. He showered and went to bed. And for the second night in a row, Maddie didn't haunt him.

CHAPTER 11

The next morning, Jake woke up ready to start the day. His shift started at 7:30, so he had two hours to kill before he had to show up at the docks. He bolted out of bed, dressed, stretched, and jogged out the front door.

Half an hour later, Lily awoke to a knock on her window. When she pulled back the curtains and looked through the basement window, she saw Jake dressed for a morning workout. She smiled, held up a finger, got dressed, and met him outside.

He was smiling. "Hey."

"Hey."

"Wanna go for a run?"

"Ah, sure. Long or short?"

"Long or short what?"

She giggled at his confusion. "Run."

"Short. I have to be at work at seven thirty."

"Then let's go. Follow me."

Jake raised his eyebrows and followed her. Winding her way to the back of her uncle's house, she started down a path through the brush. The path was narrow and Jake ran behind her instead of beside her. Not that he minded. The view was great.

He searched his brain, remembering the path and where it led. He hadn't been back there since middle school.

Jake kept the pace Lily had set. It wasn't a slow jog but it wasn't the intense, leg killing run he'd subjected her to the first day they ran together either. It was quiet out there. Neither of them spoke. He was amazed at the slight sounds of nature waking up. He saw birds and squirrels and lizards scuttling across the dirt. The smell of the ocean was strong. Salt permeated the air, the humidity was beginning to rise, and the sun peaked through overhead. It was gonna be hot today.

A mile in, they were both dripping with sweat. She slowed at a clearing, and he saw where she'd taken him. It was an old saltwater pool. The tire was still there attached to a high branch on the tree next to the bank. He used to come here when he was younger. He and his friends had their first cigarettes out here, drank their first beers. A flood of happy memories overtook him. Good memories that had been suppressed by the bad. Suddenly, he pulled off his shirt and ran toward the tree. He jumped up, grabbed the tire, swung himself out into the middle of the water, and dropped. His loud "woohoo" made Lily laugh.

"Try it!" he yelled to her, laughing as his head broke through the surface.

"What?"

"The swing. You need a running start. It's high. Grab it and jump!"

"You're crazy!"

"I know. Isn't it great?"

The admission was just what Lily needed. She stripped off her shirt so she was wearing only her sports bra and shorts. She kicked off her sneakers and pulled off her socks. Smiling wickedly at him, she crouched and took off, grabbing the tire on the first try. As she swung out to the middle of the pool and splashed in next to him, she heard his laugh. The water was cold but neither of them minded.

Jake was as giddy as he'd been when he first discovered the pool. "Holy crap, Lily! I haven't been here in years! How did you know it was here?"

"I found it the morning after I got here. I woke up early and decided to go for a walk. I was itching to take some pictures. I had noticed the path so I decided to see where it led. This is great, isn't it?"

"You have no idea. Years, I am telling you. Man, I have the greatest memories of this place. Unbelievable."

"I hadn't tried the swing when I was here before. That was fun."

"Wanna do it again?"

With the excitement in his voice, she couldn't say no. They jumped a few more times before climbing out of the water and sitting on the bank.

"Thanks, Lily. That was fun. I can't believe I haven't been here in so long. I guess kid stuff doesn't matter so much when you're a grown-up."

"Sure it does. If you don't stop and let go once in a while, the grown-up stuff can suffocate you. And besides, when's the last time that tire saw a twenty-eight year-old man? And that last flip was a nice touch."

"It was, wasn't it?"

Jake sat for a few minutes reveling in how good he felt. It was like he'd woken up that morning for the first time in a long time. "Hey, I have an idea."

Out of the corner of her eye, Lily looked at him with interest. "Oh yeah? What's that?"

"How about I call out of work today and we go back to my place and finish the deck?"

"Can you do that? You aren't giving much notice."

He frowned a minute then smiled. "True, but I haven't taken a day off in two years. I even went in once with a broken wrist."

"You broke your wrist?"

"Yeah. But listen. They won't mind. Mr. Olsen has been telling me I need some time off."

His smile was contagious. "Has he now?" she asked.

"Yeah. So what do you say?"

"Well, Uncle Billy did give me the day off, and I had nothing planned other than taking some pictures."

"So you will?" When she nodded, he yelled, "Awesome! Come on. Let's see if we can't knock this thing out today. Maybe I'll take tomorrow off, too. The house needs painting and the shutters need to be fixed."

"Hold on, slugger! Take it one day at a time. Work through today and then think about tomorrow. Come on. Let's get back. I'll shower and get dressed. I'll meet you at your house in an hour."

"Good. I'll pick up some bagels or something. Maybe I'll make sandwiches for lunch. This feels great!"

"Okay, okay. You are crazy, Jacob Morgan. Let's go."

They ran back like they were running toward something. Within an hour, Lily was at Jake's house, hammer in one hand, bagel in the other.

"So," she said between bites, "where do you want to start?"

"The floor is done, so I figure we'll knock out the steps then work on the railings."

"Sounds good. Now what should I do?"

"Let's measure out the steps then go back and cut the wood. I figure we'll have a small space over there for the steps."

"Why small? If you make the steps small then the railings will take up the rest of the space and when you sit out here, you won't be able to see anything."

"What would I need to see?"

"Jake, look around you. The trees, the dunes, the grass. It's beautiful out here. You should make the deck an extension of that beauty."

She was right. He'd never thought of that. He'd never thought about the deck as a place to really hang out. He'd used the old one mostly to hold his grill and a lawn chair. He liked the idea of creating a space he could use for more than a few minutes at a time. "That's a good idea. I never thought of it that way. I've just been so preoccupied, I never really noticed. So what do you think we should do?"

She liked the "we" when he said it. It made her feel like he appreciated her input. She walked the perimeter of what they'd built. It was twelve by twelve on the main deck with a step down to a second level about a foot off the ground.

"What if we build the steps over by the driveway first? Then extend the deck the length of the house so it meets your bedroom? Then if you ever want to knock down a wall and put in a slider, you'd have a deck off your room?"

Jake followed her thought process. He'd never thought about opening up his wall to the outside. To be honest, he hadn't thought much about changing anything over the past two years. He'd been stuck in the past and hadn't moved forward.

"You know what, Lily? That's a great idea. I'm gonna have to get some more wood but I think I might have enough to frame it out. And I think I have a couple bags of cement to start the footings. Why don't we measure that out first then go back to the steps around the driveway and backyard? I think I'm gonna return the railings. I don't think I want them. You're right. I don't want to feel closed off."

"All right. Let's go. What should I do first?"

He winked at her. "Grab a shovel."

"Why do I feel like I just made more work for myself?"

"Because you did. And it's awesome."

It was three in the afternoon before the two took a break for lunch. As they sat eating sandwiches, they admired their handiwork. The steps around two sides of the deck were in place and the concrete footings for the rest of the deck extension were dug, poured, and setting up. Jake and Lily measured out what wood they had left and made a list of what materials Jake would pick up tomorrow.

"I gotta say, Lil, I don't think I'd have been able to get this far so fast without your help."

"I am the great motivator, you know. It looks great so far. I can't wait to see what it looks like when you finish it. Tomorrow, you think?"

"Yeah, I think it'll be done tomorrow. And what do you mean 'when I finish it'? Aren't you gonna help?"

"I'd love to but I promised Billy I'd work a double tomorrow. Arlene has to take the kids to the doctor's and Marta's off."

Disappointment clouded his face and he was quiet.

"But I can come by after. If you need any help then, I would be glad to pitch in."

"Oh, yeah. That would be great."

"Good. I should be off by five or so. I can be here by six."

They finished their sandwiches and beers. For an hour, the two sat next to each other in silence on the finished part of the deck and looked out at the trees.

Finally, Jake spoke. "This is nice."

"It is."

"Thanks for helping."

"Anytime, Jake."

Jake breathed in and closed his eyes. "She left two years ago."

Lily looked straight ahead. "Why did she leave?"

"'Cause that's what she always did."

"I'm sorry."

"I'm not. For the first time in a long time, I'm not."

CHAPTER 12

Very early the next morning, Jake awoke covered in sweat. He'd dreamt of Maddie again. He dreamt of the happiness he felt when he first found out, the happiness that precluded the collapse of his world...

☙☙

Maddie had been sick for days. Her stomach rejected everything she ate. She stayed in bed for three days and Jake was worried. The morning of the fourth day, he decided she needed to see a doctor.

"Maddie, I'm gonna take you to see Dr. Anderson."

She didn't say anything, just nodded her head as she sipped the water he brought her. She looked awful and he hoped she really *had* stopped using. He'd hoped she'd really given up the drugs. It wasn't that long ago, after all, that he found her in his bathroom, high on God knows what.

Whatever was wrong with her, he wanted to find out and get her better.

Once at the doctor's office, Jake sat in the examination room with Maddie. She looked pale but at least she'd kept down the water he gave her earlier. He took that as a sign she was feeling better. This visit was more for Jake, unfortunately. He needed to know what was going on with her, and he swore to himself that if she was on drugs, he needed to make a decision. It wasn't an easy wait for him.

After a blood test, a urine test, and an overall physical examination, Dr. Anderson walked in the room with her file.

"Well, Maddie, how are you feeling? Sorry for all the tests but we wanted to cover all our bases. And it seems there's nothing wrong with you."

Relief washed over Jake. "That's terrific."

"Nothing wrong in that, well, nothing is *wrong*. I am happy to say that you two are going to have a baby."

The color drained even further from Maddie's face but Jake was too busy beaming from ear to ear to take much notice. It was as if the past almost two and a half years had disappeared. In an instant, he forgot all her drama, all her bull shit, all his pain and focused on the tiny little person growing in her belly. His hand moved to her stomach and he smiled at her. She didn't smile back.

"So all this—her throwing up and nausea is all because of a baby?"

"Yes. All women react differently and Maddie, unfortunately, seems to be especially sensitive to morning sickness."

"But I don't just get sick in the morning."

Dr. Anderson laughed. "The term 'morning sickness' is deceiving. It can happen any time of day, usually throughout the first trimester. From what I can tell, you are smack in the middle of it. About eight or nine weeks as far as I can see. You will have to make an appointment with your OB/GYN to be sure. You will need to make regular visits to her, just to make sure everything is on track."

"I can't believe it, Doc!" Jake crowed. "Thank you so much! This is such a relief. Not just a relief, a reason to celebrate!" He was over the moon. He just needed to talk to the doctor for a minute without Maddie in the room.

"Well, Jake. Madison. I am happy to be able to deliver you the good news. I am going to write you a prescription for some prenatal vitamins. You need to make the appointment with an OB as soon as you can."

Dr. Anderson stood and walked out of the room, Jake on his heels. In the hallway, Jake was torn over whether or not he should ask, but for the sake of his unborn baby, he knew he needed to.

"Dr. Anderson! Wait. Did anything else show up in Maddie's tests?"

"Anything else?"

"You know her history with drugs. Did anything show up in there? I need to know. That's my baby she's carrying."

"No, Jake. Nothing else showed up. She's clean as a whistle. The only thing that showed up was a baby."

Dr. Anderson placed his hand on Jake's shoulder. "You done good, kid. Keep her healthy." He turned and walked away leaving an incredibly happy Jake standing in the hallway.

❧❧❧

Jake sighed, got out of bed, and walked to the bathroom. He was tired of her intruding in his life. She was gone and for the first time he wished she would stay gone. Anything good that happened to him, any happy memory, was always tainted with bad. He knew he couldn't go on like he had before. He had been shown the promise of a ghost-free future. Even if Lily was leaving at the end of the summer, he was happy she was there. She reminded him what it was to be alive, to live for something. And he'd be damned if he was going to let Madison ruin him again.

It was too early to wake up fully but too late to go back to bed. He had things he wanted to accomplish this week, so rousing early wasn't totally annoying.

He'd taken the rest of the week off. Mr. Olsen seemed pleased and Jake thought it was funny that a boss would actually want an employee to take time off. There were enough people working, though, to give Jake a little leeway for a much needed few days of personal time. He planned on finishing the deck and painting the house. He might possibly even replace the shutters. But he remembered that Lily had said to take it a day at a time. Plan for today, and then tomorrow, plan for that. It was sound advice, especially since he wasn't used to planning much of anything other than showing up for work. It felt good.

He dressed and ate a leftover bagel that had gone stale on the counter. Instead of his usual morning run, he decided to get an early start on the deck. He figured the concrete was set enough to start framing the extension. It was a project he knew he could throw himself into. He'd even called his father last night and convinced him to take the day off so he could come and help. It had been a long time since Jake and his father had spent any meaningful time together and now was as good a time as any. He had his reasons for wanting to finish the deck as soon as he could.

He looked at his watch. At four-thirty, there wasn't much of a chance of anyone else being up. His father would be here at seven, so he had a couple of hours to get started. Maybe he'd be able to give his father a reason to be proud of him again.

Before his father showed up, Jake measured twice more and cut the wood he had to the lengths he needed. Once the footings were prepared with braces, and he and his father had figured out exactly what else he needed, he'd run back to the lumberyard for the rest of the supplies. He'd even measured and outlined an opening on his bedroom wall and, though it would be a stretch, maybe he'd pick up a door for that.

Jake consciously locked all memories of Madison away. She wasn't welcome here, not today. He needed to focus. He wanted to finish the deck, and he felt like a parent preparing Santa Claus's presents for his young children. He wanted to make the unveiling a surprise. He just hoped Lily would be as excited as he was.

At seven sharp, he heard tires pull into the gravel driveway. His dad was nothing if not punctual. It was a trait he'd tried to instill in his boys. Danny was better at it than Jake but he tried. A second set of tires pulled in right behind the other. Jake couldn't figure out who, besides his father, would be here this early. He walked around to the driveway and smiled.

"Hey, Dad! Danny, what are you doing here?"

"Dad called me last night and said I should take off for some family bonding time."

"You didn't have to do that."

"I know I didn't. I just figured if you thought it was important to finish this deck, I should be there to help. And I brought some extra boards from when I finished mine."

"You guys are awesome. Thanks. This means a lot to me."

Andy spoke up. "We figured you haven't been this focused on something in a long time. I'm happy to be a part of it. Come on, let's grab some of this wood from Danny's truck and get to work."

Danny smiled and held up a plastic container. "Megan made muffins."

"Say that three times fast?"

Danny was confused. "What?"

Jake smiled. "Nothing. What kind?"

"Apple cinnamon."

Jake couldn't help but laugh. "How many did you eat on the drive over?"

"I'm offended!"

"How many?"

"Four."

"Four? It's a ten minute drive."

"I was hungry."

"Maybe she's right. You should stick to the light beer."

"Come on! She never makes these! She only made them 'cause I was coming over here. A man's gotta eat!"

"You're so weird, man. How many did she make?"

"Twelve."

Jake walked over and took the container from his brother. "The rest are for me. And Dad."

As Jake opened the container, his dad walked by. "When are you two boys gonna stop goofin' off and help me empty this truck? If the deck is going to be what Jake said, we have work to do. And give me a damn muffin."

By ten, the three men had laid the floor of the deck extension. Jake's father had taken the drive to the lumber yard and picked up any materials they'd need to finish while Danny and Jake measured, cut, hammered, screwed, and laid the boards. It was shaping up when they took a break. The summer heat was turning up.

"Do you think we'll finish today?" Jake asked his father.

"Yeah. We'll finish. We may not have all the minor touches done but we'll finish the decking. We might even be able to knock that door out. You know, while we're here, I figure we can measure that out, too. Come to my truck, I got something for you."

Jake and Danny followed their father to the driveway. In the bed of the truck was a set of french doors.

"Dad, you bought these?"

"Yeah. I know you said you wanted a slider but I remember your mom always wanted french doors. I never got around to it before she passed. I figure she'd appreciate this."

"I don't know what to say."

Even Danny was impressed. "Yeah, Dad. That's really cool of you. I need a new toilet in the downstairs bathroom. You got one of those in there too?"

Andy smiled. He was glad he'd agreed to spend the time with his boys. It had been a long time since the three of them had spent any quality time together. He and Danny had remained close, but Jake had closed off not long after he and Maddie became an item. Andy thought about how upset his wife would have been, had she been alive, to see the life sucked out of her youngest son...

⁂

"Dad!" Jake ran into his father's house yelling. "Dad!"

"What? What's wrong?"

"Nothing! Nothing's wrong. As a matter of fact, everything is great."

"Well, spill it. What's so great?"

"I'm gonna be a dad! Maddie is pregnant! We're having a baby!"

Andy sat down. He wasn't prepared for this. He should have been, he knew. But he had hoped that, despite the constant break-ups and reunions, Jake would come to his senses and get rid of that girl. Now she would be tethered to the family regardless of what happened from now on.

"Dad? Don't you have anything to say?"

"It's yours?"

Jake looked shocked. "Of course it is. Why would you ask that?"

"I'm sorry. I just wasn't sure. Are you sure you two are ready for this? A baby is a big responsibility."

"You think I don't know that? What? You think I can't handle it?"

Andy saw his son losing control. "No. It's not you I am worried about."

"She's past all that, Dad. Jesus. Can't you just be happy for us? Happy for me?"

"I don't know, Jakey. I want to be. I just thought—"

"Thought what? Thought I'd dump her and forget about everything we'd been through? I can't leave her like this even if I wanted to. I love Maddie and now we're gonna have a baby. You can either be happy for us or not. Either way, she and I are stronger than ever and now we have this baby coming. She knows it's a big deal. She's done with all that other bull shit."

"I know you think so, Jake, but how many times have I, have you, heard all this before?"

They were both yelling now, Andy, out of fear for his son, and Jake, out of anger at his father.

"Damn it! Why can't you support me? Why can't you just be proud of me?"

"I am proud of you. And I do support you. Who was there first thing every time that girl broke you? Who picked you up when she tore you down? Me, goddammit. And I'll be damned if she's gonna do that to you again. Damned if she's going to do that to my grandbaby. Jesus, Jake. Think this through. Think hard. Look me in the eye and tell me you don't think she'll screw you over again."

"It doesn't matter what I say. You think what you want. When you're ready to be on my side, you'll be welcome. Until then, keep your negativity to yourself. I'm done with it. I've had too much of it over the past few years—"

"Because of her."

Jake stopped and looked at his father. Disappointment settled in both their eyes. No longer able to deal, Jake grabbed his keys and walked out the door.

∽∽∽

Danny laughed. "Dad? I was kidding."

Shaken from a memory, Andy tried to smile. "Well, let's get this thing done. For some reason Jake is hell bent on finishing this today, and if we are gonna make that happen, we don't have time for messin' around."

Jake and Danny looked at each other. They both knew where their father went just then. It's where they all went. Back to the past, back to the pain they'd just as soon forget.

For the rest of the morning and much into the afternoon, Jake, Danny, and their father worked on the deck. Once it was finished, the three gathered in Jake's bedroom and contemplated the best way to knock down the wall.

"Do you think it's a load bearing wall?"

Andy was knocking on the wall. "Not sure."

Danny was the first to make the obvious joke. "You know, if you're looking for a stud, I'm right here."

Jake rolled his eyes and laughed despite himself. "Sure if you think a stud downs four muffins in ten minutes and is relegated to light beer."

"Beer. That's what this party needs."

Danny disappeared into the kitchen and came back with two lagers and a light beer.

"Now this will help me think. I'm so freakin' tired, Jake. You owe me one, you know?"

"I know. I owe you about a dozen by now."

"That you do, Brother. Cheers!"

Andy thought for a minute. "I think we should just cut through. There's a header that runs the length of the wall. The ceiling is high so we won't need to cut into it to fit the door. You sure you want this, Jake?"

"Yeah, Dad. Let's do it. Demo is the fun part."

"All right. Let's outline the space to fit the new doors and get to work. We can have another drink when it's finished." He took out a tape measure. "

Within a few hours, they'd cut out the opening and fastened the doors in the space. After a few adjustments, they were opening smoothly.

"Gonna have to paint your room now, you know."

"I know, Dad. Thanks for all your help."

"I don't know about you two, but I am beat," Danny said. "Do you need me for anything else? Meg just texted me asking if I'd make it home for dinner."

"Nah, man. Go home. Tell Meg I said hi. And Danny?"

"Yeah?"

"Thanks, man. Thanks for everything."

The two hugged for the first time in recent memory, and Danny felt a weird emotion churn up inside him.

"Yeah, yeah. Wussy. What else ya got? Remember, you owe me!"

When he left, Jake and his father were left to admire the massive amount of work they'd completed that day.

As he drained the last of his beer, Andy said, "You done good kid."

"Thanks, Dad. *We* done good."

"Yeah, we did. I'm gonna clean up outside. You go shower and get ready."

"Ready for what?"

"That Lily is coming over, right? Isn't that why you wanted to finish this?"

"Well, yeah. Kinda. How did you know?"

With a twinkle in his eye, Andy replied cryptically, "A father always knows. Now go. I'll clean up the mess. Shouldn't take me long. We done a good job cleaning up as we went. At least you guys learned somethin' from your old man."

"Thanks, Dad."

With that, Andy went outside and cleaned up the tools, sawdust, and random pieces of wood they'd left lying around while Jake stayed inside to shower. Andy looked around at what he and his boys had accomplished and thought, *At least it's a start.*

CHAPTER 13

Lily finished her shift an hour late. After dividing her tips, she ran home to shower and change. By the time she reached Jake's driveway, it was almost seven.

Jake heard the gravel crunch under Lily's tires and walked around to meet her. She looked amazing in simple denim shorts and faded blue T-shirt.

"Hey, you."

"Hey, yourself. Well, I came dressed to work."

"We'll get to that. You hungry?"

"Starving."

"Good." Jake grabbed Lily's hand and walked her to the back yard.

"Oh my God, Jake! You finished it!"

"Well, mostly. I still have to stain it and clean up around the new door we installed but, yeah, it's finished."

The look on her face was definitely what he needed to ward off the exhaustion that was setting in. He watched as she walked around the deck and admired his handiwork.

"It's beautiful. And the door! French doors were definitely the way to go. It's like you have your own little piece of paradise. I am sure the view from your room is great. Just like a picture. I can't believe you did all this today."

"I had help. My dad and Danny came over and we worked on it since seven this morning. I really wanted to finish it before you got here."

Lily looked at him and smiled. She was both impressed with the job he'd done and flattered that he'd thought of her while he worked on it.

"You thought of me?"

"Well, sure. It was your idea, wasn't it? And besides, you helped me with the first part. It's only fitting you help me finish it."

"I thought it was done."

"Well, it is. Just one more nail needs to be hammered in place."

From behind his back, Jake somehow produced a hammer and a single nail. He took her hand and led her to the farthest extension of the deck and pointed to an "x" he'd penciled in.

"Here you go. You started with it. Now you have to finish."

Like a giddy schoolgirl, Lily took the hammer and nail from Jake and fastened the last board to the frame. She stepped back, admired her prowess with the hammer, turned around, and hugged Jake. Though this was the reaction he'd hoped for, he wasn't prepared for it. He wasn't prepared for how good it felt to be hugged sincerely by a female friend. It was a good feeling, though foreign to him at this point in his life.

"So, you said you were hungry."

"I did."

"I pulled the grill up and bought some steaks. Sorry but the seating is a bit primitive."

As he motioned toward the main deck, she noticed a rusty round table, a broken umbrella and two metal lawn chairs.

"It's perfect!"

"I was gonna get some new furniture but I have to stain the deck first and finish the trim work. I was thinking about changing the porch light, adding some solar lights—"

She grabbed his shirt. "Jake, I said it was perfect. Now feed me!"

He went inside to get the steaks as Lily lit the grill. He brought out two glasses and a bottle of pinot.

"Wine?"

Jake blushed. "I just thought, well, since we finished the deck and all, we could, well, you know…"

"Celebrate?"

"Yeah."

"Let's do it. It's a good reason to celebrate."

Lily's enthusiasm was infectious and before long Jake was grilling up two steaks, Lily was mixing a salad, and both were starting on the second bottle of wine.

"Everything looks fantastic, Jake. Thank you so much for having me over for dinner."

"No need to thank me. You earned it. I've never seen a girl swing a hammer like that. You sure you never did it before?"

"No. Really. I learn fast, you know."

"Another glass?"

Through a full mouth, she replied, "Yes. This steak is fantastic. It just melts."

"Glad you like it. Your salad isn't bad either."

"I don't even think we need it. My mom always drilled into me that a vegetable is always necessary at dinner. If she ever had a steak like this, she'd change her mind."

They talked and ate for a while before Jake began to ask Lily about her life.

"Did you play any sports in high school?"

"Yeah. Oh my God, I am stuffed. I ran track—"

"Obviously."

She smiled. "Yes, obviously. And played soccer."

"I never got into soccer. I didn't understand it. You just run and kick the ball into a net."

"Hey!" She threw her napkin at him. "Like baseball is any more interesting?"

"Well, yeah. It takes skill to be able to hit a baseball with a stick while it's hurling at you at ninety miles an hour."

"And running the bases takes skill?" she demanded.

"Yeah, you gotta run fast enough to beat the ball but slow enough to stop if you have to."

"What position did you play?"

"Pitcher."

"Pitcher, huh? And why'd you stop?"

Jake took a long swallow of his wine. "Ahh, man. My mom was sick. When she died, I declined the scholarship and stayed here to keep an eye on my dad. He was a mess."

Sorrow filled her. "I can't imagine. And how'd you handle it?"

"I didn't handle it well. Started getting into fights, started working like a beast. The only thing that kept me sane was my guitar."

"The one you threw away?"

"Yeah."

"You should play again."

"No. I don't play anymore." He drained the wine from his glass before pouring more.

"I am not gonna ask why because we are having such a good time but I just figure if it kept you sane before, maybe it would keep you sane now."

"What makes you think I'm not sane?"

"Well, not that you aren't, per se, but maybe it would fill the void in your eyes."

Jake leaned back in his chair and looked at her while he drank his wine. She kept his gaze as he contemplated her words, almost daring him to deny them.

"Hmm. Maybe."

"Maybe."

As the sun finally winked its way to sleep, Jake lit the citronella torches and turned on the porch light.

It was midnight before Lily stood up and stretched.

"Thanks for dinner, Jake. I really appreciate it. I had a great time. Everything was great, the food, the wine, the company."

"You're leaving?"

"I have to. Early shift."

She saw the disappointment in his eyes so she added, "Maybe we can run tomorrow. Six okay for you?"

"It's a date. Let me walk you out."

"Okay. Let me help you clean up first."

"No. I'll take care of that. You go home, get some sleep."

She took his hand and they walked around to her car. She fiddled with her keys for a minute, and Jake couldn't help noticing how pretty her hair looked in the moonlight. They stood there, like two teenagers at the end of a first date and neither could figure out what came next.

"Thanks again for everything." A flush rose through her cheeks as she realized how loudly the words came out.

"Anytime."

"Well, okay then…" Lily reached up, hugged Jake, and kissed him softly on the cheek.

He was too stunned to respond. Not so much that she kissed him, even if it was on the cheek, but the way the kiss lingered after she pulled away. His heart tripped up a bit and his mind clouded.

As she climbed into her Jeep, she said, "See you tomorrow, Jake."

He watched, rooted to the ground, as she backed out of the driveway and headed home. He put his hand on his cheek, almost expecting to feel something left there. When he finally moved, he walked back to the deck, sat in the old metal lawn chair, and poured himself the last of the wine. He stared out into his backyard, looked up at the moon, and finally saw himself moving forward.

The next morning, he met Lily at her house and they shared a five-mile run. Everything was so easy for him when he was around her. He was relaxed and the ghosts of the past didn't haunt him. When he thought about the fact that she was leaving at the end of the summer, he'd remove it from his head. She'd taught him to live for the day and think about tomorrow when it happened. It was something he needed to practice but it seemed to be working for him so far.

Throughout the rest of the week, Jake worked on his house. Each day began new and fresh. He was happier than he'd been in a long time and he had Lily to thank for it. She was saving him, he knew. And he thanked her silently every morning when he woke up and every night before he went to sleep.

CHAPTER 14

On the first steamy Saturday in July, Jake rolled out of bed and made his way into the kitchen. Dreamless over the past few weeks, he'd finally begun to heal. Thoughts of Madison didn't drop him to the floor like they once had. His time over the past month had been taken up by work, home improvements, and Lily.

He was amazed they spent just about every free moment in each other's company without progressing past a hug or quick peck on the cheek. He was falling for her. He wasn't pursuing more than what they were, however. Jake was becoming content with dealing with things day by day. And today, he needed to see her.

He was humming a tune he'd started to work on when she answered the phone, still groggy with sleep.

"Hello?"

"Good morning! How'd you sleep?"

"Barely. You?"

"Good actually. Thanks again for coming over last night. That was some celebration, huh?"

Her giggles set the butterflies in his stomach into a frenzy. "If I never have to hang another window shutter, I'll be fine."

"I just wanted to thank you for helping me. The deck is done, the house is painted, and the shutters are up. I can barely recognize the place when I pull up now."

"I know what you mean. Is another thank you why you called me so early? I thought we'd said no running today."

His fingers drummed excitedly on the kitchen counter.

"No, no. I just, well, I wanted to know if you wanted to hang at the beach today. Maybe we could build a bonfire, have a few beers. Whatever. But if you're busy, we could do it another day."

"Oh yeah? A girl always loves waking up to hear a boy wants to see her. What time were you thinking?"

"I don't know. You're off today, what time's good for you?"

"I have to run a few errands today. How about four? I'll bring the beer."

"Four it is."

"See you then."

When he hung up the phone, he sat back in the chair and closed his eyes. He didn't know where this was going and for the moment, he didn't really care. The fact that she was there was enough for him right now. But that thought was enough of an opening for Madison to intrude once again...

❄❄❄

In the two months since they'd found out they were going to have a baby, Jake did everything he could to make Maddie comfortable. Despite her overbearing demands and roller coaster emotions, which were apparently par for the course according to Danny, Jake was the happiest he'd been in a long time. There was no real drama, no drop-down, drag-out fights, and no issues with the baby. Maddie wasn't gaining weight like the doctor would've liked, but other than that, she and the baby were healthy.

Until they weren't.

Jake was clearing out the extra bedroom in preparations for a nursery. It was a small space and they'd probably have to move eventually. For the time being, it was a perfect place to store a crib, changing table, and all the other stuff that came along with having a child.

"Maddie. Maddie! Come in here a second."

Madison walked in the bedroom with weary eyes and a pale complexion.

He crossed the room to the doorway quickly with concern in his eyes. "What's wrong?"

"Nothing. I'm just tired. I'm still throwing up a little. I'll be okay. What did you want?"

"You sure?"

"Yes, Jake. I said I was fine. What did you want?"

Not entirely satisfied with her answer, he began, "I was looking at the room and wondering if we need to paint it now or wait until we find out what we're having? Some people paint it yellow or something and then put in some blue or pink when they find out what the sex is."

"I don't care, Jake. You wanna paint it yellow, paint it yellow. I don't really care right now."

"Maybe we should talk about it later when you're feeling better."

"What's there to talk about? You wanna paint the freaking room, then paint it, for God's sake. I don't care."

He knew something was definitely wrong. "Why don't you go lie down? You don't look too good. I'll call the doctor."

Temper flashed in her eyes. "Of course, I don't look good, Jake. I have a thing growing inside me. I'm getting fatter by the day, and all you can talk about is a fucking paint color. God. I never should have agreed to have this baby."

The bottom fell out of Jake's stomach. "Don't say that, Madison. This baby is a good thing for us. Can't you see we've been better for it? Don't say things like that, Maddie. Please, let me help you. Just lie down and I'll get you some water."

He brushed quickly past her on the way to the kitchen. When he returned with a glass of water he saw she was standing by the window. The setting sun was streaming through the glass and encasing her in a glow that made his knees weak. Her blonde hair was set off by the green sundress she was wearing. Her thin arms and shoulders made her look so fragile.

"You are so beautiful."

She turned and smiled. It was then he noticed her legs were bleeding.

"Madison, what's that? Did you cut yourself?"

"No. What are you talking about?" As she said it, she grabbed her stomach and fell to her knees. "Oh my God, Jake. It hurts. Oh my God."

Dropping the glass to the floor he rushed over to her. "What hurts? Madison, what's wrong?"

"The baby. It hurts."

The moan that escaped her lips weakened him. He lifted her up into his arms and rushed her to the car. Flipping open his cell phone, he called the doctor.

"Dr. Garmen? It's Jake. Maddie's bleeding. I'm taking her to the hospital. Please meet us there. I don't know what's wrong. God, she's bleeding."

"Calm down Jake. Just get to the hospital. I'll meet you there. Did she fall? Did anything unusual happen?"

"No. No. She was complaining she didn't feel well. We argued a minute over paint colors and when I brought her a glass of water, there was blood."

"Okay, Jake. Just get there. Be careful and I'll see you in a bit. I'm leaving now to meet you."

Without a goodbye, Jake snapped the phone shut and sped to the hospital. He drove like a maniac with Madison in the seat next to him clutching her stomach and moaning in pain.

Why can't anything be normal? Why is it always something? He quickly shoved the thoughts from his head and focused on not crashing the truck on the way.

He pulled right up to the emergency room doors, ran inside, and yelled for help. "My girlfriend's in the car. She's pregnant and bleeding. I need help."

An orderly grabbed a wheelchair and raced outside with Jake. When they got to the car, Maddie was crying and clutching her stomach. "Jake. What's happening? The baby. What's happening?"

"I don't know, sweetie. Let's just get inside so the doctor can take a look. Everything's gonna be fine."

"You don't know that."

"I do know that. Just hang on, Maddie."

Jake gingerly lifted her from the truck and placed her in the wheelchair. By then Dr. Garmen was outside with a nurse. They rushed inside as the doctor tried to figure out what was going on.

"Maddie. It's Dr. Garmen. Where's the pain?"

"My stomach. It hurts so much."

"Okay. I know it does. Did you fall today?"

"No."

"Did you hit your stomach on anything?"

"No."

"When did the pain start?"

"Last night when I went to bed."

Jake's eyes were wide. "Last night? Why didn't you tell me?"

The doctor looked sharply at Jake. "That isn't important right now. Madison, I'm gonna take a look as soon as we get you to the bed. Okay?"

Ashen, she responded weakly, "All right."

For an hour, the doctor and a team of nurses worked on Maddie. The bleeding eventually stopped and she was finally able to get some sleep. Dr. Garmen pulled Jake into the hall.

"We're gonna admit her for observation and detox."

"Detox?"

"Yeah. The process is rough for anyone, especially a pregnant woman. Did you know she was using?"

Baffled, Jake sank down onto a chair and put his head in his hands. "Detox? Using? What do you mean? What was she taking?"

"So you didn't know."

"What the hell? Of course, I didn't know."

"Her blood showed traces of cocaine."

"Cocaine? What? Are you fucking kidding me?"

Tears streamed down Jake's face. Dr. Garmen knelt down in front of him. "Jake, with her history, we knew it was a possibility she wouldn't stop with the drugs."

"Is the baby okay?"

"It seems as though he is."

Jake snapped his head up. "He?"

"Yup. A boy. We did an ultrasound to check out what was going on. It seems the placenta tore away a bit but for now, the baby is fine. His heart rate is up a little but we'll keep an eye on it. We will monitor both Madison and your son while she's here."

"A boy? I'm having a boy?"

"You are."

"Holy shit. A boy. How could I not have known she was using? Well, of course, I didn't know. I've been so wrapped up with getting everything ready, working overtime to save for when it, I mean when he comes. I just assumed everything was all right."

Dr. Garmen's words were soft. "It isn't your fault, Jake. She hasn't been eating very well either. Her iron is low, her weight is down, and she's depressed."

"Depressed? What the hell does she have to be depressed about? She's having a baby. Isn't that a good thing?"

"It is, for most. Maddie has dealt with depression in the past. She's acted out, she's used drugs, drank in excess. It's just good we caught it now. I'll be expecting her to come in weekly from now on out. I'm going to need you to keep a closer eye on her. If anything seems off, I want you to call me. Anytime. Day or night."

Leaning back in the chair, Jake closed his eyes. A mixture of anger, sadness, and disappointment bubbled inside him. A familiar sense of dread filled him. Balling his hands into fists to keep them from shaking, he looked at the doctor. "Can I see her?"

"Sure. She's asleep now, Jake. Remember. Addiction is a disease. She may not have been able to stop. This might have scared her straight. It might not have. All we can do is be supportive and help her through this. If not for her, for your son."

Sincerity poured from the doctor and Jake was grateful for it. After all the lies and secrecy he needed a dose of honesty. "Thanks doc. I'll remember that." With that he forced himself up from his chair and walked into Madison's room.

He pulled a chair close to her bed. There was nothing he could do but sit and watch and wait for her to wake up. He wasn't sure when she'd be moved out of her ER room or if she'd be awake for it.

Tears filled his eyes as he gently reached over and put his hand on her small but growing belly.

"A boy," he whispered to himself. In spite of today's drama, all he could think about in that moment was he'd get to paint the nursery blue.

‧☙☙‧

Jake's eyes stung from the memory as he stood and walked down the hall. Opening the door to the room he never entered anymore, he was blinded for a moment by the soft blue paint on the walls, the yellow curtains, and the cherry wood crib. In the corner, the rocking chair that had once been his grandmother's sat with a handmade blue and white blanket draped across the arm. A large gray elephant lay on its side in the middle of the floor next to dozens of unopened presents.

Memories of Madison always jolted him, always came out of the blue. But memories of the baby that should have been his twisted his gut. He never knew what triggered any of them, but thoughts of the baby were the hardest of all.

If he was going to get past any of this, he knew he had to open up. He needed to acknowledge the pain in order to heal.

He walked over to the drawer and, with shaky hands, opened it slightly. From inside he retrieved a tiny green hat that he'd picked up. Maddie had loved the color. Funny how one second she was happy and carefree and the next she dissolved into an emotionally-unstable mess. Funny how one second she was here and the next she was gone. As far as he'd come in the past few weeks, Madison still held tight and wouldn't let him go. Until he got the closure he needed, he figured, she'd always be there while he held tight to the memory of a child he'd never had the chance to know. A child whose life was cut short by circumstances beyond anyone's control.

CHAPTER 15

While Jake was reliving the past, Lily was looking toward the future, at least the immediate future. With camera in tow, she drove an hour on a lonely road full of natural beauty, stopping every now and then to snap some pictures. She knew the photographs would be amazing and she'd been meaning to replace those on the walls at her uncle's place with local shots instead of the ones from Connecticut.

After a couple hundred shots, Lily jumped in her Jeep and drove the twenty miles to the next town. It was small and quaint, with tourists and locals mixing seamlessly. Driving through, she noticed a cluster of shops located on what she assumed was the town's main street. She easily found a parking space at the end of the last block, checked her watch, and made her way toward the one store in particular that caught her eye.

The jingle of the opening door caught the attention of the owner as Lily walked in.

"Good morning. Can I help you find something?"

Lifting her sunglasses and resting them on top of her head, Lily smiled. "What kind of store is this? You have so much here."

"Well, some folks call it an antiques store and some call it a pawn shop. Generally, we get items from estate sales and such. Occasionally, I'll purchase something someone brings in. Is there anything in particular you're looking for?"

Lily walked to the front window. "I saw this camera. What is it? A Brownie Box?"

Impressed, the woman walked over to Lily. "You must know your photography."

"I do. I studied it in college. I have a job waiting for me in Atlanta at the end of the summer."

"Well, this here was donated a few months back. It's a little beat up and I'm not sure if it works but you're more than welcome to check it out. Price is one hundred."

"Thanks. I'll think about it. Mind if I take a look around at what else you have?"

"Be my guest. I'll just be in the back if you need anything."

Lily walked through the shop touching and holding everything she could. She loved old relics and knick-knacks. She thought the camera might be a great addition to the apartment she had waiting for her in Georgia.

When the woman walked out from the back, Lily turned. "I'll take the camera."

"Excellent choice. I'll go in the front and grab it for you."

Still looking through the store's treasures, Lily noticed something sticking up behind a pile of boxes.

Pointing, she asked the owner. "What's that?"

Putting on her glasses, the woman placed the camera on the counter and walked over.

"Oh that? It's a guitar. Gibson, I think. Are you interested? Let me check for you."

Sifting through piles of boxes to get to the guitar proved to be a little difficult for the older woman, so Lily took it upon herself to help move them.

Reaching back and grabbing it by the neck, the woman pulled it out. It looked to be in perfect condition, not that Lily knew much about guitars.

"Yes. It's a Gibson. It needs new strings but if you're interested, Walt across the street can put them on for you. He's the local music teacher. The man can play anything and has the voice of an angel. Mind you, he can't hear so good anymore."

"How much?"

"Well, considerin' it needs some strings, I'll sell it to you for, let's say one-fifty."

"For a guitar?"

The chuckle that spit from the woman's lips highlighted her amusement. "Some would say the same thing about your camera."

"I only brought two hundred with me."

"Ah, well. Maybe you can come back next time and get the guitar."

"Yeah. I guess so."

Disappointed, Lily grabbed for her wallet and took out a hundred dollar bill and laid it on the counter. As the woman reached for it, Lily grabbed her wrist.

"Wait." Lily was hit with an idea. She wanted to buy that guitar. Who cared about a silly old camera that would probably just sit on the shelf? "I want the guitar."

"But you said—"

"I know what I said. I'll take the guitar and come back for the camera."

"You sure?"

With a smile on her face, Lily laid another hundred on the counter and replied, "Absolutely."

With the guitar slung across her back, Lily made her way across the street to a gray haired man named Walt who strung up the guitar and, even with a bit of a hearing issue, tuned it beautifully.

Excited by her purchase, she ran to her Jeep and headed back. She had a few more hours until she would meet Jake at the beach and she knew just how she was going to surprise him.

Her foot heavy on the gas, Lily turned up the radio and sang at the top of her lungs. Maybe Georgia didn't look so good after all.

CHAPTER 16

By the time three-thirty hit, Jake had done what he'd always done with his memories, shoved them aside to deal with later. He didn't want anything to ruin the plans he had with Lily. These were, after all, his issues and he didn't need to bring her into them just yet.

As he checked his bag, he mentally went over what he needed. Once he knew he was square, he grabbed his keys and headed out the door. He needed time before she arrived to make everything perfect.

Lily was setting up a blanket on the beach at precisely the time Jake was leaving his house. Her stomach was churning with excitement. Fingers drumming on her knee, she decided to tamp the excitement with a quick swim. Checking to make sure the guitar was wrapped enough to look like a pile of blankets, she undressed down to her suit and dove into the waves.

Washing away the sudden anxiety in the pit of her stomach, Lily thought about the past month. She'd grown closer to Jake than she'd intended. A frown pulled at her mouth when she wondered whether or not they'd crossed into sibling territory. It wouldn't be terrible if that was the relationship they'd developed, but it wasn't what she was looking for, even if she was leaving at the end of the summer.

She shook the thoughts from her mind as she floated on her back. Every now and then she needed to remind herself to deal with life by accepting what it offered daily and not to look too far into the future. If she and Jake were meant to be, then it would happen. If not, she could at least tell herself she had met someone important.

Jake walked over the dune and saw that Lily had already set out a blanket. She was floating in the ocean, her skin sparkling with moisture. Her hair splayed out around her head reminded him of a mermaid. She was beautiful. Not just to look at but, as he'd begun to realize, everything about her was beautiful.

She hadn't noticed him so he quickly walked over to her blanket, dropped his things, stripped off his shirt, kicked off his flip-flops, and ran into the ocean. The water felt amazing. It was warm and clear and relaxing.

As he quietly swam to where she was, he noticed her eyes were closed and she had a look of pure contentment on her face. A look he was beginning to familiarize himself with again.

He quietly ducked his head under the water and swam underneath her. Reaching up he grabbed her leg.

"Oh my God! Holy shit!"

She flailed her arms, kicked her legs, and darted her eyes around for the culprit. When Jake popped up in front of her, she screamed.

He laughed. "You should have seen your face!"

Slapping him on the shoulder, she tried to be angry. "Jesus, Jake. What the hell?"

"Did you think it was a shark?"

"So what if I did? You shouldn't scare people like that. There are real enough things to be scared of in the ocean without you giving me a heart attack, you know."

His voice was teasing and playful. "Aww. Don't be mad. I was just having fun. Besides, no one's seen sharks around here in at least, oh, four or five days."

"Yeah? Well how would you like it if I scared the crap out of you?"

Treading water, Jake stared at her with an amused look on his face. Eyebrow cocked, he replied, "I don't think I scare quite as easily."

As she swam closer to him, Lily's eyes danced mischievously. "Is that so?"

"That's exactly so."

"I bet I could scare you."

"I bet you couldn't."

With one stroke Lily was nose to nose with Jake while he contemplated his words. Despite the coolness of the ocean breeze and comfort of the water, he suddenly felt hot.

She whispered. "Care to wager on that?"

He knew what was coming and she was right, it scared the crap out if him.

Lily leaned in and kissed Jake on the lips, softly at first, then with a bit more purpose. It wasn't until he allowed himself to close his eyes that he felt the healing power of her kiss. All the pain he'd buried, surfaced. He flinched inwardly at the ghosts rushing to the surface. And, as if she knew, Lily's kiss deepened. She pulled all his fear, all his pain, forward. Electricity shot through into her heart. When they finally separated, she stared into the ache that filled his eyes and the tears that threatened to overtake them. By the look on Jake's face, she knew he felt it, too.

The intensity was more than Lily had imagined. Her hand flew to her mouth as Jake pulled back.

His voice quivered. "What was that?"

"I think it was a kiss."

Staring at her with new eyes, Jake smiled. "I think it was more than that."

"I think you're right."

"Should we be doing this? You're leaving at the end of the summer. And I don't know if I—"

Lily placed a finger on his trembling lips. "Shh. It's okay, Jake. We don't have to. It's my fault. I must've misunderstood."

He watched as she tucked a curl behind her ear and replied quietly, "You didn't misunderstand."

She whispered gently, "I'm not her, Jake."

"No. You're not."

"C'mon. Let's get out of the water."

She swam the few yards to shore in long strokes, then she turned to look at him and held out her hand. As if on autopilot, he joined her on the beach.

He grabbed her hand and, before she could lead him to the blanket, jerked her around. He wasn't going to let the past interfere with this moment like it had minutes ago in the water. With his hands tangled in her hair, he returned the kiss. This time, the shock of it didn't hold him back.

His skin sang with excitement, his head threatened to explode, and his stomach tightened into a knot of anticipation. It didn't feel quite as awkward as the first kiss. There was more to it than that. With each touch of her hand, her lips, her tongue, he grew less anxious, less frightened.

Nothing needed to be said as they slowly sank to the sand. Lily matched his intensity with her own. Jake's weight on top of her covered her like a security blanket as they both let go.

Jake pushed her hair away from her face. She smiled as he kissed her forehead, her eyes, and her nose.

"Not so scary, now."

Jake returned the smile as he reached down and untied the strings of her bathing suit. "Nah. Not so scary."

Her hands pulled him towards her. "I'll have to try harder next time."

He lifted her to him. "You do that."

Their eyes locked with an anxious and heightened familiarity for a few seconds. As a small moan escaped her lips, Jake covered her mouth with his.

Neither felt the tide come in. Neither felt the temperature drop as clouds covered the sun. Neither felt the small drops of hesitant summer rain. In those moments, all they knew was each other. No past. No future. Just that moment.

CHAPTER 17

After the rain stopped, Jake walked back to his truck to grab dry blankets, smiling to himself. He changed into the dry clothes he always kept in his truck and tucked and extra T-shirt under his arm. He dropped his head against the window of his car and closed his eyes. He remembered every touch, every kiss, every feeling of the past hour. His heart lifted and opened in a way it never had. He didn't know where any of this was going, but he vowed to himself to hold on to it for as long as he could.

He turned to Lily's Jeep and opened the bag in the backseat looking for the jeans she'd said were inside. When he found them, he saw tucked underneath was a small portfolio of photographs and a letter from a magazine based in Atlanta stating how excited they were that Lily would be joining them in September. Caught up in the moments they shared, the fact that she was leaving had fallen away from him. He wasn't sure if he was enough of a reason for her to stay.

While Jake was at the car, Lily stared at the ocean waves as they rolled in and out. His touch lingered over her like soft feathers. She thought briefly about the fact that her time here wasn't permanent. The thought pierced her before disappearing behind thoughts of Jake.

"I got your jeans," he said, coming up behind her. "I also grabbed one of my shirts for you to wear. It's long sleeved so it should keep you warm enough. And a couple of extra blankets."

"I thought I had you to keep me warm."

She stood as he handed her the clothes. With a grin on her face, she said, "I'd ask you to turn around but I guess that ship has sailed."

She took off her bathing suit and pulled on her jeans, all the while keeping eye contact. He reached over and buttoned them for her as she slipped on his T-shirt.

He kissed her gently. "You keep doing that, you're gonna be the death of me."

Her laugh covered him. "We wouldn't want that, now would we?"

"Probably not. Are you hungry? I brought some sandwiches. Hopefully the short rain didn't ruin them."

"I would love a sandwich. I brought some beer."

She popped the caps off two bottles and handed one to Jake as he passed her a sandwich. They sat comfortably on the dry blanket across from each other, legs crossed. Jake rested his hand on her knee.

"So what'd you do today? You said you had errands."

"What? Oh yeah. Well I wasn't really running errands, per se. I took a drive south along some lonely road and took some pictures for my uncle. His birthday is coming up and I wanted to get some new photos for him to hang up on the wall. The ones there now are shots from Connecticut. I thought he'd like something local."

"Those pictures are amazing. I always wondered about the niece that sent them to him. I've looked at those pictures for years. You have a real talent."

"Thanks. I do mostly landscapes, nature, stuff like that. I got some beautiful shots today, then I kept driving to some small little town about an hour and a half away."

"Did you take pictures there too?"

"A couple but actually I went to a few stores. I saw an amazing camera from the early 1900's that I was gonna buy."

"Did you buy it?"

"Nope. Changed my mind. Bought something else instead."

The twinkle in her eye caught Jake's attention.

"What'd you get?"

She pulled her knees under her and leaned back on her heels. "Well, actually, I bought something for you."

"Me?"

"Yeah. I saw it and thought of you immediately. I'm not sure if you want it or need it, I just wanted you to have it more than anything."

He reached out to clutch her shirt. "Really? You didn't have to buy me anything."

"I know. And that's exactly why I did. Now close your eyes."

"It's here?"

She chuckled as his eyes darted around, looking for the gift. "Yes, now close your eyes."

He did as she asked and she laughed at the goofy grin plastered on his face. She crawled over to the blanket she had set aside now damp with rain, uncovered the guitar, and gently placed it on his lap. "Now, open your eyes."

Shock rang through him as he saw what she had done. "You bought this?"

"Do you like it?"

He was quiet as he ran his hands over the wood. His smile disappeared and she wasn't sure if she'd done the right thing. It wasn't her place to force something on him that he'd obviously given up.

She cast her eyes down in embarrassment. "That's okay if you don't like it. I just thought, well, it doesn't matter what I thought."

As she reached to take the guitar from his lap, he placed his hand on hers. She didn't lift her head as he slowly pulled the strap around his neck. The guitar felt comfortable and safe in his hands. He'd forgotten the escape that music brought him, the energy it gave him.

"Lily."

"Jake, you don't have to. I know it's not my place—"

"Lily, look at me," he interrupted and she finally lifted her gaze to meet his. "No one has ever bought me anything like this."

"But you don't play anymore."

"I haven't had a reason to play in a long time. Maybe it's time I tried again."

"Really? You really like it?"

"I love it. Thank you."

"I wasn't sure. I mean, you and I are, I mean we're just…"

He finished her sentence. "Friends?"

"Yeah. I guess so."

He pulled the guitar strap off his neck and leaned toward her. "I kinda thought, after what just happened, we were more than that. At least I was hoping we were."

Shifting her body closer to his, she responded, "I'd like to be."

"Good."

His fingers outlined her jaw and his eyes fell towards her mouth.

She planted her hands on the blanket as she moved to her knees. As he fell slowly to his back, she covered his body with hers.

She softly kissed his eyelids, ran her tongue along his jaw, before settling on his lips. His eyes locked on hers and when their lips met, they both felt everything around them disappear. When they each slowly pulled away, the want they'd felt for the other morphed into need.

Fingers tightly gripped her thighs as he pulled her knees to either side of him. Straddling him, she sat up and slowly pulled off her shirt just as the sun was setting behind her.

He moved his hands up her body. She took them in hers, interlocking her fingers in his, and leaned forward to place them on either side of his head.

Her whisper was almost imperceptible. "No touching. Not yet."

She released his hands, then her fingers played with the buttons on his shirt as she lowered her mouth to kiss every inch of skin she uncovered.

He tensed as she littered his chest and stomach with soft kisses before stopping at the top of his pants. She ran her tongue along his waistband, softly biting his hipbone, while working the button free.

Jakes hands flew to her shoulders and he pulled her to his face, cupping his hands around her cheeks.

She giggled with naughty anticipation. "I said no touching."

"I know what you said."

He dropped his hands to her jeans, easily opened them, and began to coax them below her hips.

Half-heartedly attempting to pry his hands from her, she laughed. "You don't follow directions so well. You're supposed to wait for me to give the okay."

Jake shifted his weight so they rolled over with him on top of her.

On the brink of losing control, he buried his face in her neck and gently cupped her breasts in his hands. "I don't want to wait."

Her body responded to his tongue on her stomach. When his hands finally pulled her jeans away, he tossed them to the side and settled himself between her legs.

She reached down and slipped his pants over his rear and he kicked them off. She shifted to allow him inside and it was his turn to smile wickedly.

"Oh no. Now it's your turn to wait."

She lost control as he explored her body with his fingers. Her head exploded with pleasure as his mouth took over. And just as she thought she'd die from his touch, he crushed his mouth over hers and plunged inside her. The sun winked away, promising a new beginning.

CHAPTER 18

In the morning, Jake awoke first, tangled under the warmth of her body. Contentment washed over him as he studied her face, soft with sleep. He felt alive and free and finally awake.

He'd wondered if God had gone away or if he was just losing his mind, and he'd begged for a sign that he'd be able to feel again. For every day of sun and warmth, he'd felt at least two of sadness. Just as he became comfortable with the thought that hell would have to freeze over before he'd have feelings again, Lily came into his life. Full of energy and spirit, and without an ounce of pretension, she'd slowly taken over the void left in his heart.

Then again, where he came from, a man didn't become a fool for love after only one night. But this wasn't just sex. He truly felt the closeness they shared. As he lay on the beach with her hair in his face, with locks of curls swimming in the light breeze, he thought of her plans to move down to Georgia and wondered if she'd take over the world. And if he'd ever feel this good again.

He shifted, careful not to wake her, and reached for his pants. Standing, he pulled them up before bending to reach for the guitar. Holding it out in front of him, he realized the gift was an invitation to move forward. But he knew he couldn't, not without letting Lily all the way in. Not without telling her everything.

Lily woke to the sound of Jake strumming the guitar. The melody was soft and beautiful. She lay there for a few minutes with her eyes closed, allowing the music to fill her.

When she finally sat up, holding the blanket to cover herself, she saw him deep in thought with his eyes closed and a pencil between his teeth. After a moment, he took the pencil from his mouth and leaned down to scribble on a pad of paper.

"Whatcha writing?"

He looked up and smiled. "Good morning. Something just came to me, and I wanted to write it down. I didn't have anything to write with so I took this out of your car. I hope that's okay."

"Of course," she said as he shifted over to kiss her. "Can I hear more?"

He grinned sheepishly. "Sure. If you want."

"I want." She lay back down on the blanket and listened to him coax out the melody.

"No words?"

"Some. But I have to organize them first. For now, I just have the tune in my head."

After a few more minutes of playing, Jake put the guitar down and lay on his stomach next to her.

She turned to look at him. "What's the last song you played?"

His voice suddenly hoarse, he replied, "It was a lullaby."

"Did you write it?"

"I did."

"I'm sorry."

Wrapping her hair around his fingers, he said, "No need for you to be sorry for anything. Do you have any plans today?"

Stretching, she smiled and he wondered what he did to deserve her.

"Not really," she said. "I was thinking about taking some more pictures. Why? Do you have any plans?"

"Well, I did tell Mr. Olsen that I'd stop by the docks later. He wanted me to stock one of the boats for tomorrow. The guys are going out for a twelve-hour run and need to be ready to go by four in the morning. But I was thinking after, maybe we could do something."

"What did you have in mind?"

"Maybe we could run over to Bill's and get something to eat. Maybe rent a movie or something. I gotta be at work early tomorrow so I have to get to sleep early."

"Poor baby needs his sleep. What time do you have to be there today?"

Looking at his watch, he frowned. "In about an hour."

"An hour doesn't give us much time."

A wry smile played on his lips. "Much time for what?"

"Breakfast! I'm starving."

They laughed easily. He reached over and threw her his T-shirt and her jeans.

"Well, get up then. I have just the place."

She dressed quickly as he grabbed the blankets and bags and threw them in the bed of his truck.

Within an hour, Lily was pulling her Jeep into her uncle's driveway, and Jake was pulling into the lot at work. Danny pulled in after him.

"What are you doing here?"

Danny responded, "I'm loading the boat. What are you doing here?"

"The same. I guess Olsen really needs it done today."

"What's with that look on your face?"

Jake pulled together his best poker face. "What look?"

As Danny pointed at Jake, he laughed. "You were smiling."

"No I wasn't."

"You were! Holy crap! Call the newspapers. Jake woke up happy today."

"Don't be an ass, Danny. I can't win. You bust my balls for smiling, you bust my balls for not. Geez. Give me a break."

"Relax. I was only—Wait a minute. Wait a minute. Stop the presses."

"What?"

Clapping his hands together, Danny's eyes danced with excitement as he wiggled his eyebrows. "You got lucky."

Jake pushed his brother out of his way and walked toward the docks as he said, "Get out of here."

"No. No. You did. Look at you! You can't stop with the teeth. I haven't seen you look like that in forever!"

"Shut up, Danny."

"Was it that girl Lily?"

"What? No. Yes. Maybe. Just leave it."

"No wonder Billy wanted you to stay away from her. Who woulda thought it'd take Jake a whole month to get a girl in bed. You're losing your touch man."

Jake stopped walking. "Stop. It isn't like that okay. I wasn't trying to, it just happened. She's different."

"Dad was right."

"Dad was right about what?"

"You and her. He said he knew something was up. I told him he was wrong but he knew. He said she'd save you."

"Save me? What the hell are you taking about? And besides, she's leaving at the end of August to go to Atlanta. She isn't staying. I'm just taking this for what it is right now."

"Yeah? Then why did Billy tell Dad she'd stay if she had a reason to?"

Jake's heart tripped up at Danny's words. It was hard enough to understand why a sinner like him had an angel like her even give him another glance. There were times, in the past, that he'd felt evil, but whenever he was around her, he'd felt redemption. He doubted for a second that he would be the reason she'd stay, but as the day went on, he grew more hopeful that he'd be enough.

Later that night, as he sat on the couch with her head in his lap, he said, "I got something for you today."

"You did? What is it?"

"Well, it's not much but I think you should have it."

She smiled as he echoed her own words and watched as he walked to the back of the house. When he returned his hands were behind his back and she was sitting up.

"Now close your eyes." He laughed as she grimaced and did what he asked. "Hold out your hands."

He laid his gift in her open palms and when she opened her eyes, confusion plagued her. To Jake, it was the most amazing reaction ever.

She held up his gift between two fingers. "A toothbrush?"

"Yup. You like it? It's pink."

"I can see that. A toothbrush? Really, Jake. You might need to take a class on Gift Giving 101."

He'd known that was going to be her reaction and his smile broadened.

"You see I got you a pink one because, well, mine is blue and in the morning I wouldn't want to confuse the two."

"In the morning?" Her head tilted in a way that made Jake smile.

"Well, yeah. I figured that maybe, if you wanted to stay here, tonight, you might be happy if you had one of those."

"You're asking me to sleep *here* tonight?"

"Yeah. Tonight, tomorrow night. Anytime you want. I mean, you don't have to. This is a just-in-case gift."

Her eyes wide, he saw the confusion slip away into something else.

"You know Jake, you're pretty amazing. I happily accept this toothbrush. Shall I go put it in the bathroom?"

"Sure."

He knew as she skipped away that he was losing himself again. But this time, he was losing himself in happiness without any fear to tether himself to.

CHAPTER 19

A week later, Lily was helping Jake de-clutter his house. It was neat enough at first glance but when she saw the piles of stuff stacked in his closets and basement, she convinced him it was time to clean house.

"How can one person have so much stuff?" she inquired one rainy afternoon.

"I don't know. I'm kind of like my mom was. I don't throw much away."

"Well, my friend," Lily said with her hands on her hips. "I think it's time to let go of some of this. Reorganize, you know? Figure out what you want to keep and figure out what you want to throw away."

Jake looked up from his baseball game. "Yeah. I guess so."

"You guess so?" Lily walked over and straddled his lap, interrupting his focus on the game. "In seventy years, someone is gonna come in here and find you lying in a pile of stuff. C'mon. Let's fix it. You fixed the outside of the house, now let's give the inside the TLC it needs. And once we get it all done, we can paint your bedroom like you wanted to do."

It was hard to deny her logic. Jake was starting fresh with everything else. What could it hurt? Besides, maybe he'd be able to get organized enough to do some updating in there.

He reached his hands around her hips and squeezed her rear. "All right."

She clapped. "That's the spirit! Let's grab some garbage bags. Where do you want to start?"

"The basement?"

She leaned forward to give him a quick kiss before jumping up and pulling him up with her. "Excellent choice!"

The two walked down stairs, armed with garbage bags and a plan. Two piles, Lily had explained—stuff to keep and stuff to throw out.

In four hours, though they'd only organized half of the basement, Jake was impressed. The number of garbage bags with things he'd thrown away had cleared out more than he thought.

"See, Jake? All you have to do is throw one or two bags out a day and before you know it, your house will be clutter free."

"I gotta say I wasn't sure I'd be able to get rid of so much stuff."

"Well, you don't get rid of things with memories attached like pictures, trophies, and such. You just have to get rid of the junk. Like this flannel shirt. It's full of holes." She poked her finger through a hole in the sleeve. "Do you really need to keep it? When's the last time you wore it?"

"I don't know. High school?"

"Right. You don't need it. Toss it." She threw it, hitting him in the chest.

"But I like this shirt."

"Really?"

With her hands playfully placed on her hips, she looked as if she meant business. With a salute, he tossed the shirt in the throw away pile. "Yes, ma'am."

Throwing all this stuff away was cathartic for Jake. He knew it all needed to go, but he'd never been able to figure out how to move past it. He'd held onto the past for so long, letting it go gave him a new sense of freedom.

"And this. Your brother or sister-in-law must've left this here. Wanna toss it? I don't think they need it anymore what with their kids too old for it now."

He glanced at what she was holding up. It was a blue baby rattle. He knew immediately it hadn't belonged to his nephews. It hadn't been Danny or Meg who left it here.

Jake forced the bile in his throat back down to his stomach and held on tight to the present. He couldn't let Maddie in here, not now. He needed to be alone for that. And he knew she'd come, no matter how hard he tried to keep her out. The blood drained from his face and sweat formed on his brow. Memories of her always made him feel claustrophobic.

"Jake?" Concern filled Lily's voice.

"Ah, yeah. Keep it. I'll give it to them later. Maybe they'd want it for, you know, memories."

Lily noticed the strain in his voice and the paleness of his face but she didn't mention it. She figured he'd tell her when the time was right, when he needed to get it out. For now, she smiled and put it in the "keep" pile. She was savvy enough to know he needed to be alone, and as much as it pained her to admit it, there were some demons he had to face on his own.

She looked at her watch. "All right. Well, I think that's enough for today."

He nodded his head in agreement as he walked over and picked up the rattle.

"Jake, I don't know what I'm supposed to do here."

He lowered himself to the floor and leaned against the wall, turning the rattle over and over in his hands. "Stay."

Lily walked over, sadness in her heart at his obvious suffering, and witnessed, for the first time, Jake fall into the past.

As she sat down next to him and pulled his head onto her breast, she squeezed his hand, kissed his cheek, and worried about him as he unraveled a silent memory...

❦❦❦

"Surprise!" Everyone in the bar yelled as Jake walked Madison into Billy's place. It was decorated with storks, blue balloons, and gifts wrapped in baby boy paper. She was due in eight weeks and they had been working hard transforming the second bedroom into a nursery. But they still had nothing to fill it with. The shower was Meg's idea and by the look on Maddie's face, it was perfect.

"Oh my gosh, everyone! I had no idea!"

"Glad you like it." Meg walked up and hugged her sister. "How are you feeling?"

"I feel great. My belly's getting big and other than growing out of my pants, I'm terrific."

"Let's get you something to drink."

"Okay. Thanks."

Jake walked Maddie around the room as they thanked everyone for the wonderful surprise. She was glowing. Her smile stretched from ear to ear and she looked calm and happy. He was happy, too. After all the stress and garbage they'd been through, they were going to have a family, and a little boy, at that. Everything was almost perfect. There was one thing he still wanted to do and that surprise would have to wait until right before they cut the cake.

They dined on a lunch of finger sandwiches and small bite-sized appetizers before opening gifts. Everyone was so generous. The couple now had all they needed to complete the nursery, including a crib. Jake didn't even mind that he'd probably spend the next two months putting everything together. As Mrs. Olsen declared it was time for everyone to have some cake, Jake stood up.

"Before you do that Mrs. Olsen, I have a gift for Maddie."

Of course, all the women in the room swooned with excitement at the gesture as Jake faced the woman bearing his child.

"Madison Olsen. What can I say? We've traveled a bumpy road to get where we are today and I couldn't be happier. You're an amazing woman and I am proud to say you're having my child. I'd like to give you this gift. Something for both you and our baby boy."

He held out a small rectangular package wrapped in light blue with a white bow. She took it gently from his hand and began to open it. When she pulled the lid from the box, she looked inside and a shade of disappointment passed quickly across her face. Jake smiled despite it. Nestled inside was a small blue baby rattle.

"It's a rattle," she said with confusion.

"I thought the baby would need a rattle to play with. Take it out. Give it a shake."

Maddie lifted the toy from its box. A blue ribbon was attached to it, and attached to the ribbon was a sparkly diamond engagement ring. When she looked up with tears in her eyes, Jake was kneeling in front of her.

"Maddie, I know it's a little late to be asking this, considering we already have a baby on the way, but would you do me the honor of becoming my wife?"

There wasn't a dry eye in Billy's place that afternoon as Madison jumped up and said "yes."

✥✥✥

When Jake shook himself free of that day, he was crying. He allowed the memory to overtake him and didn't fight it as he had before. He let the sadness and anger wash through him as Lily held him tight—let himself cry and feel something other than emptiness.

When he fell asleep in her lap with a small blue baby rattle clutched in his hands, Lily took all the pain he'd released and allowed it to wash over her. Only when he was asleep did she cry for him.

Jake opened his eyes. The moon was keeping watch and Lily was asleep with the wall at her back, dried tears on her face. He quietly tucked the rattle in his pocket and lifted

Lily from the floor. She barely stirred as he walked up the stairs into his bedroom and laid her down on his bed, kissed her head, and covered her with a blanket. Sitting on his bed, he turned the rattle over and over again in his hands, much like he'd turned that memory over and over in his mind. It was time to let go of the past, he knew, but he just couldn't bring himself to release that one. Not yet, anyway. So he tucked the rattle away at the bottom of a drawer and closed it. It was something he'd have to revisit—later.

CHAPTER 20

At the same time Jake was tucking away a memory, Lily quietly lay in his bed, careful not to let him know she was awake. She hadn't wanted to disturb him, remembering the look on his face when he saw the baby rattle in her hand. She'd been replaying the scene over and over in her mind. This wasn't a part of him he was ready to share with her. Though he'd slowly begun to open up, she knew there were some big memories he kept for himself—and this was one of them.

She'd learned early on not to push him. He'd let her in on his own time and open up he did. The things he'd told her, the pain he allowed to trickle out and evaporate, made her sad. She had yet to hear one good memory, one sliver of why he'd held onto someone like that. The puzzle pieces didn't always fit.

Earlier, the look on his face and the pain in his voice let her know she was one step closer to figuring out why Jake was the way he was. It was true, she mused, that much of the emptiness that filled his eyes had slowly become replaced with life but there were still shadows left.

She wasn't sure if she'd ever know the whole story but she now knew a baby had been a part of it. Where was the baby now? Where was Madison? When did she leave? Lily was curious by nature and it was hard for her to refrain from digging deeper. But while she respected Jake's privacy and his need to heal at his own pace, she couldn't move forward with a man trapped in the past.

Her feelings for Jake were complicated, even for her. She wasn't one to fall in love. She'd had a few boyfriends over the years but none of them long term. She'd never felt the spark, the connection, that she needed to for anyone. She was too much of a free spirit, too focused on living in the now, to be much use to anyone looking toward the future. She wasn't one to settle. Her affair with Jake, for the first time, had her looking towards a future. Without her consent, without her knowing, she'd begun to fall in love with him. Despite herself, she started to plan for the future.

In the short time they'd known each other, they'd become more than friends, more than lovers. Their relationship was both comforting and terrifying. Because of this, she contemplated heading for Atlanta early. It was only the middle of July but she wasn't sure she could handle another six weeks of coaxing the past out of Jake just so he could look to the future. It hadn't started out that way. In the beginning, he was just a lost soul she'd wanted to befriend. But over the past month and a half, he'd become more to her. Her uncle saw it, she knew, but he'd refrained from talking about it. Maybe he'd hoped, like others did, that she would be the one to save Jake. Even his father and brother had become tentatively hopeful that Jake was finally breaking free from Madison.

She couldn't leave. She couldn't handle it and she knew Jake couldn't. Even before the beginning of their romantic relationship, the two had become inseparable. Many nights were spent lying in the grass, staring at the stars. Mornings were spent running and swimming in the ocean. She'd begun spending nights at his house. They'd made love. She'd fallen in love and she was sure he had, too. She'd seen the Jake that people wanted him to be again.

Thoughts like these were foreign to Lily. She'd never really met anyone like Jake before. She'd never met anyone she'd wanted to fight for. But how could she fight against a memory?

She shook the thoughts from her head and closed her eyes. She felt him slide into bed and wrap his arms around her as he settled in behind her. She hoped he'd open up to her, but she wasn't going to allow him to wallow. She had a feeling this particular memory would close him off from embracing the beginning of what they were becoming.

By six-thirty Lily woke to the sound of Jake shuffling around in the kitchen. She wasn't sure if she should mention what happened yesterday. She played in her head what she was going to say but nothing sounded right. She didn't want to scare him off, push him away, or make him think she'd given up on him.

The first thing she noticed when she walked into the kitchen was Jake staring out the window with his shoulders slumped.

"Jake?"

When he turned, she saw the lost look in his eyes return. She moved to stand in front of him and grabbed both of his hands with hers.

Despair filled the room even as promise circled them. He sighed and dropped his head.

"Jake it's okay. It's me. What do you want to tell me?"

His eyes held hers. When they met, he hadn't been planning on doing this—telling her any of this. "Well, before you came, and even after, I'd been holding onto ghosts. For the first time in two years, those ghosts haven't haunted me like they did. Because of you, I see that I might be able to get past them, but I can't do that without telling you everything."

Lily held his hands tighter, knowing that whatever he was about to say would either break the wall he still kept or rebuild it higher and stronger.

He blew out a breath and began with what she already knew. "Her name was Madison. She left two years ago."

He didn't tell her everything, that day but he told her enough to find himself again for a few hours. Little by little, over the next few weeks, Jake told Lily more about Madison. How they first met and the day he first decided she really might have changed. Lily was patient with him. She could feel his uneasiness and never once pushed for him to let it all out. So she waited, day by day, as each piece of the puzzle was laid into place.

Like photographs from an album, he'd walked her through his agony. She learned of a man tormented by a woman who didn't deserve him. She learned of his faults and his recklessness. She learned of Madison's selfishness. Lily longed to pull the pain from him. Some days she would cry with him and others she just held him as he relived the past for her.

Eventually, every memory that haunted him was set free. It wasn't until he finally told her about the baby that he choked up. Lily didn't interrupt once. She let him keep talking until he was too exhausted to continue. By the time the story was done, tears were streaming down her face. The pain he felt was obvious and raw. To be hurt like that was incomprehensible to Lily. To be the one to cause the pain was unforgivable.

She knew he had one more story to tell. He hadn't yet confided the hows or whys of Madison's departure or the fate of his child. If the ghosts he'd introduced her to were any indication, she was sure this would be the biggest revelation of all, and she'd have to brace herself for the fall.

None of this was something Lily had asked for, but it was something she accepted. With each day they grew closer, stronger. And with each day the end of August loomed larger, though Atlanta retreated farther away.

CHAPTER 21

By the time the beginning of August came around, John decided to give Jake a second chance on the boat. Though content to work the docks, Jake was happy for the opportunity given him.

"I appreciate you giving me another chance on the boat, Mr. Olsen. I won't let you down."

Placing his hand on Jake's shoulder, John forced himself to forget the past. It wouldn't do anyone any good. "I know you won't, Jake. This chance was a long time coming. Truth be told, I should have given it to you long ago."

Jake looked him in the eye, without the shame that had plagued him since the job was taken away. "No. You did the right thing. I wasn't able to hold on to that responsibility. I needed to be able to move out of the past. For the first time since Madison left, I feel like I am able to. Somehow, this summer, I've been able to find some sort of closure."

Pride swelled inside and a small piece of the burden John had carried around lifted from his shoulders. He hadn't heard Jake utter his daughter's name in two years. He couldn't remember the last time Jake allowed anyone to talk about her, to mention her, without falling apart. Maybe it was time they all took Jake's lead and pushed forward.

"We all need closure. Every time I think about what happened and I begin to go down the path of what-ifs, I remember, out of all of us, you are the one who has the most reasons to question."

"It will come, Mr. Olsen. I never thought it would come for me but it has. I have Lily to thank for that."

John knew Lily was the reason for Jake's turn around. The whole town knew the story and had waited for Jake to open his eyes. It was beginning to happen. After all the prayers and sadness, Jake was letting go.

"Well, you'll start Monday. Finish out the week on the docks and brush up on what you need to. How about you come by this weekend? Sunday, Mrs. Olsen and I are having a little barbeque. Nothing fancy, just winding down the summer. Your brother's coming with Megan and the boys, and I'll invite your dad. Bring Lily along, too, if you want."

Jake smiled. "Sure, Mr. Olsen. I think it'd be fun. I'll call Lily to make sure she has the day off."

While he watched Mr. Olsen walk off the docks, Jake flipped open his cell phone and called her.

"Good morning, handsome."

Lily's husky morning voice was the only pick me up he needed. Since he'd begun to open up to her, they'd gotten closer than he'd thought possible.

"Good morning, beautiful. What are you doing on Sunday?"

"Lunch shift. Why? What's up?"

"Well, John Olsen invited us over for a barbeque. Nothing fancy. But I was wondering if you'd like to go."

"Sure. I get off at three. Can I meet you over there?"

"Yeah. No problem. I'll tell him we'll be there."

"Cool. Should I bring something?"

"I don't think so. I'll ask. Guess what?"

"What?"

"Mr. Olsen is putting me back on the boat."

Lily knew how much it meant to Jake and she shared his excitement. "That's great! I'm so happy for you."

"I start Monday. I have a few things to clean up on the docks before I'm ocean bound. You coming over later? Maybe we could celebrate."

"Don't I always?"

"Okay then. See ya later."

"Bye, sweetie. Have a good day at work."

When she clicked off, he was overcome with feelings of contentment. This is exactly how a relationship was supposed to be. It only took him twenty-eight years to figure it out.

Lily disconnected, smiling and still holding her phone in her hand. But the smile disappeared from her face as she checked her watch. She had two more minutes before she'd have an answer she wasn't sure she wanted.

Atlanta loomed over her head. She had to make a decision soon. Long distance relationships didn't seem to work out for anyone she knew. Now, with Jake getting his job back on the fishing boat, she couldn't ask him to leave.

He would if she asked. But it wasn't fair to ask him to give up his life for her. While she'd always been happy to move on and had always accepted the challenges of doing so, he wasn't built that way. He'd never left the comfort of his hometown, even when parts of it threatened to choke the life from him. He was a long-hauler. And Lily had never before been comfortable with the idea of remaining in one place too long—until now.

She thought of what her life would be if she stayed. Would she and Jake be as happy down the road as they were now? Would she resent him for her missed opportunities? Could she live her life in such a small town?

That's the problem of planning for the future. There were no answers for anything. Just what-ifs. Definitely foreign territory. But, then again, wasn't the lack of concrete answers the same as living day to day?

Blowing out a long, unsteady breath, Lily checked her watch again. It was time. She walked into the bathroom and checked the stick she'd placed on the sink. She was only a few days late but she needed to know. When she saw the results, tears immediately began falling down her cheeks. With shaky hands, she picked it up and stared until her vision went hazy. Slowly, she backed up against the wall and sank to the floor, the pregnancy test still in her hand. Dizzy, her head wouldn't allow her to decide if she was happy or not. It wouldn't let her think about anything other than the answer presented to her. Her head dropped to her chest as she tried to control her breathing. *How could this have happened?* Jake had always used a condom. There was that one time that it broken, but he'd pulled out immediately. Could that have been enough for her to get pregnant? Oh, God, what was she going to do now? What did she want to do?

She closed her eyes and focused on every second she'd spent with Jake. Every word that had been said, every touch that lingered over her body, and she knew how she felt about all of that. What was going on in this bathroom, however, she still needed to figure out.

She grabbed her camera and headed for the door. If she focused through the lens, maybe she'd clear out enough space to gauge her feelings about this.

Jumping in her Jeep, she drove down the main road and out of town. She needed to escape, if only for a little while. She'd sort all this other stuff out later. With dread in the pit of her stomach, she continued to allow the tears to fall until she reached her destination.

About an hour outside of town, Lily pulled over to the side of the road. The location was familiar. This is where she'd stopped the day she'd bought Jake the guitar. Pulling her keys out of the ignition and checking her camera, she got out and began walking through the open field. Just on the other side was a path that led into the woods. She hadn't had time to explore it last time and figured now was as good a time as any.

As she walked, she stopped every now and then to photograph random flowers, trees, and leaves. It wasn't until she entered a clearing about a mile in that she saw what she came for.

In the middle of the clearing was a farmhouse. It was old, abandoned, and spectacularly beautiful. Though the paint was weathered and peeling and the shutters were falling off the windows, the house made Lily feel at home.

With her lens, she wanted to capture all it used to be. In her mind she saw mothers and daughters and fathers and sons. She saw births and happiness, deaths and mourning. Through her lens, she saw life.

As if walking through time, she saw what could be by imagining what once was. Every stone on the path, every board on the porch, and every tree that stood watch told her a story. It wasn't with pen a paper that she would retell it. It was with film and a lens.

She saw the promise of a future in the peeling paint. She saw the love that would be tangible in the overgrown gardens. As she walked around into the backyard, she saw the life that could be hers etched into the headstones of the family that had been buried there.

As she had hoped, Lily lost herself in her muse. For hours, she explored and discovered. And with each click of her camera, she grew more comfortable with what was to come. It wasn't until the sun began to set that she bid farewell to the house that had given her a reason to plan for the future.

CHAPTER 22

When Lily pulled into Jake's driveway, she had resolved to revisit her thoughts tomorrow. She needed a break from all the thinking. She didn't want to be the downer to Jake's celebration. And she needed to forget herself for tonight.

Walking into Jake's house, she stepped out of her shoes and placed her camera on the table. She could hear him singing in the shower as she tiptoed down the hallway. Carefully nudging the door open, she entered the steamy bathroom and listened. It wasn't a song she was familiar with. She wondered if it was the one Jake had been secretly writing over the past few weeks. Whatever it was, it was beautiful, heartfelt, and perfect.

Pulling her tank over her head and slipping off of her shorts, she pulled back the shower curtain just enough to step inside. He was so lost in whatever song he was singing, he didn't notice her until she softly kissed his chest.

"What the—Hey, you."

Wrapping her arms around his neck, Lily playfully licked his shoulder. "Hey, yourself."

"I wasn't expecting you for another hour."

"I know. I just needed to see you."

Massaging soap onto her back, he knew exactly what she was feeling. He'd just been thinking the same thing.

"What was that song you were just singing? Shampoo, please."

He reached up, grabbed the shampoo off the shelf, and handed it to her. "Oh, just something I've been working on. It's almost ready."

She dropped her hands to her sides as he took over washing her hair. This is what she needed most. She needed to wash away all the fear and indecision of the day and just be. With Jake, she'd always been able to be herself and that's how she wanted it to stay.

While she rinsed the shampoo from her hair, she felt his hands on her as he washed her body. With tiny movements and soft touches, he filled her stomach with anticipation. His hands moved down her arms to her stomach. She drew in a sharp breath as he massaged her, bringing her to the edge. He guided her to the wall of the shower lifting her leg to his waist. Holding onto him, she closed her eyes as he entered and filled her with promise and love. Breath heavy, she buried her face in his neck and her nails in his back. This time, it was her turn to clear her mind of what plagued her as he brought her to the top of the mountain and she leapt off the edge.

CHAPTER 23

On Saturday, Jake wanted to take a drive. He decided it was time to give Lily the last piece of the puzzle, and he didn't have much time before she left for Atlanta. They hadn't talked much about her leaving. She seemed to be acting a little funny the past few days, and he figured if he finally cleared the air, she'd know exactly how much she was saving him.

"Where are we going?"

"I need to tell you the last of it. I need to finish the story about Madison and the baby."

Anxiety twisted in her gut. She couldn't figure how to tell him what was going on with her and this certainly wasn't the day to do it. She had no idea where they were going, but she knew he was going to talk about his son. Her issues could wait.

They drove in silence. She could tell Jake was running things over in his head. For the time being, she was content with taking in the morning. The sun was shining and the pavement was still wet with rain from the night before.

Humidity had not yet taken over and Lily rolled down the window to breathe in the salty air. She closed her eyes and allowed her mind to empty of everything that weighed heavily on it. It wasn't until she heard the crunch of gravel that she dared open them. When she realized Jake had pulled into the cemetery, her eyes immediately filled with tears and her hand flew to his.

"Jake?"

"It's okay, Lily. It's been a long time coming. I need to get this off my chest. I need you to help me."

He reached into the bed of his truck and produced a simple bouquet of yellow daisies. He held her hand as they walked through the gravestones, to the last row. All the way at the end was a small cross. Jake walked towards it, knelt down, and placed the flowers across the base of the cross.

As he traced the inscription with his fingers, he began to speak. "We named him Joseph Paul Morgan, after Joe DiMaggio. Silly, I know, to name your kid after a baseball player, but I loved the idea and Maddie was okay with it. Of all the things she fought me over, you'd think she'd fight me over the name of our kid, right? But no, Joseph Paul was his name and I was so freaking happy."

With a sad smile, he remembered. He was quiet and Lily didn't interrupt. She figured if he was going to get it all out, he didn't need her prodding questions. She was sure they'd be answered, anyway, so she sat in the grass next to him with her hand in his and her eyes on the gravestone.

"I told you we almost lost him once. That's when I found out we were having a boy. I should've seen it in her face. I knew her better than anyone, but I just figured that she'd come around. She had that depression women get when they find out they're pregnant. I just attributed everything to that.

"Sure, she was happy most of the time but there were other times I swear she resented him growing inside her. Then I asked her to marry me. I figured, 'Hey, we were having a baby, we should get married.' You know? God, I knew we were no good for each other but maybe that would make everything all better."

Lily squeezed his hand in encouragement. Jake turned to her and smiled slightly before sadness took over again.

"We got married real quick. We both thought a baby should have parents that were married. So we did it in front of Judge Collins. She was eight months along. Everything was going great. She seemed so happy. I was over the moon. The nursery was ready. And then she went into labor. It's not like he was that early but he still ended up in the NICU. Something about his lung development 'cause she, you know, used when she was pregnant and all.

"Madison had to come home before he did. What's weird is she never went to visit him in the hospital. I went every day, sometimes I slept there but she never did. It bothered me but I figured she was still dealing with post-partum depression or whatever they call it. I tried getting her there but she always had an excuse. I shoulda known then she wouldn't be good for either of us."

Lily needed to reassure him. "Jake, you couldn't have known."

"Yeah? You weren't there. I definitely should have."

He dropped his head and plucked blades of grass, mentally forcing himself to get through this. Just because most of the people around him knew what happened, didn't mean *he'd* ever confronted it. Now he finally felt like he had the strength to get through it. If he couldn't do it now, he knew he'd never be able to.

"So anyway, it was a week or two before I could even hold him. When I finally did, his fingers were so small and his feet were so tiny. He was just so small..." Jake trailed off, remembering. "I could swear he smiled at me even though I knew he couldn't yet. I'll tell you, I never felt anything like that in my life. It was like, all of a sudden, I had a purpose. If I did nothing else in life, I was going to take care of that little boy. God help me. I was going to do everything I could to make his life amazing because he'd already made mine perfect."

Tears fell from Jake's eyes onto the ground and, with fists clenched, he fought to retain his composure.

"And then the doctor's said he could come home. We were told in the afternoon that he could come home the following day. For some reason, I called Billy and asked if I could come in and sing. I wanted to share with everyone that my boy was coming home. I had written a song for him and played it that night. It wasn't the first song I wrote, but it had the most meaning. I only played it that once but I hear it every day of my life. You'd think I'd hate the sound of it but with Madison haunting me, that lullaby is the only light I see in the darkness.

"The next day, I took off from work and Maddie and I went to get him. But when we got to the hospital, something was wrong."

Jake's face crumbled and his tears were no longer silent. Lily pulled him to her, put his head on her shoulder, and waited for him to find a way to continue.

"They were in his room and there were machines beeping and nurses and doctors running all over the place. We weren't allowed in the room."

"Shh. It's okay, Jake. It wasn't your fault."

"But it was! Don't you see? I should have been there that night instead of singing a stupid song at Bill's. If I had, then maybe he'd still be here today."

"What happened?"

"Something with his lungs. The doctor's thought he'd be all right. He was off oxygen for a week and they said he was well enough to come home. I'd even fed him bottles and changed his diapers and slept in a room next to him. He was *fine*. They said he was fine."

Lily placed her hand on her stomach and flinched.

"It's okay, Jake. It's okay." She didn't know what else to say. There were no words for the pain she felt for him. She let his head fall to her lap and cried with him.

Jake couldn't contain himself. Tears that he hadn't let himself cry in two years fell to the ground. And for the first time in a long time, he allowed himself to remember...

୧୬୧୬

"What's wrong? What's happening?"

Jake let go of Madison's hand and ran into his baby's room. Nurses and doctors were rushing around screaming orders and codes, hovering over his tiny little boy.

"Somebody talk to me!" Panic stole Jake's heart.

Peggy, one of the nurses, noticed Jake standing in the middle of the chaos and directed him out of the room. She pulled up a chair and sat him down. The look of terror on his face did nothing to ease her tired mind.

"Jake. Look at me."

His eyes were wide and looked everywhere but at her. She saw Madison standing feet away from the door, staring at the room. Peggy walked over, put her arm around Madison, and steered her towards Jake.

"I need you both to listen to me. Joseph is having a hard time breathing on his own right now. His heart and his lungs aren't as strong as we thought. We thought he was out of the woods, he's been responding so well. Then a few minutes ago, his heart started racing and he was having trouble breathing. That's why all those people are in his room right now. They are doing all they can to help him. Do you understand what I'm saying?"

Madison looked as though she was going to throw up, and Jake stared straight ahead, barely blinking away the tears that slipped down his face.

When Madison tried to speak, nothing came out. Her hands were shaky from both fear and withdrawal. Jake's mouth hung slack, he didn't dare try to vocalize what he was thinking. The sounds of the frenzy in the room were almost too much for him to handle.

Peggy placed her hands over theirs. "I'm going to go and see how it's going. I will be right back to let you know."

When Jake nodded, she felt sure that they'd heard and understood her. She just hoped it wouldn't be bad news she came back with.

Over the next few hours, Peggy returned with a few, grim updates. Neither Madison nor Jake ever made a move that night to comfort each other, she noticed. Jake had come and slept at the hospital every night, except last night. Madison hadn't been to visit her child for more than an hour or two each of the handful of times she'd made it to the hospital. Madison was hollow, whereas Jake was being wrenched from the inside out.

When she came out the last time, Peggy saw that Jake had fallen asleep in the chair and beside him sat his brother and father. She was glad she was able to get a hold of them. Jake needed someone right now.

Madison was sitting at the other end of the hallway, face ashen and hands shaking. Peggy brought her a glass of water.

"Madison, drink this."

"I don't want it."

"You need to drink something. You look dehydrated."

Madison took the glass and drank it down in a gulp.

"Do you want to know how your baby is?"

"Is he dead?"

Surprised, Peggy had to compose herself quickly. "No. He isn't dead but he isn't doing well. I was thinking you might want to go over and sit with Jake. I think the doctor is going to come out to speak with the two of you shortly."

"I can't do this."

"Do what?"

"Forget it."

"No, Madison. I'm here. What do you need?"

"Nothing. I'm fine. I have to go to the bathroom. I'll go sit with Jake soon."

Madison stood and rushed to the bathroom. Peggy dropped her head to her hands but was jolted by a hand on her shoulder.

"Jake? I thought you were asleep."

"I wasn't. I just closed my eyes for a few minutes. I heard you talking to Madison."

"Is she alright, Jake?"

"I don't think so, Peg."

With that, he walked back to his seat and waited. His father and brother sat beside him, hands wringing, with ashen faces of sadness. It wasn't long after until the doctor stepped into the hallway, pulled up a chair right in front of Jake, and looked down to the floor. "Where is Madison?"

"She went to the bathroom. She should be back soon."

"Peggy," the doctor motioned for her to join them. "Please, we need Madison here. Could you go get her?"

Jake stood. "No. I'll go."

Shoving his hands into his pockets to keep them from shaking, Jake walked down the hall to the ladies room. Knocking garnered no response so he walked in. But Madison wasn't there. No one was there. Walking over to the sink, he stared at himself in the mirror and forced himself not to cry. He knew she was gone, even before he saw the envelope lying on the shelf.

> *Dear Jake,*
> *I truly am sorry for all the pain I've caused you. You deserve more than I can give you. And in light of what's happened with little Joey, I don't think I'd be good for either of you.*

> *There should be a bond between me and Joey but there isn't, as hard as I have tried. But there is one between the two of you and, truth be told, I'm terribly jealous of that.*
>
> *I've realized I am way too selfish to be a mother. Too wrapped up in my own head to be a good wife. So I figured the right thing to do is leave you both. I'm just not cut out for any of this. I hope one day, the two of you will forgive me.*
>
> *I've already found a place and will be gone by the time you get home. Don't try to look for me. I don't want to be found.*
>
> *Take care of each other. I will love you forever, Jake.*
>
> *Love,*
> *Madison*

Jake walked out of the bathroom, handed the note to his father, and sat down in front of the doctor.

"Please. Tell me what's going on with my son. Madison is gone, and she won't be coming back. Just tell me what I need to do to make him better."

The doctor looked into Jake's eyes with overwhelming sadness.

"There is nothing you can do. You need to say goodbye."

Fists clenched and eyes shut tightly, Jake whispered, "What happened? Why do I need to say goodbye?"

"His heart isn't strong enough. His lungs aren't working as they should be. At this point the only way to keep him alive is to hook him up to machines. He's too small to live that kind of life. He isn't strong enough for surgery. He doesn't have much time left, Jake. It could be hours, it could be minutes. You need to spend that time with your son."

Andy reached over, hugged his son, and watched him fall apart. Danny pulled them both in close and quietly cursed the woman who'd destroyed his brother.

As Jake rocked his child through the night, rain fell against the windows of the hospital room. Madison's sister and parents were out looking for her but Jake knew they wouldn't find her. Madison had left long ago, but he had refused to see it. He wasn't sure if he'd ever see her again, and he wasn't sure if he wanted to. For now, he settled into the reality of the present.

Andy had called in a priest, and Joey had been given his Last Rites. Doctors and nurses walked in and out of the room while family and friends hovered in the halls and waiting room. And just as the sun peaked through the morning clouds and the rain stopped, Joey's tiny heart gave out and he took his last breath, wrapped in the loving arms of his father.

CHAPTER 24

It was almost nightfall before Lily pulled Jake's truck into his driveway. His exhaustion from the day was contagious. She walked around the truck, opened his door, and held his hand as he quietly stepped out. His grief was visible. Every brick in the wall that surrounded him had crashed to the ground when he'd opened up.

She walked him into the house and into his bedroom. He sat on the bed with his head hung low while Lily undressed him. Guiding him onto his pillow, she covered him with a blanket and lay down next to him. He reached behind him, grabbed her hand, and pulled it around his shoulders. His breath not quite even, he closed his eyes willing the day to end.

Lying perfectly still, he felt Lily's warm breath on the back of his neck. He felt her lips move close to his ear as she whispered, "I love you." He didn't respond. Instead, he closed his eyes and let her words wash over him.

She waited until she knew he was asleep before allowing herself to close her eyes. Visions of Jake's anguish swirled in her head. She slept fitfully with pictures of babies and hospitals and graveyards plaguing her dreams.

When she finally woke in the morning, Jake was still sleeping soundly. Careful not to disturb him, she got out of bed and walked to the kitchen to make herself a cup of coffee. Looking at her watch, she realized she needed to be at work in a couple of hours. She didn't want to leave him but knew he needed some time alone.

Finishing her coffee, she set the cup in the sink and rummaged in the drawer for a pen and paper.

> *Jake,*
> *I hope you slept well. I'll be at Bill's early and should finish up around 1:30. Let me know if you want me to meet you here. Call me if you need anything. Bill will understand if I need to leave early. Talk to you soon.*
> *Love,*
> *Lily*

She quietly walked into his bedroom and set the note on his nightstand. Leaning over, she brushed back the hair that had fallen into his eyes. He hadn't gotten his hair cut since they'd met. It had gotten shaggy and she wondered why she hadn't noticed it almost covered his eyes now. His skin was tanned from working at the docks. She'd have to remind him to wear some sunscreen when he finally went out on the boats. She kissed him softly on the forehead and watched him sleep for a minute before leaving the room. Grabbing her keys and purse from the couch, she made sure to lock the door behind her.

It wasn't until she was in her car that she allowed the tears to flow freely. She cried for Jake, for his son, and for a future she was unsure of. By the time she pulled into the driveway of her uncle's house she was dazed by the rush of emotion she'd finally let herself feel. When she walked into the house, Bill was sitting at the kitchen table reading the paper.

"Hey, Lil."

When she didn't answer, he looked up and saw her wipe her face as she walked to the door of her room.

"Everything okay?"

"Fine. I'll be fine."

Standing quickly, Bill walked towards her. "What happened? Did Jake do something?"

"No. No. It wasn't like that. He took me somewhere yesterday. The graveyard. He told me everything. How can one person hold so much pain inside?"

"Aw, Lil." Billy knew Jake would tell her eventually. He walked over and pulled her into a hug. "It will be all right. Jake's a strong kid. I'm glad he told you. I was wondering when and if he would."

Through tears, Lily held her uncle tightly. "I just don't understand. The stuff with Madison was bad enough, pain enough for anyone to feel in a lifetime. But to take his child? How does that happen? Why does that happen? And Madison left him to deal with that alone? She didn't even go to her own child's funeral. What kind of a person would do that?"

"Jake wasn't alone, honey. He had all of us. We're his family. Everyone in town, pretty much. Believe me when I tell you he wasn't alone. As for Madison, we all knew she was no good but none of us could ever have predicted her leaving when she did. No one, not even her family, will ever forgive her for that."

"And she hasn't been back since then?"

Stroking her hair, he could feel her calm down. "No. But if I know Madison, and who knows if I do, she'll be back. She will find the worst time to come back and that's when she'll show up offended that we all remember her the way we do."

Through loud sniffs, Lily replied, "I think I'd punch her if she ever came back."

Bill laughed that big laugh that always made her smile. "You do that, sweetie. You do that."

She stepped back. "I love him, you know."

"I know."

Walking to the counter, she poured herself a cup of coffee. She took a breath. "I don't think I want to go to Atlanta."

Bill could see she was serious. "You can stay here as long as you want. Whatever you decide, you'll always have a home here."

"I haven't decided anything yet."

"Yes, you have."

Smiling over her cup, she said, "I haven't said anything yet."

"Do you need me to cover your shift today?"

"No. I have to go. If I stay here, I'll go out of my mind thinking about everything. It'll give me a few hours to push it back."

"If you say so. Going to the Olsen picnic later?"

"Yeah. You?"

"I might try to slip out of there for an hour or so. You okay?"

"I'm good, thanks. I have to take a shower. I'll meet you there in about an hour or so."

"Alright, kiddo."

Lily slipped downstairs to her room and Billy stood in the kitchen with his hands in his pockets staring at the spot she just vacated.

"Damn it, Madison. Why can't you just go away?"

He picked his keys up and walked outside to his truck and took off for the bar.

CHAPTER 25

Lily worked through the rest of her late morning shift and rushed home to change her clothes. She'd left Jake at his house that morning and though he seemed a little better than he had the night before, she was worried about him.

Thinking about how he lost his son tied her stomach in knots. From her point of view, no one was to blame for his death. Of course, that fact didn't make it any easier for anyone to handle. Somehow, though, in spite of his evident grief, ease began finding its way back to Jake. There wasn't a heaviness blanketed on top of him as there had been before he shared the story.

She knew it took a lot out of him to share his pain. He wouldn't have shared if he didn't trust her fully. And Jake wasn't one that trusted easily. She had a feeling that trait was evident even before Madison crashed into his life.

Lily knew there was more between her and Jake than a passing summer fling. Whether or not he was ready to admit it was another story. Of course, if she didn't get the proverbial green light, she would be Atlanta bound in a few weeks. That is, if the doctor's appointment she had set for Tuesday came up with nothing. And that was a conversation she'd have with Jake if, and when, she needed to. No use screaming fire when the match wasn't lit yet.

When Jake pulled in to her driveway, she checked her watch. They still had an hour or so before they had to be at the picnic. She thought they'd agreed to meet at the picnic. Confused, she met him on the porch.

"I thought we were meeting at the Olsen's."

"We were. You look pretty."

She twirled the skirt of her blue sundress a bit for him. "Thanks. You look pretty cute yourself." And she kissed him on the nose.

"You don't mind that I came here, do you?"

"Of course not. Come on in. I just have to dry my hair."

"I didn't feel like sitting at home by myself, you know?"

Lily grabbed his hands. "I know."

The way he felt when he was with Lily was like nothing he'd ever felt before. After all the garbage he'd been clinging to, he finally felt free of the bullshit. Free of the guilt. He wanted to tell her, convince her to stay, but he wasn't sure he had enough to offer her. The job she was taking in Atlanta sounded perfect for her, and she was really excited. He didn't want to ruin it. In his mind, he thought that the distance might not be so bad but in his heart, he knew he needed her closer. But still, he kept silent, not knowing Lily wanted him to express just that.

"Give me five minutes and I'll be ready."

"No rush."

Jake walked around her room, looking at pictures, carefully lifting them by the edges and admiring her skill.

He had to raise his voice over the sound of her hair dryer. "These pictures are fantastic, Lil. When did you take them?"

"Those are the ones I told you about. Remember when I bought the guitar? I took those then."

"I've never been there. We should go sometime."

"Yeah. Let's do that. I'd like to go in the morning, when the sun comes up. I have some of the sun setting. It'd be nice to see it in a different light."

He sat in her desk chair. Her date book open to the week. Today's date was circled with a heart and she'd written "picnic with Jake" in bold red letters. He smiled to himself. Tuesday, he noticed, she had a doctor's appointment at noon. He wondered briefly why she would be going to the doctor's here instead of waiting a few weeks when she moved to Atlanta.

"Ready."

He took a moment to appreciate what he saw. Her hair cascaded down her back and her eyes sparkled with happiness. Every time he looked at her, he couldn't believe how beautiful she was, how full of life and honesty. He silently thanked whoever was responsible for bringing her into his life.

He quickly walked over and brushed a stray strand of hair away from her eyes. Lily leaned in as he cupped her face in his hands.

"You are amazing, Lily Burns."

Her breath hitched like it always did when he was about to kiss her. The feeling never diminished, it only grew stronger with each passing day. She only needed to hear two words from him, *Don't go*.

"I wanted to thank you for yesterday."

"Jake, you don't have to—"

"No but I want to. I don't think I've ever opened up to anyone quite like I did yesterday. Just you being there for me meant so much."

"Well, you're welcome. I'm just sorry you had to, have to, go through that pain. If I can do anything to take even just a little bit of it away, tell me and I'll do it."

For a moment he thought about asking her to stay here with him, asking her not to go to Atlanta but he felt like he'd already asked too much of her. So he kept his wishes silent.

"Just being here helps me step away. Somehow, you've helped me unload some of the guilt, some of the sadness. I don't know if all of it will ever go away but I don't think it will haunt me like it has. I just wish I could repay you."

Lily thought about letting him know she wanted to stay with him but she wasn't sure if it was the right time, if he was just feeling this way because the pain from yesterday was still raw.

Smiling, he reached for her hand and pulled her closer. "Let's go."

The short drive to the Olsen's house made Jake anxious. He couldn't quite pinpoint the reason for his anxiety other than the fact that he hadn't really spent much time with them in the last couple years. Madison had driven an invisible wedge between Jake and the people that mattered to him. He was now determined to remove that wall and get on with his life.

"Do I look okay?" Lily asked as she pulled down the visor to apply her lip-gloss in the mirror.

When Jake looked over, he saw the most beautiful woman he'd ever met, both inside and out.

"You look great."

When she smiled, his heart tripped up a bit and he resolved to talk to her about Atlanta, a conversation they'd both been avoiding. He couldn't let her leave without at least telling her how he felt. Even though he thought it was obvious, the words somehow seemed important, too.

As they pulled into the driveway, the first person they saw was Mrs. Olsen carrying a huge bowl of potato salad out of the house. "Jake, Lily! You made it. Thank you for coming."

"I wouldn't miss your potato salad for anything in the world, Mrs. Olsen. Let me get that for you." He leaned in and gave her a kiss on the cheek.

"You give me too much credit, Jakey. You always have."

"Impossible."

"Thanks for inviting me, too. Jake's told me so much about you."

"And we've heard all about you, mostly from your uncle. Jake's always been quiet when it comes to his personal life. Happy to have you dear. Now, both of you, go mingle. Jake, I think your father and brother are over by the food. You can put that on the table next to the other salads."

"Where else would they be?"

Abby laughed and hugged Jake—the first real hug they shared in two years. It felt good for both of them. He grabbed Lily's hand and they walked across the yard, stopping to say hello to everyone they knew before meeting up with Andy and Danny, filling their plates with picnic food.

"Jake! You made it!" Danny expressed his gratitude through a mouth full of chicken.

Jake placed the bowl on the table. "Does Megan know you're eating that? I thought she had you on a diet."

"I get the day off. I mean, why come if you can't eat. Right? Is that potato salad? Hey, Lily. You look great."

Laughing, Lily grabbed a napkin and wiped barbeque sauce from Danny's chin. "Thanks Danny. Have you lost weight?"

He scooped a large spoonful of potato salad onto his already overloaded plate. "From your lips to God's ears. Jake, where have you been hiding her?"

"Away from you. Why don't you slow down? We wouldn't want you to choke before the desserts come out."

Andy stepped out from behind Danny. "Glad to see you made it. Wasn't sure if you would. Hello, Lily. Danny's right. You look great."

He leaned in to kiss Lily on the cheek. It was a small gesture that made her feel like she belonged in this small town.

"Thanks, Mr. Morgan. What have you got there?"

"Please, call me Andy. And this here is the best bean salad anywhere. It was my wife's recipe."

"Well then, I think I might have to try it."

"You come with me, young lady. We'll get you a plate."

"I'd love to."

Lily squeezed Jake's hand and kissed him on the cheek before she followed Andy to the other side of the table. When Jake finally turned his attention back to his brother, he had to smile. Danny's eyebrows were wiggling like bushy caterpillars.

"What?"

"You know what."

"No, I don't."

"You've got a girlfriend."

"She's not my girlfriend. She's leaving for Atlanta in two weeks, anyway."

Between bites of potato salad and fried chicken, Danny asked, "Have you told her how you feel?"

"Not exactly."

"You gotta grab the bull by the horns, Brother! How do you think I got my woman?"

Just as he said that, Megan walked up and smacked him on the butt. "Excuse me?"

Jake laughed as he watched his brother back pedal. "Hey, sweetie. Jake and I were just talking about how lucky I am to have you."

"Better be careful. This bull might point her horns where the sun don't shine. Hi, Jake. Glad to see you could make it."

Jake leaned over and kissed her on the cheek. "Thanks Megan. I plan on showing up a lot more often."

"Good to hear. Maybe you can put this bullfighter in his place. Oh geez! I'll be back. One of the kids just discovered the Jell-o. Excuse me! What do you think you're doing?"

Megan walked across the yard to her oldest who was, apparently, throwing cubes of bright red Jell-o at some of the other kids.

"You have a good family."

Danny set his plate down and put his arm around his brother. "I know man. I'm a pretty lucky guy."

Nodding his head and looking across the way to Lily, who was involved in a conversation with his father, Jake smiled. Lately, he'd been feeling lucky, too.

"Danny," he said, clapping his hand on Danny's stomach, "I think I'd better get some food before you eat it all."

Danny picked up his plate and filled the empty spaces with more drumsticks, biscuits and potato salad. "Try the chicken. It's freaking amazing!"

Jake quickly filled his plate and walked over to Lily and his father. Something he said had her laughing hysterically.

"What's so funny?"

"Oh nothing. Your dad was just telling me about the time you decided to paint the bathroom walls with your mom's red nail polish."

"Thanks dad. Like she needs to hear stuff like that."

Andy clapped his hand on Jake's shoulder. "Aw Jake. At least I didn't tell her about the time you ate the dog's food and ended up painting the walls with something else."

The twinkle in his father's eye caught Jake off guard. He realized he hadn't seen his father this relaxed in a long time. As a matter of fact, his self-imposed isolation kept him from seeing a lot of things. That was all going to change.

"I'm sure I could come up with a story or two to tell her about you, too, you know."

Lily watched Jake interact with his father and enjoyed how easily they slipped into what she assumed was an old routine. She was close to her parents, but they were a bit stuffier than most people. She wasn't sure where her free spirit came from, but Jake, his family, and the rest of this tiny town welcomed it with open arms.

"You two are so funny. I feel like I've known you my entire life. I feel so, I don't know, comfortable, around all of you."

"Well, darlin', if you ever decide to come visit when that big city gets you down, you'll always have a place here."

Jake caught Lily's eye. Sadness and promise swept through each of them.

"Then again, maybe that big city could wait a bit." Andy winked and walked away leaving Jake and Lily a bit speechless.

"Don't mind my dad."

"Oh, no. He's very kind."

"Yeah but sometimes he sticks his nose in where it shouldn't be."

"It's fine, Jake."

"Well, okay." He shifted his body not quite sure where to take the conversation.

"Actually, I've been wanting to talk to you a little bit about that."

He put his plate on the picnic table. "About Atlanta?"

"Yes."

"I've been wanting to talk to you about it, too."

"Do you think after this, after the picnic, I could come over? Maybe we could talk then."

"Of course. You can come over anytime you want. You do have a toothbrush there, you know."

Lily smiled. "I do know."

As she looked down, she realized she was wringing her hands raw. She couldn't understand why on earth was that particular decision was proving so difficult for her. Anticipation of the conversation to come left her breathless.

Jake reached over and gently covered her hands with his. "Hey. It will be all right. We'll talk and everything will be fine. I promise."

She looked up at him and knew he was right.

"Son of a bitch."

Danny's whispered words pulled Jake and Lily out of their shared world. Soon, everyone at the picnic hushed and all eyes focused on one spot. Lily looked up and wasn't sure what the fuss was about. It wasn't until Jake turned his head in the direction of the stares that she felt him tense.

"What's going on?" Lily whispered.

Jake had lost his voice. No words could describe the emotions that made him feel like he would immediately collapse. Torn between hatred and sickness, he squeezed Lily's hand. He'd hoped she would be able to provide the strength that rushed away from him.

Lily squeezed back.

"Well, hey, everyone. God, I'm famished. The food looks great."

The small blonde woman searched the silent crowd until her gaze finally came to rest on Jake and woman holding his hand. The blonde raised an eyebrow and smirked. With her heart about to explode, Lily finally figured out what was happening.

She watched the woman walk purposefully across the lawn until she was within inches of Jake. Lily cringed as the she reached up and hugged him. Motionless, Jake turned back to Lily, and the fear, sadness and grief, that had once promised to leave him, magnified. A small tear fell down his face, breaking Lily's heart. She could see the wall go up, she could feel his heart harden, and when he closed his eyes and let go of her hand, distance spread between them.

"What's the matter, Jakey? Didn't you miss me?"

"What are you doing here Madison?"

CHAPTER 26

Stepping in front of Lily as if to shield her, Jake looked Madison square in the eye. Hatred burned from him and she flinched like she could feel it.

"Jake—"

"Answer me, Madison. What are you doing here?"

"Can't a girl stop in to visit her family?"

"You never just stop in anywhere. Why are you here?"

"Can we talk in private?"

He jerked away from her touch. "No."

She lowered her voice to a whisper. "Jake, please. I came back for you. I wanted to talk to you about, well, about everything that happened."

"You think you can walk back into town and *talk to me* about everything that happened? You're fucking delusional."

"Jake. Stop. Just listen to me."

He turned back to look at Lily, and she saw something in his eyes that she'd never seen before. He really looked like he was going to lose it. It scared her.

Danny caught the look, too, but he'd seen it before, and he *knew* Jake was about to lose it. He walked up to Lily and took her elbow. "Lily, we should go. You don't want to see this."

She looked at Danny, saw the pleading look in his eyes, and turned back to Jake. For an instant, sadness filled his face before it twisted back to hatred. She allowed Danny to pull her away from them.

"You stop, Madison. No one wants you here. Just go back to whatever filthy hole you dragged yourself from and get out of my sight."

He turned his back to her and she reached out and grabbed his shirt. "You listen to me, Jacob Morgan. You and I have to talk about this. I will stay here and meet you around every corner until you talk to me."

He knocked her hand off of him. "Don't touch me. Don't you ever touch me again. You're a lying whore and I want nothing to do with you."

Mrs. Olsen walked over. "Jake. Please don't. Just hear her out."

He looked at her like he hadn't heard correctly. Mr. Olsen stood beside him.

"Leave him alone, Abby. Madison, haven't you caused enough trouble?"

"Dad?"

"Honey, I love you but come on. What's going on? Why are you here?"

Jake had heard enough. He stormed across the yard towards his truck.

"Damn it, Jake. Don't walk away from me."

"Fuck you, Madison."

He jumped into his truck, started the engine, and peeled out of the driveway. Lily stood back, with Danny, Megan and Andy, and watched him leave. Anger and confusion filled her. She'd just realized Danny was still holding her elbow. She quickly pulled it away and walked towards Madison.

"Lily, don't..." But Danny's words trailed off as everyone in the yard stood still watching the drama unfold.

Madison looked at her father and started to turn around, but Lily was in her face before she could.

"What is wrong with you?"

Shocked, Madison replied, "Who the hell are you?"

"It doesn't matter who I am. Haven't you caused enough pain?"

"Oh, I see. You're Jake's flavor of the summer, right? Well, let me tell you something, sweetheart. I'm not leaving until Jake talks to me. So if you want to get rid of me, convince your *boyfriend* to give me a call. I'll be staying with my parents."

"Why are you doing this?"

"Because I can. He is my husband, after all."

Madison looked around at the people staring at her and smiled sweetly before turning and walking into her parent's house, slamming the door loudly behind her.

Tears welled up in Lily's eyes. *Husband?* Her voice was small. "Danny, what is she talking about?"

Andy walked up, took her hand, and steered her away from prying eyes. When he finally pulled her far enough away, he sat her down on an old tree stump. "Look at me."

Barely a whisper, she asked, "What is she talking about, Andy? What does she mean *husband*? I thought that was done."

Rubbing his hand over her face, he silently cursed Jake for not coming clean with her. It wasn't his place, after all, to talk to Lily about this, but he was going to have to clear it up.

"Lily, he filed for divorce not long after Madison left. The only problem is, no one could find her. She moved around a lot, and when she would call her parents, she never gave a concrete location. Technically, they are still married."

The thought made her want to vomit. Clutching her stomach, she bent over, tears streaming down her face.

"Oh my God. He's married?"

"No, listen. It's been over for two years. In his mind, they aren't. Unfortunately, he was never able to get her to sign the papers. He didn't tell you any of this?"

"No. No he didn't. I mean, yesterday, we went to the cemetery. I thought that was everything."

He leaned back. "So he told you about Joey."

She looked up at him and saw his eyes water. "Yes. He told me all of that."

"Lily, he hasn't talked about that with anyone, ever. Not me, not his brother. The fact that he opened up, that he told you about that, just proves what I've known all along."

"What's that?"

"That he loves you."

She looked away. "How he was with her today, how he spoke to her, how he looked, I've never seen him like that."

"She brings it out in him."

"I didn't like it."

"Can you blame him?"

"I guess not."

Andy reached out and grabbed her hands. "Hey. It will be all right. But if Madison says she isn't leaving until she talks to him, then take her at her word. She's the most stubborn—"

"You want me to convince him to talk to her?"

"I think you are the only one who can."

She thought for a moment. "You think she'll leave?"

"I know she will. Sadly, she doesn't care enough for anyone here to stay."

"All right, Andy. I'll see what I can do."

"Good. You wanna leave? I'll drive you home."

"My Jeep is at Jake's."

"I can take you there."

"No that's okay. I just want to be alone right now. If I gave you my keys, do you think one of you could get it for me and drop it at Billy's?"

"Sure. Whatever you want. I'll make sure it gets there. Come on. I'll go tell Danny I'm taking you home."

"Thanks Andy. I'll meet you at your truck."

Andy stood and began to turn away before glancing back to Lily. He looked as though he wanted to say something but had thought better of it. Shoving his hands into his pockets he walked off to find Danny.

Lily wiped the tears from her eyes and walked around the side of the house to Andy's truck. While she was waiting, Madison walked out of the house with a drink in her hand and lit a cigarette. She noticed Lily right away and started walking towards her. Lily squared her shoulders and tried to look like she didn't care.

"So, you're Jake's girlfriend now, huh? I guess he told you about me."

"He did."

"Did he tell you how much in love we once were? Did he tell you we were happy once?" Her voice dripped with sarcasm.

"He told me all about you. He told me pretty much everything."

Taking a long drag of her cigarette, Madison smiled. "Ahh, but he didn't tell you we were still married."

Lily didn't know what to say so she watched Madison gulp the caramel colored liquid from her glass. She dropped her lit cigarette at Lily's feet and stepped over to put it out.

Lifting her chin, she whispered in Lily's ear, "Well then. I guess there's still hope for me."

Just as Madison walked away from Lily, Andy walked around from the side of the house. He saw the last part of the interaction but didn't hear what was said. All he saw was Lily's pale face and shaking hands.

"Madison! Leave her alone."

"Hello, Andy. You're looking well."

"Did you hear me? Leave her alone."

Tossing a glance over her shoulder, she saw what he saw. Lily looked like she was going to faint.

"Relax. We were just catching up. It really has been too long."

"You're still the same, aren't you? You haven't changed."

"And you're the same poke-your-nose-in-other-people's-business, nosey body. Listen. Just make sure Jake calls me. Or else, I have a feeling I could get used to being back."

Madison walked away, back into the house. Not knowing what to do, he walked over to Lily.

"Are you all right?"

"No. I just want to go home."

"Okay. Okay. Let's go."

Andy pulled into Bill's driveway. Getting out of the truck, he walked around to the passenger side door and opened it for Lily. She stepped out of the truck, stood up straight, and looked him in the eye.

"Thank you."

"You gonna be okay?"

"Absolutely."

She leaned in and gave him a little kiss on the cheek before walking into the house. Andy pulled out his phone, called Billy, and gave him the run down on what happened at the picnic before climbing back into his truck and heading over to Jake's.

CHAPTER 27

Lily waited until she was in her room to lose it. She kicked her shoes across the room and threw her purse against the wall. Collapsing on the bed, she stared at the ceiling, willing herself not to cry.

Thinking over the past few days, she tried to see the silver lining. She loved Jake, but she wasn't sure she could handle it if Madison stayed in town. The look on his face when she showed up more than conveyed how he felt about her. But then again, the look is what scared her. It was full of rage and pure hatred. He had every reason to feel that way, but that fact did nothing to ease her mind. She wasn't sure how she should react to it. What she knew for sure was she needed to talk to Jake.

Picking up her cell, she dialed his number. Frustrated that it went straight to voicemail, she clicked off without leaving a message. She dialed his house but he didn't answer that either. She stood and began pacing her room when all of a sudden, she felt dizzy. Sitting quickly she dropped her head between her knees. Then hand covering her mouth, she rushed to the bathroom. She barely made it before she threw up.

Leaning over the sink, she splashed water on her face and brushed her teeth. When she stood and looked into the mirror, she was pale. She knew without a doubt what was wrong. With her hand on her stomach, she thanked God she only had to wait two more days to see the doctor.

After that, decisions had to be made. Would she stay or would she head to Atlanta? How would Jake react? She wouldn't blame him if he freaked out. It was a big deal, certainly not one she had anticipated. But if what she thought was happening really was, then she'd have to deal with it. With or without Jake.

Dropping her head, she silently cursed herself for assuming he wouldn't be happy about this. True, they hadn't known each other for very long, but she loved him and felt he loved her, too. At least until she watched the wall rebuild itself right in front of her eyes. It couldn't be permanent. After all, just yesterday she watched the last brick fall.

CHAPTER 28

Madison stormed into her parents' house and watched Andy drive away with that girl. This wasn't going exactly how she planned. Then again, she didn't plan any of this out. Not sure of what pulled her here other than the fact that she'd woken up yesterday with the urge to come back. Well, she knew exactly what made her come back. Not that she wanted to deal with it.

God knew she'd avoided coming back here for the last two years, purposefully not disclosing her whereabouts to anyone, not even her parents. She was living fine, with no responsibility, no drama, no dead babies. It hurt, still, to think about the day she'd found out...

❧❧❧

Holding the phone, Madison finally decided to dial. It was on the fourth ring before her father answered.

"Hello?"

"Dad?"

"Madison? Where are you? Are you okay?"

"I'm safe."

"Where the hell have you been? It's been two weeks without a word. Your mother and I have been worried sick."

"Dad, I'm okay. Just wanted to call and let you know I'm not coming back for a while."

"What? Why not? You have to come back. You missed the funeral. How could you miss the funeral?"

Her head spun. "Wait. What funeral?"

Silence on the other end stretched for what seemed like an eternity.

"Dad. What funeral? What are you talking about?"

"Aw, Madison. You need to come back. Jake is a mess. We're all a mess. Honey, Joey died."

The phone clattered to the floor as every nerve in her body screamed in protest.

"Madison? Are you there? Madison?"

Staring at the phone, she felt as if everything moved in slow motion—like she was watching herself react. Watching her arm stretch to the floor. Watching her hand grip the phone. Watching herself lift it back to her ear.

"Madison?"

"I'm here."

"Did you hear what I said?"

Silent tears fell down her face. "Yeah, Dad. I heard you. What happened?"

"What happened? He died just hours after you left. That's what happened. What the hell, Madison? What the hell is the matter with you?"

"What's wrong with me? Dad, I couldn't take seeing him like that. I couldn't take Jake and everyone looking at me like *I* was the one who did something wrong. The doctors, the nurses, they wouldn't even let me hold him."

"You didn't want to hold him. How many times did you go visit that poor baby in the hospital?"

"It wasn't my fault!"

"Jesus, Madison. When are you gonna grow up and stop blaming everyone else? You know what, you stay where you are. Give Jake time to grieve. God knows he can't do that with you here."

She felt like she'd been kicked in the stomach. If anyone had always stood by her, it was her dad. She'd expected this reaction from her mother, but not him.

"Fine, Dad. I'll call you later."

She hung up the phone and walked over to the coffee table that sat in the middle of her tiny apartment. It wasn't much, but it was all she could swing at the time. Leaning over the table, she picked up a rolled dollar bill and inhaled her sanity.

CHAPTER 29

Jake sped away from the Olsen's' house in a fury. He was a few miles away before he began to think clearly enough to realize he'd left Lily there. Punching the steering wheel, he thought about turning back but he knew he couldn't. He was inches from going completely ballistic and he was embarrassed enough that Lily had seen him in the state she did. The shock and sorrow on her face was too painful.

He hated when he acted like that. And it was always Madison that sent him over the edge. For the life of him, he couldn't figure out what the hell she was doing back here and what the hell they would have to talk about. He needed to avoid that conversation. The two of them were too combustible, too unstable when they were together. It wasn't like that with Lily.

When he was with Lily, he felt none of the drama, none of the sadness that he'd felt when he was with Madison. He hadn't been sure he'd ever feel normal again. Then he met Lily. She was all sunshine and smiles and had no ulterior motives. What you saw was always what you got with her.

He'd heard her, last night, when she told him she loved him, and he'd wanted to say it too but couldn't form the words. In the two short months they'd know each other, he'd fallen in love. She was everything he'd hoped for.

Not knowing exactly where he was going, he kept on driving. He needed to get away from everything he'd thought he'd left behind. He should have known, Madison would never leave him alone, she'd never let him be happy. And just when he finally thought he could be.

"Fuck!"

He yelled out as he steered the truck off the road. Punching the steering wheel, bloodying his knuckles on the dash, he collapsed forward with his head on the wheel and let the tears fall.

Much like he did the day before, he let everything rise to the surface and did what he could to expel all the negativity. He barely heard his phone ring. Without even looking at it, he switched it off.

He thought about Lily leaving and the tears fell harder. He thought about Madison and he cursed. He thought about his child and he wept. And with every tear, the cracks in his heart grew wider and he wondered if he'd ever be whole again.

CHAPTER 30

Andy pulled up to Jake's house and walked up to the door. He knocked a few times before walking around to the back.

"Jake! Jake! You here?"

Jake's truck wasn't in the driveway so he walked to the garage and opened the doors. The truck wasn't there either. He knew his son needed some breathing space. Still he pulled out his cell phone and dialed Jake's number. It went right to voicemail.

"Jake, it's your dad. Call me when you get this. I hope you're okay."

He switched off knowing Jake wasn't okay. He was walking back to his truck when Danny pulled up.

"Dad. Jake there?"

"Nope. Don't know where he is. Where are Megan and the kids?"

"I left them at her parents'. What the hell was all that?"

"I wish I knew."

"What the hell is she doing back here?"

"No idea. Her intentions were never good, though."

"Did you see Lily walk right up to her? That girl's got some balls, that's for sure."

Looking down the road for any evidence of Jake, Andy was distracted. "What? Oh, yeah. Balls."

"Dad, he'll be okay. He's Jake. This isn't the worst thing that's happened to him. He'll come through. Lily will convince him to talk to Madison then she'll go away. And hopefully, Lily will decide to stay, or Jake will go with her and leave all this mess in the past."

"I hope so."

"He has to, right?"

Andy looked at his oldest son and saw the hope in his face. Sadly, he couldn't reciprocate that hope.

"I don't know. He's barely held it together since it all happened. I just hope Lily's been able to help put him back together enough that this doesn't break him. C'mon. Let's go back and get your family."

"You go. I'm gonna drive around for a bit and look for him."

"He might not want to be found."

"I know. If I find him, I'll give you a call. If I don't find him in an hour, let Megan know I'll be back."

"Good luck."

"Thanks, Dad. Don't worry, okay?"

"I'll try not to."

Andy climbed into his truck and drove back to the Olsen's. It was time for him to find out what the hell was going on.

CHAPTER 31

Danny thought he knew exactly where Jake was. He pulled out of the driveway and headed towards the docks. A few miles down the road he saw Jake's truck and pulled into the parking lot behind him. Calling his father, Danny let him know he'd found him. Grabbing the backpack from the passenger seat, he took a deep breath and stepped out of his van.

He saw Jake slumped over, shoulders shaking, and his heart dropped. She'd finally done it. She'd finally shattered him into pieces small enough to lose. He wondered briefly about calling Lily but thought better of it. Better for him to know what they were dealing with before he called the cavalry.

Knocking on the window, he startled his brother. "Jake. Open the door."

Jake looked like he'd aged ten years in the past hour. His eyes were a blank void and his hand was bleeding.

When Danny heard the lock click, he opened the door, reached in, and took the keys from the ignition.

"Jake, what are you doing?"

"Nothing."

"You left Lily at the Olsen's'."

"Is she still there?"

Danny reached into the bed of the truck and pulled out the first aid kit. "No. Dad drove her home. She was pretty shaken up. When you left, she went up to Madison like a bat outta hell and asked what the hell her problem was."

"What?"

"Yeah. Unfortunately, I don't think Lily has a mean bone in her body and Madison sliced her pretty good."

Jake dropped his chin and balled his fists. No matter what Madison did to him, she had no right to go near Lily. It was his fault for leaving her there without fully realizing what she was dealing with. "Is Lily okay?"

"I think so. Dad said she's stronger than that." Danny pulled Jake's bloody hand free and wrapped it with gauze, taping it securely. "I don't think Madison can hurt her in the long run. But you do need to talk to her."

"I don't want to talk to her. I don't want anything to do with her."

"Not Madison. Lily. You need to talk to Lily. Square it up, you know?"

"I just don't want to be around anyone right now."

"I know. Get out of the truck."

"Why?"

"'Cause I need a cigarette. Let's go sit on the docks. Talk it out."

"I don't want to talk."

"Then don't. Come sit with me while I fill my lungs with carcinogens."

Reluctantly, Jake followed his brother around the building to the docks. There the two sat in silence for what seemed like hours before Jake finally spoke again.

"What's in the bag?"

Danny had forgotten all about the backpack. Smiling, he unzipped it and pulled out two baseball mitts and a ball.

"I thought we could throw a bit. When we were kids and had a problem, we used to do this all the time. Eventually everything worked out."

Slipping on the glove felt good to Jake. He opened and closed it a few times before realization dawned on him.

"Is this my old glove?"

"Yup."

"I thought I threw it out after mom died."

Danny paused and looked at Jake. "You did."

He adjusted the strap on his wrist. "Huh." Jake wasn't surprised his brother had pulled it out of the trash.

"Wanna start long?"

"Sure," Jake said as he jogged to the other end of the dock.

The glove felt like second skin and the ball felt good in Jake's hand, despite the bandage. He'd forgotten how much he'd missed it.

The two of them tossed the ball back and forth for a while, taking steps closer to each other every so often. It felt like old times and it was exactly what Jake needed to calm down. With every throw, he got looser, calmer. His head cleared and he began to think straight. When they were close enough to talk it out, Jake asked the question no one but Madison knew the answer to.

"Why do you think she came back?"

Danny thought about it for a minute. "I don't know man. She wants to talk. That's all she kept saying. It can't be good, that's for sure. I mean it's Madison, you know?"

"Yeah, I know. Was she ever a good person or was I blind the whole time?"

"I think she wanted to be a good person. She didn't know how. And the two of you, together? Lethal. It was like watching a car crash over and over. Brutal."

"But we had to have had good times, you know? Otherwise, why the hell would I have let her get under my skin for so long?"

"Honestly? You weren't thinking with the right head. She was pretty and you fell hook, line, and sinker. And then, well, I thought you two were finally gonna wake up."

"And then?"

"She got pregnant. No way were you gonna leave her while she was pregnant. You married her, supported her, and you two had a baby. Of course, you weren't gonna leave."

Jake knew his brother was right. No matter the issues they had, Joey had brought the promise of a new beginning. Jake held on with both hands, despite Madison pulling away as hard as she could. Regardless of the outcome, it had been the right thing to do. Who knew if he would have been able to spend any time with him before he died? If he'd let her go, he'd probably never have known what happened to Joey.

The sound of the ball hitting the mitt distracted him and for a minute, he forgot where he was and threw a fastball Danny was barely prepared for.

"Hey!"

"Sorry. I forgot where I was."

"Well, you better come back to earth, Brother. Live in the now. You have got to stop all this shit, living in the past. It's fucked you up."

"You're right. I've just been so damn stuck, so stuck to *her* that I've forgotten how to live, man. And then Lily comes along and I feel so, I don't know, alive, whole. She's amazing, you know. Nothing like Madison."

"I know. She is pretty amazing. Everyone thinks so. I can't find one person to say a bad word about her and believe me, I've tried."

"You've tried, huh?"

Danny smiled and Jake saw the crow's feet suited him. "Of course. Gotta look out for my little brother."

"I can't believe I left her there. She really yelled at Maddie?"

"Scolded is more like it. Honestly, I was hoping she'd punch her but I don't think that's Lily's style."

"I don't think so either. You know where she is?"

"Lily? She's at Bill's."

Catching the ball barehanded, Jake took off his glove and stuffed the ball inside. He walked over, folded up the mitt, and handed it to Danny.

"I gotta go."

"On your knees."

"What?"

"When you apologize, do it on your knees. Girls love it. Gotten me out of a lot of shit with Megan."

"You're sick, you know that?"

Arms outstretched, Danny yelled to Jake as he jogged back to his truck. "Whatever man. It works! Good luck."

Jake two-finger saluted as he peeled a U-turn out of the parking lot and headed for Lily's. His mind raced with things to say and by the time he reached the front door, he was no surer of how to approach this than he'd been the moment Madison showed up.

He knocked and it took Lily a few minutes to open the door. Eyes puffy and red, cheeks stained with tears, she looked so sad. In that moment, the only thing he knew to do was step into the house and wrap his arms around her.

"I'm so sorry you had to see that. I'm so sorry."

Not knowing what to do or say, she did what felt natural. She hugged him back, standing in the doorway between confusion and safety.

CHAPTER 32

Lily untangled herself and stood in front of Jake. "You have to talk to her."

He shook his head, not sure if he heard her right. "What?"

"She won't leave unless you do."

"What if she doesn't?"

"You won't know that unless you try, right?"

He reached for her hands and felt them tremble in his. Everything he felt for her rushed to the surface and he suddenly felt like he was going to drown.

He pleaded. "She can't touch us, Lily."

She blinked away a fresh set of tears that threatened to fall. "She already has, Jake. She's everywhere. And if you don't deal with this, at least get some closure, she'll be around forever."

He felt himself slipping under the water. "No. That's not true."

Pulling her hands away, Lily looked at him with an ultimatum in her eyes. "It is true. She has this hold on you.

I know you made a breakthrough the other day at the cemetery. I am so sorry for all the pain you've had to deal with, all the loss. But this is one last hurdle you have to jump before you can truly move on. Before we can move forward, you need closure. And you have to do it by yourself."

Jake stepped into the living room and sat down on the couch with his head in his hands. He wondered how everything had become so complicated. He was fine until Madison stepped back into his life. He was haunted but dealing when Lily came along. All he'd ever wanted was to be happy. The one woman who denied him that was back, threatening to take away the one woman who showed him the way to peace. His insides were twisting into knots. He didn't know what to do.

"I don't know how to talk to her. Every time I look at her, I see a woman who left her dying son and her husband and didn't look back. I don't want to hear her excuses. I don't want her to ask for forgiveness. I can't give it. I don't want anything to do with her."

Sitting across from him on the coffee table, Lily lifted his chin and searched his eyes. "She did leave you. She did leave Joey and you don't have to accept her excuses. You don't have to forgive her just because she asks for it. You may not want anything to do with her but she's here and she has something to say. What that is, I can only imagine. You have an opportunity to end this, for good."

Lily felt suddenly nauseous and she paled for a moment, holding her hand to her stomach. *Not here. Not now.* "Just promise me you'll talk to her."

Closing his eyes, he took a deep breath and blew it out slowly. This time, his hands were trembling. "Don't go."

Despite the fact that he uttered the words she'd been waiting to hear, her stomach was twisted more with each passing minute. She felt her skin begin to moisten with sweat. The room started to spin a little bit. "What?"

"I don't want you to go to Atlanta. Stay here. Stay with me."

Holding down her lunch, Lily nodded. "Talk to her." She stood and opened the front door. "Talk to her first. You and I have time to talk about Atlanta."

Taking his cue, Jake walked over to the door and gently kissed her on the cheek. "I will."

She closed the door behind him, rested her head on the smooth wood, and held her stomach. Eyes watering from the bile rising in her throat she couldn't contain anymore, she threw up on the floor. The nausea brought her to her knees as the sickness continued. For a moment, she felt as if she was dying, then eventually it subsided.

She was in the kitchen grabbing paper towels and a glass of water when Billy barged into the house. He looked down as he stepped in the mess she hadn't cleaned up yet.

"Lily? What happened?"

"I'm sorry. I threw up. I was just about to clean it up. I just needed a minute to find my bearings."

She looked pale enough to worry him. "Are you alright?"

Smiling weakly, she replied, "I'm good. No worries."

"Let me help you with that."

He rushed over and grabbed the paper towels from her. As he cleaned the mess, she sat at the kitchen table wringing her hands. When he finished, he placed another glass of water and some stomach relief medicine in front of her.

"Take this."

"That's okay."

"It will make you feel better."

"I don't think it will."

"Is this about Madison? Did that bitch say something to upset you?"

"That," she began as she nodded toward the entryway, "was not about her. We had words but I am sure my stomach issues have nothing to do with her."

"Are you sick? I can call the doctor."

Looking down, she realized she'd turned a napkin into confetti. "That's ok. I already have an appointment on Tuesday." She blew out a long breath. "With Dr. Garmen."

She said it without meeting Billy's eyes and instead continued to shred the napkin.

"But Dr. Garmen is an obstetrician. Why would you…" When she finally lifted her head to look at her uncle, more tears fell down her face. Reality punched him in the gut. "Oh, Lily. Does Jake know?"

She shook her head and picked up a second napkin.

"How did this happen?"

The look she gave him made him blush.

"Well, right. That's not what I meant. How long have you known?"

"A week or two. I wasn't sure at first. Then I was and I made an appointment."

"Are you going to tell him?"

"I don't know what I'm going to do. I have to see the doctor first."

"Are you still going to Atlanta?"

"I don't know."

"What do you need me to do?"

"Nothing. Really. I'll figure this out."

Holding her hands in his, he said, "You don't have to figure anything out by yourself. You can stay here as long as you like. I can help you out with anything you need. This isn't a decision you need to make on your own. I'm here for you."

His sincerity blanketed her with security and she pushed back from the table. "Thank you, Uncle Billy. What I need right now is to sleep. This whole day has wiped me out. I just want to forget it ever happened."

"Go right ahead, sweetie. If you want, I can drive you on Tuesday."

"That would be great, thanks."

Before she headed downstairs, Billy asked, "Did you really confront Madison?"

"Yeah. I guess I did."

"You should have punched her."

A knowing smile spread across her face. "I'll remember that for next time."

She closed the door behind her and headed to the bathroom. While she brushed her teeth, she turned sideways in the mirror pulling her shirt tight over her stomach, examining her profile. She knew it was too soon to tell but she imagined anyway. Imagined a life here with Jake. Imagined life as a mother. Imagined life with all the happiness she'd ever wanted. While she imagined, a face floated in her mind. The one person who she knew could destroy it all. Madison.

CHAPTER 33

The vibrating anger Jake had felt earlier subsided, replaced with a need for reason. He wasn't sure if he should go to the Olsen's now to get this talk over with or if he should clear his head for a bit before confronting Madison head on. His mind was swimming in a million different directions. Eventually, he figured out he was not in the right state of mind. He picked up the phone and called his dad.

"Dad?"

"You okay son?" Concern filled Andy's voice.

"Yeah. I will be. Listen. Could you come over?"

"Sure. I'll be there in five minutes."

"Thanks, Dad."

"Anytime."

When he clicked off, Jake felt a glimmer of hope spread through him. Lily was right. He needed closure. He needed to find it by himself, and if anyone knew how to steer him in the right direction, it was his father.

Never one to be late for anything, Andy was standing in the driveway waiting for Jake when he pulled in. He wasn't surprised.

Hopping out of the truck, Jake said, "Hey. Do you want a beer?"

With his hands in his pockets, Andy replied, "Sure," as he walked over to the fridge.

The two men walked into the house. Jake dropped his bag on the table. Reaching into the fridge, Andy pulled out two bottles and opened them, setting one on the counter in front of Jake.

"Tough day, huh?"

"You could say that."

"So, what's up?"

"Just wanted to talk."

"Have you spoken to Lily?"

"Yeah, I did. She was pretty upset. She said I needed closure."

"Smart girl."

"I know. The thing is, I don't how to do that."

Andy turned away from Jake and headed out the back door, making himself comfortable on one of the lawn chairs on the deck. Jake followed, settled in the chair beside him, and waited. He knew his father was a man of few words and always chose the right ones. He wouldn't speak until he had an answer.

Together they sat, listening to the croaking of frogs and the chirping of crickets. Stars shined above them as the heat of the day faded to the cool of night. The weight of it all began to fall away when Andy finally spoke after the third, slow beer.

"I think," he began, pausing to choose his words carefully, "you need to get past what happened. You haven't spoken about it. Yesterday when you finally opened up to Lily it was a breakthrough but you still haven't dealt with it. You've refused to notice the pain the people around you were feeling. You closed yourself off from all of us and refused to acknowledge what was going on around you."

Jake nodded in agreement, grateful for his father's honesty.

"When your mother died, I was destroyed. I felt like my whole world collapsed. I remember lying in bed, praying for God to take me, too. I was so sure I wouldn't be able to live without her. Then I realized I had to. You and your brother needed me to be strong. I realized it wasn't just me that was hurting, you two were as well. And your mom would have been pissed if I didn't take care of you.

"So I wallowed in self-pity for a bit. I tried to keep most of the pain from you. I had to come to terms with her passing, as much as I hated it. Sure she was my world, but so were you and your brother. I couldn't live in the past if I was going to help you move on. Do you understand what I'm saying?"

Jake finished his beer and sat for a moment, taking in what his father had just said. "I guess I forgot I wasn't the only one who lost someone when Joey died. Madison didn't just hurt *me*."

"You can't forget something you didn't know existed. You just couldn't look past it all."

"You're right. It wasn't intentional. I just didn't know how to handle it. I still don't know how."

Andy nodded before walking back into the house to grab two more beers. When he returned, Jake continued. "If I don't make peace with everything, then I can't be there for the people that need me."

"Like Lily."

"Like Lily. And you and Danny and everyone else I pushed away."

"You need to talk to Madison. Square it away. Put it away. Don't forget, don't ever forget. Just allow it to fade. The past doesn't need to haunt you. You can embrace it, learn from it, and move on. And I'm telling you, it's not fair to Lily if you don't. If you love her, you won't imprison *her* in *your* past. It's not her burden to carry."

Sitting quietly, Jake thought about what his father said. He was right, of course. Jake decided he'd think about how to approach Madison and call tomorrow to figure out when and where to talk. He wasn't going to let her choose the place and time. He wouldn't let her have control over this situation. For once, he needed to take charge and show her she couldn't affect him like she once had.

"Let me ask you a question."

Jake turned to his father. "Shoot."

"What do you want?"

"What do you mean?"

"What do you want to get out of all this?"

"With Madison?"

"With Madison, with Lily, with life in general. What do you want?"

The question wasn't easy for Jake to answer. It wasn't one he'd ever been asked before and certainly not one he'd thought about.

"I don't know. I just want to finish this thing with Madison. I want to tell Lily I love her. I want her to stay here. I want to live a normal life with the happiness I think everyone should have. I think I deserve some peace."

"I don't think you understand that you can control all of that. Madison is here. You have the opportunity to finish it, on your terms. As for Lily, open your damn mouth and tell her. Don't wait for her to leave. Tell her. If she leaves, at least she'll make an informed decision. Normal life? Don't we all wish for that? Happiness? Make your own. If it's with Lily, the docks, the guitar—make your own happiness and stop waiting around for someone to hand it to you. The only thing you deserve is what you give."

Jake cringed as he was smacked in the head with the brutal honesty in his father's answer. "Tell me how you really feel."

"Look. You're my son and I love you. But for Christ's sake, Jacob. Wake up. Life is passing you by. Where the hell have you been for the past two years? Not here, that's for damn sure. Everyone has figured out a way to move on but you. And then suddenly, a beautiful, amazing woman walks into your life and you're too afraid to hold on to her? That's not the son I raised, and I can't sit back and let you do this anymore."

With nothing more to say, the two men sat in silence until Andy checked his watch. Realizing it was after midnight, he stood.

"You leaving?"

"Yeah. I think you know what you need to do."

Jake hugged his father tightly, the first real hug they'd shared in a long time. "Thanks, Dad."

"No problem. Let me know if you need anything."

Jake walked his father around the house to his car. "I will. I think I'll sleep on it and call tomorrow. I'll have this hashed out in a day or two."

"All right then. See you at work."

"See you tomorrow."

Jake banged on the hood as his father pulled out of the driveway then he walked back into the house.

Throwing away the empty beer bottles, he paused. The melody he'd been mulling over in his head, since Lily gave him the guitar, finalized. He walked over to the closet and pulled out the guitar. Settling back out on the deck, he began to play as words materialized from nowhere. Before sunrise, the song he'd wanted to write for Lily was complete and he'd figured out how to handle Madison.

He placed the guitar on the stand in his room instead of hiding it in the closet. It belonged there now. Lily had given him a second chance and he was done running away from it. He wanted Lily to be a part of his life and he'd do whatever it took to make sure that happened.

CHAPTER 34

When Lily woke up the next morning, Billy had already left for the bar. He'd told her last night she could take the day off. Sitting home alone was the last thing she wanted to do. She'd thought about grabbing her camera and heading for the beach but even that wouldn't be enough to distract her. Jake didn't call last night and she wasn't sure when he would. Just another thing she didn't feel like thinking about.

She straightened up the house for a bit before hopping in the shower to get ready to go to work. Billy would protest but she needed to face the day. A lot of the people from the picnic would probably end up at the bar today, and she needed them to know she wasn't going to let what happened yesterday dictate her routine. And she needed to not think about tomorrow until she had to.

Despite the fact that her stomach protested, she choked down a piece of dry toast and a banana before heading out the door. At the last minute, she pulled her cell phone out of her purse, turned it off and left it on the table.

She walked in the back door of the bar, grabbed an apron, and headed towards the office. Billy was sitting at his desk, face buried in paperwork—his usual spot on a Monday morning.

"Hey."

Leaning back, Billy tossed his glasses on the desktop and rubbed his face. "What are you doing here? Didn't I give you the day off?"

"Yeah. I didn't want to sit home and think all day. Besides, you can't afford to give me the day off. Two of your waitresses are sick and another one's on vacation. You need me."

He seemed to think it over before replying, "Fine. You can stay. But the second you don't feel like you can handle it, the moment you start to feel sick, you promise me you'll go home."

Lily smiled. "Of course."

"Promise."

Crossing her fingers over her heart she promised before heading out to the floor.

The lunch crowd started early today, she noticed so she got to work taking orders and making small talk with the customers. For the most part, the day was moving quickly giving her a much-needed break from her thoughts. It even got busy enough for Billy to help out in the kitchen. Before she knew it, she was running around like a mad woman. She didn't even notice Madison walk in and sit in her section.

Without looking at her customer, Lily pulled out her pad and pencil. "What can I get you?"

Placing the menu on the table, Madison looked up at her waitress in surprise. A smirk curled across her mouth. "Well, well, well. Fancy meeting you here."

Lily gripped her pencil so tightly in her hand that it threatened to snap. "Madison."

"You remembered! Look, I'm sorry about yesterday. It wasn't my intention to get into it with you."

"I'm sure."

"No really. I didn't even know you existed until yesterday. Imagine my surprise."

Anger balled in Lily's stomach. "You're surprised? Are you for real?"

Madison looked genuinely insulted. "How was I supposed to know Jake had a girlfriend? Really. None of this has anything to do with you."

"You have got to be kidding me."

"I'm not. Truce?" Madison held out her hand.

At that moment Billy walked onto the floor. A number of other patrons had stopped to watch the exchange. When he saw Madison sitting at the table, he headed right for her. It wasn't until he was halfway there that he realized Lily was standing next to the table.

"Aw shit," he muttered to himself.

A hand reached out to stop him from moving any further. "Leave her be, Bill. She can handle it."

Billy did as Mrs. Jones told him and continued to watch the exchange.

"You can stuff your truce and take it back with you to wherever you came from."

"Look, Lily. My issue isn't with you. I came here for Jake and when I talk to him, I'll go. I won't ruin the nice little thing you have here."

"Maybe he doesn't want to talk to you."

"Oh, he does. He just doesn't know it yet. You know what? I'm not hungry. Just tell Jake I'm looking for him."

"Tell him yourself."

"Maybe I will. Just take this advice. Be careful. Jake doesn't know how to care about anyone but himself."

"Screw you. You don't even know him."

"I know him better than he knows himself."

With that, Madison, stood and left the bar, leaving Lily standing with nothing to do but watch her go. When she finally turned around, she saw her uncle and a number of customers watching her. Suddenly self-conscious, she ducked her head and headed to the back. Billy followed her.

"You okay?"

"Fine. She was just looking for a reaction. I don't believe for one second that she didn't know I was here."

"You handled her well."

Throwing her hands up, she yelled, "I shouldn't have to fucking handle her!"

Billy smiled.

"What? What are you smiling at?"

"You. Don't let her rile you up. That's what she wants. You stood up to her. That's not what she wants. Let her do her thing and leave. Jake can handle it."

Taking a deep breath and blowing it out slowly, Lily calmed down. "Sorry."

"Don't apologize to me. You did great."

Smiling despite herself, Lily nodded, gave Bill a quick kiss on the cheek, and walked back out with a small spring in her step.

"Hey Mrs. Jones. What can I get you?"

"A set of balls like yours."

Lily almost dropped her pen. "Excuse me?"

"Someone needed to put that girl in her place. Glad it was you."

She didn't know how to respond. "Well, thanks, I guess."

"You're welcome. Now, I'll have a burger, medium, hold the tomato. And an iced tea. Bill makes the best iced tea."

"I'll get right on that. Thanks again."

Mrs. Jones was reading the paper and didn't hear her. Lily smiled to herself and went back to work taking orders, feeling somewhat better about the whole situation than she had earlier. Maybe she was stronger than she thought.

CHAPTER 35

Madison waited until she left the bar to storm to her car. She wouldn't give them the satisfaction of knowing she was pissed. She needed everyone to think she was in control, even when she was going off the rails.

She'd hoped to intimidate Lily a little bit, but all she did was embarrass herself. Everyone was looking at her with pity, and she didn't need their sorrowful glances. She wanted them to look at her like they looked at Lily. She wanted them to stand up for her like they stood up for Lily. No one ever did anything but feel sorry for her. She'd come back hoping that had ended. Now she felt even more like an outsider than she had two years ago.

"Screw all of you," she muttered and yanked the door open.

Getting in her car, she vowed to talk to Jake if it killed her. As the thought crossed her mind, her cell phone rang.

"What?"

"Madison? It's Jake."

She wasn't happy that he sounded so abrupt but she turned on her sweetest voice.

"Oh, hey. Wondering when I was gonna hear from you."

"You said you wanted to talk, right?"

"I did."

"What do you want to talk about?"

She frowned, momentarily annoyed with the way he was talking to her, as if she didn't matter. Like she was some random annoyance he needed to deal with.

"If I told you that, then we'd have nothing to talk about later."

"No games, Madison."

"I would never. How's tonight sound?"

"Fine. I—"

She cut him off. "I'll meet you at your house at seven."

She hung up the phone before he could protest and quickly shut it off, tossing it in her purse. Pulling down her visor, she freshened her lipstick in the mirror. This was going to be on her terms whether he liked it or not. She held the cards, and she wasn't about to give any of them away.

Backing out of the parking lot, she drove back to her parents' house. She wanted to make sure everything was perfect when she met up with Jake tonight.

When she drove up to the house, her father was outside, mowing the lawn. Her mother was in the flowerbed, weeding. Not much had changed, she thought as she walked up to the porch and sat down.

Abby looked up. "Where have you been?"

"Oh, out. Here and there. Stopped at Billy's for a bite to eat but realized I wasn't hungry."

"You stopped at Billy's?"

"Yeah, why?"

"Well, didn't your father tell you last night that Lily worked there?"

Looking everywhere but at her mother, she replied lazily. "Did he? I don't remember."

"Was she there?"

Focused on her fingernails, Madison was determined to keep control. "As a matter of fact she was. Nice girl."

"Please leave her alone, Madison. She's never done anything to you."

"Come on, Mom. Give me a little credit. I'm not the same person I was. I've changed."

Exasperated, Abby stood up finally pushing back against her daughter. "How many times have we heard that, dear?"

Madison stood to face her. "Jesus. You and Dad never could take my side. She came up to *me* yesterday. She started yelling at *me* and yet, here you are, defending *her*. Thinking I am going to do something awful to her. I guess nothing has changed."

Abby watched her daughter stomp into the house and shook her head. Madison had always been a drama queen, had always been up to something. There was nothing they could do for her then, and Abby was sure there was nothing they could do for her now. As much as she hated to admit it, life was much simpler when Madison wasn't around. They'd all have to wait, though, until Madison decided it was time for her to move on. It wasn't easy having a daughter who flitted in and out whenever she pleased, but Abby had to accept it.

John turned off the mower and walked over to his wife. "What was that all about?"

"Nothing. Just Madison being Madison. You know her."

"Yeah." He reached over, put his arm around his wife, and kissed her on her head. "Unfortunately I do know. I just can't figure where we went wrong."

Grabbing his hand for comfort, Abby leaned into him. "We didn't do anything wrong, John. She is just who she is and we have to accept that."

"I know. You're right. I just wish I could get through to her. She's always been so unreachable."

"Always. And that's why we have to just accept her. It's not like she's changed from who she used to be. From the daughter we raised."

"I hate it. I hate the fact that I'd rather her be anywhere but here. It makes me feel like a shitty father, the fact that I don't want anything to do with my own daughter. All she does is cause drama and pain."

Squeezing his hand for reassurance, Abby looked into her husband's eyes and saw the torment, the sadness that lived there.

"It doesn't make you a shitty father. It makes you a human being."

John said nothing more. He kissed his wife on the head and started up the lawnmower again, resolved to lose himself in mundane normalcy. He refused to get caught up in Madison's nonsense.

Abby watched as her husband walked away with his shoulders slumped. She knew exactly how he felt because she felt the same way. The difference was she'd decided not to let it steer her anymore. Madison was a grown woman. Abby was done making excuses for her.

CHAPTER 36

Jake's first day back on the boat was uneventful, other than the fact that he dreaded seeing Madison later that night. It wasn't easy to focus on what he needed to do in order to get through the day safely. His head swimming with dread, he finally stepped onto the dock with his stomach in a knot. His nerves were on edge and he couldn't shake them out. Checking his watch, he realized he had some time before she'd be at his house, so he went into the locker room and changed into running clothes.

Plugging in his ear buds with his iPod on the fastest playlist he had, he stepped outside, stood for a minute in late afternoon sun, and then ran. It took him some time before he was able to fall comfortably into a rhythm but when he did, he was able to clear his mind of all the cluttered junk and focus. Everything began to stream as smooth as his stride.

Madison.
She's coming over to talk.
What could she want? Whatever it is, it can't be good.

Divorce papers on the table. Make her sign them.
Tell her to leave. I want nothing to do with her.
Close the door on her, for good.
Lily.
Ask her to stay. Convince her if I have to.
Build a life.
Be happy.

He kept reminding himself that he was stronger than the last time he saw Madison. Hell, he was stronger than he was three months ago. Lily had helped him find himself and he wasn't going to let the past break him down. One day, he mused, he wouldn't have to remind himself of that on a daily basis.

He made his way to the beach for a while before heading back to the docks. Sitting and staring into the horizon always filled him with peace. He let the sunlight and the warm breeze wash over him and he closed his eyes. He turned off the music and let the sound of the crashing waves fill his ears.

He didn't hear Lily walk up behind him. It wasn't until she sat next to him and blocked the sun that he opened his eyes and looked around.

She was next to him on the sand with her head turned towards the sun, soaking it in. He gently reached for her hand and interlocked his fingers with hers. A tiny smile played on her mouth. He stared at her, trying to memorize every curve of her face, every eyelash, the slope of her neck. Today she looked different. If it was possible, she looked even more beautiful than yesterday. There was a warmth pulsing off her and he wondered what was different.

Her tone was matter-of-fact when she spoke. "You should have told me."

Knowing exactly what she was talking about, he acknowledged his mistake. "I know. I just don't think of myself married to her. I'm sorry."

"It wasn't easy to hear coming from her. I would have understood if you had told me."

His fingers tightened around hers. "I know."

Shading her eyes with her free hand, she turned to him. "Is there anything else I need to know?"

Meeting her eyes, he replied, "Nothing else. You know everything."

She continued to watch his face for a few moments. "Are you going to talk to her?"

"Yes. Tonight."

"You better get going. We can talk tomorrow, okay?"

"Okay. Lily?"

She stood and dusted the sand from her clothes. "Yeah?"

"I'm so sorry you had to deal with all this. It isn't fair."

"I know you are. And it isn't. But I can deal. Just talk to her and we'll figure out the rest."

She leaned down and kissed the top of his head before walking off. Her touch lingered, forcing him to stand and make his way back to his car. It was time for him to face this head on and finish it. He was tired of living with all the ghosts.

By the time he made it back to his truck, it was later than he thought. Madison would be at his house in less than half an hour. Though he'd mentally prepared himself for this, he wasn't sure what kind of curveball she'd throw at him.

Once he was home and showered, it wasn't long before there was a knock at his door. Counting backwards slowly from twenty before answering, he walked over to the door and opened it.

"Hey, handsome!"

Madison was standing there, obviously dressed to impress. Not a hair was out of place. Her face was flawless and her clothes hugged her in the places she'd wanted to highlight. Jake wasn't impressed.

"Let's get this over with."

He opened the door wider so she could step in but she managed to brush against him, anyway. Rolling his eyes as he shut the door, he walked immediately over to the kitchen table and sat down. Madison walked over to the couch and sank comfortably onto the cushions.

"Love what you've done with the place. Certainly better than when I lived here."

"I've made some changes."

"Of course, you have. So have I."

"How many times have I heard that?"

"Enough, I would suspect." She stood and walked over to a picture hanging on the wall, studying it.

"What do you want, Maddie?"

"My goodness, Jake. You haven't even offered me a drink."

"Fine. Do you want a drink?"

"Sure. What was it we drank that first night? Whiskey?"

Lying, he replied, "I don't remember."

Her eyes glinted when she looked at him. "Sure you do."

He took two glasses from the cabinet and set them on the table. He poured them each a drink. He finished his and was pouring another before she walked over to pick hers up.

She watched him over the rim of her glass and noticed the gray in his hair and the crow's feet forming around his eyes. He sat bouncing his knees and fidgeting with a pencil and she laughed.

"Jesus, Jake. Relax."

"I don't want to relax. I want you to tell me what the hell you want."

"No small talk? No catching up? No 'where the hell have you been'?"

"Fine. Where the hell have you been?"

"Florida. I left right before, well you know. I was staying with some friends for a while, trying to get clean."

"Trying?"

"At the time I was trying. I'm clean now. Have been for a long time. None of that AA stuff. I have a job, an apartment, and friends. I'm doing what I should've done right after school."

"And what's that?"

"Starting over. People only know the new me there. There are no funny looks, no whispers behind my back. None of that nonsense I got while I was here."

"So you want to talk about how happy you are now? How wonderful your life is now that you've left me and your dead son behind?"

Madison pulled out a chair and sat across from him. She set her glass down on the table hard enough to get his attention. Running her hands through her hair, she felt she was beginning to lose control of the conversation. She wanted a different reaction and it suddenly hit her, she wasn't going to get it, not from him.

"This isn't going the way I'd planned."

"Oh? And what exactly did you plan? Were you gonna stroll back into town and swoon when everyone welcomed you back with open arms?"

"Don't be a dick."

"You don't have a right to tell me what or who to be. And I have every fucking right to be a dick. You fucking walked out on me, on our baby, while he was in *the hospital*. Who does that? Who walks out on their sick kid?"

"I know. I'm sorry."

He stood so fast, his chair toppled over. "Sorry? You're fucking sorry? Yeah, well, I don't forgive you. You can keep your fucking sorry. Joey died *in my arms*. *I* was with him when he died. Not you. You left."

She was shocked into stillness. She could feel the emotion pouring out of him. Emotion she hadn't let herself feel until now. Swallowing the rest of her drink, she reached for the bottle and poured herself another.

"I didn't know. At least not then. I thought he was going to be okay. It wasn't until a few weeks later that I found out."

"He wasn't okay. I buried him five days after you left. I couldn't wait for you to come back so I buried our son without you. You didn't even have the decency to call, to check up and see if he was all right."

Jake was shaking with anger. Without thinking, he picked up his glass and threw it against the wall. Madison jumped and knocked over her own glass.

"Jake. What the hell? Not this shit again. Can't we have a normal conversation without any of this crap?"

Clenching his fists, Jake turned away from her and willed himself to calm down. He hadn't allowed himself to feel this out of control in a long time. It wasn't a welcome feeling.

Madison, at least, knew enough from their past to leave him to himself for the moment. The last thing she wanted to do was get in his face when he was like this.

When he finally turned back to face her, he saw her broken eyes overflowing with tears. "No! No! You don't get to cry. You don't get to shed a fucking tear over him."

"Stop! Look, I'm sorry. I made such a mess of everything. That's why I am here, to apologize, to make amends. I haven't even been to see where he's buried."

"And you want me to take you? Fuck you."

"You have to forgive me."

"Why?"

"Because..." She wasn't able to finish her sentence. Truthfully, she couldn't think of a good reason for anyone to forgive anything she'd ever done.

"Because?"

She whispered. "Nothing."

"That's right, nothing."

He picked up a folder from the counter and threw it across the table. "I've been trying to get you to sign these for two years."

Picking up the folder, she opened it and began to read. It wasn't surprising, really. She'd have been surprised if he hadn't filed for divorce by now.

"You want me to sign these."

He handed her a pen. "Yes."

"Jake, listen—"

"No, you listen. I've been walking around broken for two years. Two years! All because of you. I've finally begun to heal, and you waltz back like nothing ever happened. I want you gone. Out of my life. Have a little self-respect. Sign the damn papers and leave. Go back to Florida."

"Jake, I'm dying."

Stepping back, he put his hands up in front of him. "What?"

"Brain tumor. I've only got a few more months. That's why I came back. I can't die knowing all the pain I caused is still so raw."

"I don't believe you."

"It's true. I found out a few months ago. I haven't told my parents yet."

"Sign the papers, Madison."

"I will. I just want you to understand where I'm coming from."

"I don't care if you die on the floor right now, I'll never forgive you."

"You don't mean that."

"I mean it more than I've ever meant anything in my life."

"How would Lily feel if she saw this part of you? How do you know it won't come out around her?"

"She's different. I'm different when I'm with her."

"People don't change that much, Jake."

"Oh, but you'd like people to think you have."

"Brain cancer puts things into perspective."

"So does love."

Leaning back in her chair, Madison contemplated his words. "Touché."

"Sign the papers. Please, Madison. And get out of my life."

A fresh set of tears rolled down her face and she rolled the pen between her fingers before signing her name. Silently, she picked up her purse and walked out the door.

Finally free of her, Jake allowed himself to crack. With shaky hands, he picked up the papers and read her signature over and over until it began to sink in. He'd figured he'd be happy that it was finally over. Instead, he felt even more lost than ever.

CHAPTER 37

Madison drove up to her parents' house and sat in the driveway. She didn't want them to see her like this. She hadn't stopped crying since she left Jake's house. She knew she'd probably deserved every cruel word he'd spoken but it didn't make the cracks in her heart any smaller.

Not sure why she thought there might be a different outcome, she leaned her head back on the seat. The moon was full and the wind had picked up. A summer storm was threatening the night sky. Closing her eyes to the uncomfortable, dull headache that threatened to overtake her, she focused on her breathing. She knew it was only a matter of time before the pain would become so unbearable that she wouldn't be able to walk. But still she sat. Reliving the day.

When the passenger door opened, she didn't look over. Instead, she smelled the familiar aftershave her father had been using ever since she could remember.

"Hey, Dad."

"What are you doing sitting out here in the dark?"

"Trying to forget."

"Didn't go so well today, did it?"

"You knew it wouldn't."

"So did you, sweetie. I don't understand. What was so pressing that you had to talk to him? Why couldn't you just let it lie?"

It was then she opened her eyes and looked at her father. He was getting old. There was no longer any brown in his hair, just a shiny mop of silver. The wrinkles around his eyes had deepened. She reached out and touched his face.

"I signed the papers."

"What papers?"

"Jake had divorce papers waiting for me."

"Oh, that."

"Yeah, that."

"So that's why you made such a big stink? To sign divorce papers?"

"Yes. No."

"I don't understand, sweetie. Help me understand."

Eyes shut against the pain in her head; she rubbed her hands over her face. "Aw shit, Dad."

"Maddie, you're my daughter and I love you, but you have to stop this. You have to stop hurting people."

"You don't think I know that? That's why I came back. To make it right. I just can't seem to do anything right. I just make it worse."

"Why now? Why make amends now?"

"Dad, listen. There's something I'm going to tell you and I don't want you to get all weird on me. Just let me tell you what I came to say and then we can move on. Deal?"

John looked at his daughter and noticed that she'd aged more than she should have over those past two years. The drugs didn't help, but the lines on her face were too deep, the ash in her skin too gray, and the pain in her eyes too intense.

"What's wrong?"

"I was getting headaches, really bad migraines. Every time I got them, they'd get worse, you know? So I went to the doctor. We tried meds and stuff but nothing worked. He sent me for some tests."

"And?"

"And, well, I have a tumor pressing on some lobe in my brain."

Silence filled the car as John felt the air rush out of his lungs. "What?"

"A tumor. Inoperable. Fatal. So I came here to make everything all better. Part of my own twelve-step, I'm-gonna-be-dead-soon, plan."

When she laughed, John felt sick to his stomach. How could she joke about something like that? Why hadn't she told them before? Every bone in his body shook. Every hair stood on end. Pain like he'd never felt before permeated every inch of his heart. Guilt wracked his nerves, and he punched the dashboard. Madison jumped.

"That was pretty much Jake's reaction."

"You told him?"

"Yeah. He called me a liar and kicked me out of his house. Nice, right?"

"How can you make jokes?"

She couldn't stand to watch the tears fall from her father's eyes so she looked quickly away.

"Not much else to do, Dad. Karma's a bitch, huh?"

"Son of a bitch, Madison! This isn't one of your jokes. This isn't one of your games. You're telling me you're going to die, and there is nothing anyone can do about it?"

"That about sums it up. Look, I've had time to process this. Though I haven't quite come to terms with it, I've been dealing with it. I've had second and third opinions."

"What about treatment options?"

"They'd buy me a month or two, tops. And I'd be sick the whole time. I don't want that. Dad, look, I'm fine. I didn't handle coming back well. I should have done things differently. But that's me. An A-Plus screw up. Take it or leave it."

"We have to tell your mother."

"I was hoping you could tell her."

"No. You need to have this conversation with her. No running away. No leaving. You will talk to her, to us. We will make plans, we will help you."

"I don't need any help."

"I don't give a shit what you think you need. Damn it, Madison. When are you going to grow up and think about someone other than yourself?"

"It's easier this way. If I don't care about what other people think, then I don't have to feel bad when I hurt them. And I will hurt them. I always do."

"It's never too late to change."

"For me it is."

"No. It isn't."

She fought against the pain. When she started shaking, John reached over and held her. She let go and collapsed against him, feeling the comfort of her father's love.

He barely heard her whisper, "I'm so scared."

Stroking her hair, he heard his own voice crack. "I know, honey. I'm scared too."

As the rain began to fall, Madison pulled away. "Is Mom asleep?"

"Yeah, I think she is."

"Should we wake her up?"

"No. Let her sleep. You and I can hang on till morning."

"It sounds silly, but would you make me some hot chocolate?"

"Sure. C'mon."

He walked around the car and opened the door for his daughter. With their arms around each other, they walked into the house ready to face whatever life was going to hand them.

CHAPTER 38

Lily woke late the next morning full of nerves. Her appointment with Dr. Garmen was in a couple hours and Uncle Billy was taking her. She wasn't sure what to expect, she wasn't sure how she felt about all of this. She just wanted confirmation. She wanted to know she wasn't reading the tests wrong. She wanted to know everything would be all right. She wanted to talk to Jake but knew she couldn't until after the appointment, when she knew for sure there was something more to talk about. Then she would go from there.

After she showered and dressed, she made her way to the kitchen where Billy had made a full breakfast of eggs, bacon, toast, and orange juice. He was moving through the small kitchen like he was on fire. He was just as nervous as she was.

"Good morning."

Caught off guard, he almost dropped the plate of bacon. "Hey. How are you feeling? You ready for the appointment? I know it isn't till noon but I figured if we get there a little early, maybe he'd see you sooner. I made breakfast. You should eat something. You look so pale."

His energy was both reassuring and nerve wracking.

She sighed. "Sure. That sounds like a good idea."

She sat at the table. He pushed a plate full of food in front of her and told her to eat up. She did as she was told, despite the protests from her stomach. Today was not the day she needed Billy to freak out, even though she appreciated the sentiment. No, what she needed was calm.

"Hey Billy. You're making me more nervous than I already am. Why don't you sit down and eat with me?"

Smiling gently, he grabbed another plate and filled it up before sitting across from her.

"How'd you sleep?"

"Fine, actually. Surprisingly well."

She watched him carefully as she chewed. His hands were shaking and beads of sweat formed at his temples. His eyes darted around the room.

"You okay?"

"Huh? What? Me? Yeah. I'm good. Nervous as hell but I'm okay. Never had to deal with baby stuff before. Never had any of my own, you know."

"I do know. It's gonna be okay. No matter what happens today, no matter what the doctor says, it's all gonna be okay."

He finally settled his eyes on hers. "Jesus, look at me. I'm acting like a fool and here you are all grown up, so calm. I should take my cue from you, you know. I can't believe what a wonderful woman you've turned into. God, I remember when you were just a baby."

Lily placed her hand on his. "Billy. I promise. It will all work out. Here, let me clean up here. You go get ready. We'll have to leave soon if we're gonna be early."

"I just hope Jake knows what he's got."

She didn't say anything, just smiled before clearing the table.

She was finishing up the last of the dishes when Billy walked in.

"You ready?"

Frozen with fear, nausea threatening to overwhelm her, she swallowed it down and straightened her shoulders. "Yup. Let me get my purse."

Her head buzzed with what-ifs and unanswered questions. She wasn't following the advice she'd given Billy. Eyes closed, she took a deep breath and blew it out slowly before turning to face her uncle.

"Let's go."

The ride to the doctor's office was quiet. Neither knew exactly what to say to the other. Billy didn't want to make her any more nervous than she already was and she didn't want to worry him.

They checked in twenty minutes early and sat in the waiting room until her name was called.

"I'll be right here if you need me kiddo."

"Thanks. I'll be back in a jiff."

She walked stiffly through the door with the nurse and Billy proceeded to wring his hands raw.

The nurse smiled softly and handed her a cup. "I'm going to need a sample. The bathroom is down the hall and to the left. You can just bring it into room number four when you're finished. I'll wait there for you."

"Okay." Lily took the cup and walked into the bathroom. She met the nurse in her room when she finished.

"Here you go."

"Thanks. I'll go take this to the lab while you get undressed. The gown is on the table. Dr. Garmen and I will be back in a few minutes."

"Thank you."

"No problem, sweetie. Don't worry. Dr. Garmen is the best."

Lily undressed and lay down on the table. After a few moments, a small knock on the door pulled her out of herself.

"Come in."

"Hello, Lily. I am Dr. Garmen."

"Hi."

"So it says you're here because you think you might be pregnant."

"Right."

"Have you taken any home pregnancy tests?"

"Yes. Three."

"And they were all positive?"

"Yes."

"Well, they are pretty spot-on nowadays. I don't see why they wouldn't be correct in your case, but we'll check anyway. How have you been feeling? Any morning sickness? Tired?"

"Some sickness and I have been feeling pretty tired lately."

"When was your last period?"

"About two months ago."

"Two months? Are you usually regular?"

"Like clockwork."

"While we're waiting for the test to confirm it, let' see what we have here. Lie back." Dr. Garmen felt her stomach for a bit before asking, "Does this hurt?"

"No. Just feels weird. I have a bit of a stomach ache."

"That's normal."

Tears began to stream down the side of Lily's face.

"But before we get ahead of ourselves, I'd like to take an ultrasound. Do you know what that is?"

She nodded tightly.

"Okay. You hang tight. I'll be right back with the machine and we'll see what's going on."

"All right."

He placed his hand on hers before walking out of the room. When he returned, the nurse that had helped her earlier was pushing in the ultrasound machine.

Settling onto his stool, the doctor looked at her. "The test is positive, Lily.

"I'm going to use the machine to take a look at the baby. Okay? It won't hurt but the gel might be cold."

He opened her gown to reveal her stomach. She inhaled sharply as the cold gel touched her skin. She heard a few beeps and clicks before she felt the wand roll across her belly. All she heard were weird swooshing sounds. She closed her eyes as she focused on them.

"Lily, your baby looks just fine. From what we can tell, probably no more than six weeks."

The first time she and Jake slept together.

Eyes flying open, she jerked her head towards the monitor. The doctor laughed when she squinted at what she saw.

Tracing his finger across the monitor, he said, "Your baby is here. Right now it's really tiny, maybe about an inch, inch and a half."

"Is that sound the heartbeat?"

"No. It's too early to hear the heartbeat. That's just the sound the machine makes. Your heartbeat, your breath sounds."

"So it's definitely in there? I'm definitely pregnant?"

"Yup. Measuring at six weeks on the button."

Her hand flew to her mouth. "Oh, God." More tears flowed as the nurse handed her a tissue.

Sitting back, Dr. Garmen contemplated her for a moment. "I take it this wasn't a planned pregnancy."

"No. It wasn't planned."

"Well, there are a few options to consider. You have some time to make those decisions."

Before she thought about it, she answered, "No. I'm keeping it."

"You're sure? Like I said, you have time."

"I'm sure. Thank you." Suddenly, that much of this was clear. She was going to keep the baby.

"All right then. I would recommend you come back in another six weeks to check on the baby's progress. Here's a prescription for some vitamins. Be sure to stay away from raw fish, alcohol, cigarettes…"

"I don't smoke."

"Well, then that's something you don't have to worry about." He smiled as he handed her the script.

"That's it?"

"That's it. Call me if you have any questions. Congratulations, Lily."

Dr. Garmen walked out behind the nurse and left Lily to dress. When she walked out into the waiting room, Billy stood. He didn't need to ask, the answer was etched on her face.

"Let's go home."

She said nothing, just nodded in agreement and allowed him to steer her out of the office.

They drove in silence. When they arrived at the house, Lily walked downstairs to her room and curled up under the blankets of her bed and cried herself to sleep.

Upstairs, Billy grabbed an early beer from the fridge and sat on the couch wondering how he could help her. It wasn't necessarily his place but he'd help her in any way she needed. She was the closest thing to family he had. He'd just hoped he wouldn't be the one to break the news to her parents.

Finishing the bottle in a few pulls, he rubbed his hands over his face and looked at his watch. He should head over to the bar soon but he'd hold off as long as he could before leaving, just in case Lily woke up and needed something. The bar had been there so long, it could pretty much run itself.

He'd seen her tears fall as they drove home, saw her shudder as she tried to keep her composure. Her shoulders slumped as she walked down to her room. At this point, he wasn't sure what she was going to do about the baby. He figured Jake needed to know but, again, it wasn't his place.

She was a grown woman with a solid head on her shoulders and she would do what was right.

He busied himself with straightening up a bit and making Lily a sandwich for dinner. He covered it and placed it in the fridge before writing her a note, letting her know where he'd be. Satisfied he'd done all he could, he carefully opened the door to her room and walked down the stairs. Halfway down, he looked over at her bed and saw she was sleeping soundly. He smiled.

He placed the note on the kitchen table, picked up his keys, and headed to the bar. When Lily heard the sound of his car back out of the driveway, she opened her eyes. Momentarily unclear, the day flooded back to her in an instant. Her hand on her stomach, she felt a feeling of urgency.

Sitting up, she picked up her phone and dialed. She needed to hear Jake's voice.

When he didn't answer, she left a message. "Jake. It's Lily. We need to talk. Call me when you get this. I was hoping I could see you when you finish work today."

Ending the call, she forced herself to stand up and walk around. The situation wasn't any different than what it was yesterday. The only difference was that a doctor had confirmed what she'd known all along.

Upstairs she found Billy's note and the sandwich he'd left in the fridge. Her appetite was back in full force. She made another sandwich after she ate the first one and made her way back downstairs. There was another phone call she had to make.

Cell phone in hand, she closed her eyes for a moment. Breathing slowly, she dialed the number. "Hey, Mom."

"Hey, sweetie. We miss you."

"I miss you, too. Is Dad there, too? I have something I need to talk to you both about."

"Sure, sweetie, hang on. Let me get him."

Lily's cuticles were bleeding by the time her father got on the line with her mother.

"Hey, Lil. How's South Carolina treating you?"

"Good, good. Listen. I have to tell you both something. You may not like it but you have to know that I always make good decisions, right?"

Worry echoed from the other end of the line. "Lily what's wrong? Did something happen?"

"You could say that."

CHAPTER 39

It was early afternoon before Jake dragged himself out of bed. After Maddie left, he drowned himself in the rest of the whiskey. At least he'd had the forethought to leave a message for John that he wouldn't be at work.

Head throbbing, he staggered to the kitchen and poured himself a glass of water and popped two ibuprofen. Standing at the kitchen sink, he dropped his head into his hands. *A tumor?* Every cell in his brain told him she was lying but then again, he saw the look in her eyes when she'd told him. There was a truth in them he'd never seen before.

He needed to know. He needed to go over there and see for himself. He turned up the hot water in the shower and stepped in, willing the steam to erase his hangover.

By the time he'd gotten dressed and headed to the Olsen's, it was almost three. Banging on the door, he had to wait a minute before anyone answered.

When Mrs. Olsen answered the door, her eyes were red from crying and she looked broken.

"Mrs. Olsen. Is Maddie here?"

"Jake? I don't think now is a good time."

"I just need to know if it's true."

Fresh tears spilled from her and Jake's heart hitched.

"Please, Mrs. Olsen. Let me see her."

"She's sleeping. The headaches. She gets bad headaches."

"Let me see her. I won't make any noise, I promise."

"Abby, who is it?"

John appeared at the door with the same sad, red eyes as his wife.

"Jake?"

"I just want to see her."

"She's sleeping."

"I know that. Just let me look at her."

"I don't know."

"I just need to see for myself. I'll know it's true if I can just see her."

"Fine. You have two minutes. Don't make any noise. She needs her sleep."

"I know. Thank you."

"She's in her room. Two minutes."

Jake stepped to the back of the house and slowly opened Madison's door. Her hair was still wet from a shower and her face was clear of any make-up. The gray tinge to her face was highlighted by the brittleness of her body. He didn't know why he hadn't noticed it before. She looked sick. He'd been too busy hating her to actually notice her.

He rested his head against her door and stared for longer than the two minutes he'd been given. He didn't know what to feel. He was supposed to hate her, to despise her. And now, here he was, feeling sorry for her. Feeling *something* for her.

John walked down the hall and watched as Jake stood, stiff as a board, in the doorway. As he watched, Jake slumped against the door. He could feel the conflict warring inside him. He stepped over and put his hand on his shoulder. Jake turned around and held John's gaze for a moment before walking out of the house.

Reaching into his pocket for his cell phone, Jake realized he'd left it at home. He knew Lily had off from work today, and he just hoped she was home.

Lily answered the door on the first knock.

"What's wrong?"

"Can we talk?"

"Sure, come on in. I wanted to talk to you, too."

"I was hoping we could go for a walk."

"Sure. The swimming hole?"

He nodded as she stepped out onto the front porch. When he held her hand, she noticed his was damp and clammy.

Walking through the wooded path helped calm him down. She was bursting with the news she wanted to share with him, but that would have to wait. Clearly, whatever was plaguing his mind needed to be freed.

Once they walked into the clearing, Jake turned as Lily inhaled sharply.

"I'd almost forgotten how beautiful it was here."

He squeezed her hand and led her to the bank where she slipped her now bare feet into the warm water.

"So, what's on your mind?"

"I talked to Madison last night. She signed the papers. I just have to call my lawyer and drop them off to him."

"That's great! Was it as difficult as you thought?"

"Yes and no. She came in playing her usual games. She tried to be evasive. I pretty much lost it."

"Lost it?"

"Yeah. I got so mad, I threw a glass at the wall."

Lily looked away from him as the dread in the pit of her stomach grew. "I just realized I've never seen you angry. Is that a normal reaction?"

"With her it is. I could never get that angry at you."

She momentarily froze at his words before turning back to him. "How do you know? We've never had anything to be angry about. Nothing, so far, to fight about. Maybe in a month you won't like the way I vacuum the carpet, and you'll flip out and throw something."

Hands up in protest, Jake took a few steps back. "No. No. I wouldn't do that."

"It seems to me, Jake, that we don't know each other very well. And despite it, I've fallen in love with you."

"I'm in love with you, too. I want you to stay here with me. I want to know where all this is going."

"And if it doesn't work? If it doesn't go anywhere? What then?"

"Then, I don't know. I don't want to think like that. When I look at you, I see the future I've always wanted. You are the best thing that's ever happened to me."

When she didn't say anything, Jake started skipping rocks into the water. He felt his world closing in on him. Emotions he didn't know how to deal with surfaced.

"Madison is dying."

Lily pulled her hand from his. "What?"

"She has a brain tumor. She doesn't have much longer to live. She came back to make amends."

"Okay. Is she telling the truth or is this one of the games she plays that everyone has told me about?"

"I thought she was lying, and I told her so right before I kicked her out of my house. Then I went over there today, right before I came to see you."

"And she was there?"

"Yeah. She was sleeping. Her parents had been crying. I walked into her room to see for myself and I saw what I had been too angry to notice before. She's pale, fragile looking. She looks sick. For the first time, she looked vulnerable."

He wasn't fighting back his tears as well as he'd hoped. The last thing he wanted to do is cry about Madison in front of Lily. He was beginning to think she was going to start looking at him like he was some sort of emotional wreck and run away.

Lily couldn't hide from the fact that Jake wasn't ready for her news. No matter how much she wanted him to be, she wasn't sure if he'd ever be ready. Not as long as he was hung up on Madison and her illness. The thought made her feel selfish.

"Do you need to spend time with her?"

"No. I don't think so. She has her parents, her sister. She'll probably go back to Florida or wherever she lives now. She doesn't need me."

His word choice made her uncomfortable. *She doesn't need me.* For some reason she thought he should have said something else but then again, that was probably the selfish Lily talking.

"So what are you going to do?"

"What do you mean?"

"About Madison. Did you get the closure you needed?"

"I think so. I wasn't prepared for her to tell me something like that. I could have sworn she was lying again. I wouldn't put it past her."

"Right."

Lily stood and walked over to the tree, leaning her head against it as she took in her surroundings. It was peaceful here.

"So, what did you have to talk to me about?"

As she closed her eyes and placed her hands on her stomach, she turned to him and smiled. "Nothing that can't wait. I'm just happy you've finally put that part of your life behind you. We can move forward. We'll talk about Atlanta and all that another day. Today you should just go home, relax and finish dealing with your feelings."

"I'm fine, really. I don't need to deal with anything else. I thought we could spend the day together."

"I know. But you should go. I haven't been feeling well. I think I'm coming down with something. All I want to do is go to bed. It's okay, really. We'll talk tomorrow."

Jake felt something was off, there was something she wasn't telling him but he couldn't quite put his finger on it.

"Are we okay?"

"Yeah. We're okay. Ready to walk back?"

She reached for his hand and he pulled her in for a hug. He felt something putting distance between them and he hoped he wasn't losing her. Whatever it was, she was definitely distracted and he thought it would be better not to push.

"You know, none of this changes how I feel about you."

"I know. And it doesn't change how I feel about you either. We have time. I promise."

Jake couldn't shake the feeling he was losing her.

Lily couldn't run from the fact that he'd never be truly free from his past. She wasn't sure if it was cruel of her to expect him to be. One thing was certain; she needed to sort out her thoughts and feelings before she pressed him. It wouldn't be fair to ask him for something she wasn't willing to give back in return.

CHAPTER 40

For someone that was used to being alone, Jake didn't like the feeling. He'd always been one to ignore phone calls and text messages, hole himself up in his house for days, and avoid contact with others. It wasn't that he was anti-social, he just liked being by himself. Even when Madison lived with him, he'd find ways to escape. Usually that meant playing his guitar at Billy's or spending extra time at the docks. Now, he wanted nothing more than to have Lily near him. Even if they didn't speak, didn't touch, just knowing she was there made him feel comfortable, made him feel something. The fact that she seemed distant made him antsy.

He'd already gone through his contact list and called everyone he could think of. His father wasn't home, his brother was watching the kids while Megan dealt with her sister, Billy was working the bar. A few of his other friends were either unreachable or unavailable. After two years of forcing himself not to think, that was all he could do while shuffling aimlessly through his house.

His mind moved from memory to memory, awash in hopes, dreams, and regrets. Thoughts of his mother punched a hole in his heart and though it'd been years since she passed, every color, every wind shift, every memory of her flooded his mind. Just as quickly as the wave washed over him, it receded, and he was overcome by memories of baseball, college scouts, and lost dreams. It wasn't long before visions of Madison plagued him.

Every minute detail of their doomed relationship spun him until he was dizzy enough to throw up in his sink. Soaked with the sweat of ignored issues and suppressed emotions, he was forced to face everything he hadn't, everything he didn't. Everything he wouldn't. He was forced to face his role in it all, his faults, and all the blame he placed elsewhere.

Had he not been so complacent, had he played things differently in the beginning, could they have survived? Would he have felt the same? Would he have loved her, anyway? Was it the drama and pain and disrespect that was their glue? Had he changed enough since then to move on to a healthy relationship with Lily?

Images of Lily whisked in, replacing the darkness of Madison. Rays of light, crashing waves of hope and freedom followed her. But was it real? Was it doomed to fail much like everything else in his life? Would he screw everything up? Was he waiting for the other shoe to drop? Could he survive more heartbreak? Overwhelming failure filled him as he fought to remain upright. Hand pressed up against the wall, he clutched his chest as the next wave crashed.

In a panic, he picked up his keys and headed for the door. Jumping in his truck and slamming it into reverse, he peeled out. His tires screeched black lines into the pavement as he changed direction. He needed to see her. Even if she didn't want to see him, he needed to know he wasn't crazy. That everything would be okay.

CHAPTER 41

As Jake was jumping into his truck and rushing off to see Lily, Madison stirred from her sleep. The headaches that greeted her every time she woke up were becoming an unwelcome regularity but this time it felt different. The distant throbbing she was used to quickly morphed into sharp pain. It wasn't long before it moved behind her eyes and she was seeing stars. She needed her meds.

Voice weak, she tried to yell, "Dad?"

When no one answered, she tried rolling to her side, like her doctors had taught her. It was easier for her to sit up from a sideways position than it was lifting herself straight up. It alleviated the pressure on her head, and she didn't feel like she was going to vomit every time she tried to get out of bed.

"Dad? Mom? Meg?"

She struggled to turn over to the side but her body wasn't cooperating, and her vision was blurring. What began as short, sharp bursts of light in her eyes soon raged into seizure inducing flashes. Closing her eyes to ward off the pain, she crossed her left arm across her body and felt for the edge of the mattress. Her fingers gripping as hard as she could, she struggled to pull her body over on its side. The effort alone had her gasping for breath. This wasn't like anything she'd ever experienced before. This was much worse. Her doctors warned her to expect something like this, but it was something she shouldn't have needed to be prepared for at least another couple of months.

Beads of sweat began forming at her temples, and she continued to squeeze her eyes tight. Goosebumps littered her body. A sudden flash of heat was quickly replaced with teeth chattering cold. She could hear the sound of her heartbeat pounding in her ears, every breath an echo. A dog barked outside, and she could have sworn it was right next to her. Every sense was heightened, every nerve screamed itself raw.

She forced her legs to drop over the side of the bed. Tingles raced up from the tips of her toes to her hips. Mouth dry and tongue thick, she used the same hand that had pulled her over to push herself up to a sitting position. On the first attempt, she collapsed into a trembling heap. After the third try, she gave up, grabbed the edge of the mattress and used every ounce of strength to pull the rest of her body off the bed. If she couldn't walk, she was sure as hell gonna try crawling.

With a grunt, she managed to roll off the bed. Her legs failed to support her, and she smacked her head on the side table as she fell. Momentarily disoriented, she slowly opened her eyes and tried to blink away the blood that dripped into them. Reaching up to wipe it away, she started to shake uncontrollably. Her head smacked back against the bed frame, causing the bursts of light to intensify like fireworks. In a fit, she bit through her tongue, but she didn't have the capacity to cry out. As her mouth filled with blood, rust colored tears fell to the beige carpet. She was aware of everything that was happening to her but helpless to do anything about it.

When the seizure finally subsided, she lay on the carpet, barely able to take stock of the situation. Her mouth was bloody, her tongue bleeding, and she had a gash on her forehead. She thought she might have she cut the back of her head on the bed frame as well. It was a moment or two before she realized she emptied her bladder all over herself. She was still coherent enough to be embarrassed, but she was determined to get out of that room. Unfortunately, when she tried to lift her arms to start dragging herself, she realized one of them wasn't working. Try as she might, she couldn't move her left arm. She couldn't move her fingers. Fear ripped through her and her heart began to beat wildly.

Mustering up the energy to call out one last time, she found her voice no longer worked either. Digging the fingernails of her right hand into the carpet, she bent her right leg and pushed and pulled herself across the floor. Three of her nails snapped in the process and her fingers bled. Vomit poured from her mouth as she dragged herself toward the door. A trail of blood and urine followed her. She shook in fear and exertion before finally collapsing in the middle of the room. Eyes closed, she drifted off to unconsciousness to escape the pain.

CHAPTER 42

As Jake left his house, Lily was in the kitchen making a second sandwich when she felt the first pinch. Briefly touching her side, she mostly ignored it, picked up her plate, and walked over to the table. Tossing the knife in the sink and capping the mustard, she stepped back across the kitchen. The second pinch came as she opened the refrigerator door. This time, the pain was sharper than the last. She stood up straight and rubbed her hand across her stomach, breathing deeply. When it subsided, she reached in, placed the mustard on the door, grabbed a bottle of water, and went back to her sandwich.

She thought about Jake as she chewed, deciding to drive over to his house later. He needed to know about the baby. She needed to see his reaction before she made any decisions. As it was, she wasn't going to Atlanta right away. After she'd spoken to her parents, they'd all decided she should go back to Connecticut, at least for a while. At least until she figured out what to do next. And much of that decision rested on how Jake took the news. In her heart, she knew he'd be happy, but her head warned her against fairytale endings.

On the table next to her was her phone so she turned it on and noticed a she had a new voicemail message. More concerned with hunger pains than voicemail messages, she tossed the phone back on the table and cursed to herself as it slid away and onto the floor. Looking from her dinner to the fallen phone, she arched her eyebrow, pursed her lips, and picked up her sandwich.

She was halfway through her meal when a stabbing pain ripped through her abdomen. Crying out, she shoved herself back from the table and dropped her head between her knees. The pain intensified before it subsided. A bit disoriented, she finally stood. Her pants felt damp, like she had wet herself.

Reaching down between her legs, she felt something sticky. She lifted her hand to her face and saw that her fingers were red. It took a moment before she realized it was blood. Eyes wide, she looked down at the chair she'd just vacated. A dark stain marred the seat cushion.

"Oh my God," she whispered as she covered her mouth with her hand. She was reaching for the table to steady herself, when another pain ripped through her abdomen and dropped her to her knees. Looking around the kitchen, she saw her cell phone lying on the floor on the other side of the table. She couldn't get her body to cooperate enough to get to it. Instead, she sat on the floor and slid back far enough to lean on the cabinets. Focusing on her breathing, she closed her eyes and accepted the pain until it abated.

She was finally able to pull herself up, even out her posture, and retrieve her phone. When she bent over, another jolt ran through her. She cried out. On her hands and knees, she picked up her phone and dialed Jake.

"Lily."

"Jake. I need you to come here. Something's wrong."

"I'm pulling into the driveway now. What's wrong? Are you okay?"

"Just get here. Please."

When he heard her moan on the other end, he barely took the time to put his car in park, let alone take the keys out of the ignition. By the time he burst through the front door, Lily was lying on the floor in the fetal position.

"Oh my God, Lily! What happened?"

She looked at him through tears as he held her head and checked her for injuries.

"What happened? What hurts?"

She lifted her hand and showed him the blood. "The baby."

"Baby? What baby?"

He looked around and saw her pants were wet. Touching them, he noticed she was wet with blood.

"Lily? A baby?"

Nodding, she buried her head into him and sobbed.

Thoughts raced around him as he tried to understand what she was saying. Her baby. His baby. Their baby. Blood. He picked her up, rushed her out to the truck, and took off for the emergency room. He'd already lost one baby. He wasn't about to lose another.

CHAPTER 43

John walked into the kitchen from the backyard, dirty from yard work and exhausted with grief. He poured himself two fingers of bourbon and settled at the kitchen table. Abby finally fell asleep on the couch hours ago, and John hadn't wanted to disturb her. Megan left an hour before. He used the silence to catch his breath and process the past few days. He hadn't had the chance to comprehend the magnitude of what a brain tumor meant for his daughter. He'd been too busy holding up Abby, consoling Megan, and taking care of Madison. For the first time, he sat alone with nothing but his thoughts to occupy him.

What any of this meant for his family, he didn't know. He was certain that the time spent estranged from Madison was needless. When it came down to it, he was a family man and he was ashamed he'd ever turned his back on his daughter.

Standing, he crept into the living room, careful not to wake his wife, lifted a photo album from a shelf, and returned to the kitchen table. Slowly leafing through the memories, John remembered a simpler time when the kids were younger, before Maddie was sick. He looked at photos of a young Abby holding a newborn Megan, John lying in the grass with Madison and first days of school. Sadness crept through him as each forgotten moment came into focus.

Closing the album, he leaned back and poured the last of his drink down his throat. The smooth burn calmed his nerves, and he walked down the hall to Madison's room. Knocking softly, he whispered her name. There was no answer so he slowly cracked open the door. He thought it odd that she wasn't on her bed but then he looked closer. The blanket was disheveled. The sheets were torn from the bed. It was a moment before he realized enough to be alarmed. He pushed the door a little more and took in the room. There was no sign of her. Looking up and down the hallway, he wondered for a moment if she'd gone to the bathroom. He opened the door enough to step inside her room. His stomach dropped when he found her lying on the floor.

"Oh my God!"

His daughter's body was limp and awkwardly pale against the beige carpet.

"Madison! Madison! Wake up. Wake up baby."

He rolled her onto her back and lifted her head into his lap. Using his shirt to wipe the blood and vomit from her face he screamed for his wife.

"Abby! Abby! Come quick! Call an ambulance."

He rocked her back and forth trying to figure out what to do. She was still breathing but her pulse was weak.

"Abby!"

Abigail ran into the room and screamed. She grabbed Maddie from her husband.

"John, what happened? What happened to her? My baby!"

"I don't know. I found her lying here on the floor."

"There's blood everywhere. She must've thrown up. What the hell happened?"

"I don't know, I don't know. I just came in to check on her."

Abby pleaded, "Oh my God, John. Do something!"

John ran from the room and called the ambulance. When he returned, Abby was bent over, cradling Madison in her lap.

"They're on their way."

"Did you hear her? Did you hear anything?"

Rubbing his hands over his face, he sat down on the floor with his wife and daughter. "No, I didn't. I was outside doing yard work. I didn't hear anything."

"Well, you would have if you weren't outside," Abby snapped.

John lowered his eyes. The guilt he already felt deepened. He should have heard something. He'd known Abby was asleep, Megan left. He was the one who was supposed to be taking care of Madison. But he couldn't take sitting in the house waiting for whatever was supposed to happen. He'd needed to take his mind off of it. He hadn't thought taking an hour for himself outside would matter.

Eyes on his daughter, he began to cry. "I'm so sorry."

Abby reached over her unconscious daughter and placed her hand on her husband's. "No. I'm sorry. It's not your fault. None of us could have known. I was asleep on the couch, for God's sake."

"She'll be okay, Abby."

"And if she isn't?"

"She will be."

The sound of sirens drawing closer pierced the silence. Leaning over and kissing Maddie on the cheek, he stood and ran to meet the paramedics.

Not sure what else to do, Abby busied herself combing her fingers through Madison's hair while John waited outside. Using her skirt, she wiped Maddie's face. She heard the front door, voices, and hurried footsteps grow closer. The first paramedic through the door knelt beside her and carefully pulled Maddie out of her arms. He laid her down on the carpet and began to check her vital signs. Another stood off to the side with John asking questions about Madison's condition and overall health. Questions and answers floated through the air and disappeared like bubbles.

"Age?"..."Do you know what kind of brain tumor?"..."We just found out."..."How long has she been unconscious?"..."Her pulse is weak."..."Is she taking any medication?"

Figures moved through the space in slow motion. People rushing in and out, Madison lifted onto a backboard, placed on a gurney, carried out of her room, out of the house, placed into the ambulance, and whisked away.

"Ma'am? Ma'am, are you okay?"

The voice grew louder with each word and Abby searched for where it was coming from.

"Abby?"

John's voice shook her free.

"John?"

"Are you okay?"

"I think so. I'm not sure."

"Ma'am, let's get you back into the house. I'd like to check you out for a minute."

"No, I'm fine. I just need to go with Maddie."

"Honey, we'll go. Just listen to the nice young man. Let him check your blood pressure or whatever he's going to do and then we'll go. I already called Megan, and she's on her way to the hospital now."

Allowing herself to be guided back into the house, Abby sat on the couch and allowed the medic to shine a light in her eyes, wave his fingers in her face, wrap a cuff around her arm, and listen to her heart. She politely answered his questions. Meanwhile, terror was coiling itself in her stomach, snaking around her heart, and threatening to burst out of her if she didn't get to her daughter. Her eyes were focused on the door, and as much as she tried to pay attention to the young man, it was all she could do to keep from jumping up and racing after the ambulance. With every minute that passed, Abby couldn't help but feel a piece of herself falling away.

CHAPTER 44

Racing down the road, Jake tried to punch Billy's number into his phone but his hands were shaking too much to dial properly. Frustrated he threw the phone on the floor and looked over at Lily. With her head leaned up against the window, her complexion took on a ghostly appearance.

"You okay?"

She didn't speak, just nodded slightly.

"So how long...the baby. When did you know?"

Turning her head slightly, she responded, "Two weeks."

"You've known for two weeks?" His voice was panicky, and he knew he shouldn't be mad right now. It wasn't the time. Focusing on her was the priority, not the sudden anger he felt for being left in the dark. He was sure she'd had her reasons for not saying anything. But was she ever going to tell him? The question looped in his head liked a scratched vinyl record. "I'm sorry. We can talk about that later. You sure you feel all right? Are you going to be sick? You can throw up in the truck. I don't care."

He was babbling but couldn't stop. She just closed her eyes and continued to lean against the window with her hand on her stomach. He noticed a stray tear slip down her face. Putting more pressure on the accelerator, he nearly doubled the speed limit through town. As he crossed through the intersection, he failed to notice the ambulance speeding through a turn.

Time slowed as he slammed on the brakes. He could feel his body push forward and he reached out to stop Lily from doing the same. The sound of colliding metal was deafening as each vehicle rolled to its side. A shower of shattered glass blew in and rained over them like hail. The ambulance siren wailed and its tires continued to spin. Smoke billowed from under the hood of Jake's truck as he hung suspended by his seat belt.

Dizzy from whiplash, he took stock of what happened. Airbags deployed. Windshield cracked. Other than a few bumps and bruises he was okay. Turning his head to find Lily, she was unconscious and bleeding from her head. She'd taken the brunt of the accident as the car had flipped to the passenger side and her head hit the window hard.

"Lily?"

She didn't answer when he spoke her name and she didn't stir when he reached over to rouse her. Panic began to build as he jiggled his seatbelt buckle but it wouldn't budge.

"Lily ,wake up."

He searched his surroundings for anything that would get him loose. His keys were jammed in the ignition and he couldn't reach the glove box where he kept his Swiss Army knife. Gripping the steering wheel, he tried to pull himself forward enough to get at least one foot on the car seat. He managed to shift his shoulder through the locked belt but it was too tight against his lap for him to do much else.

"Lily. You have to wake up."

Reaching over, he jostled her shoulder to wake her up but her body flopped like a rag doll.

"Help! Somebody help us! Help us!"

∽∽∽

The ambulance driver saw the pickup truck at the last minute but there was nothing Dave could do to avoid the collision. The brakes did little to slow the slide into the other vehicle. The sound of metal twisting in on itself was deafening. As the siren wailed, Dave turned the wheel attempting to prevent flipping over but as he watched the pavement approach through the driver's side window, he braced for the impact. Lunging for the other seat, he held on as they slid to a stop at the side of the road. He quickly grabbed the radio and called in the accident.

"Marty! You okay?" he yelled to his partner in the back. "Marty, how's the patient?"

There was no answer. Dave unbuckled his seat belt. Repositioning his grip on the seat, he pulled himself up and through the passenger side window. He ran to the back of the ambulance and opened the door. Marty was bleeding and his arm was bent at an odd angle. Dave checked his vitals and quickly pulled him out onto the side of the road. Marty was breathing and his pulse was shocky, but fine.

Pulling a blanket from the back, he covered his partner to keep him warm.

The patient, however, was a different story. She was strapped to a backboard and gurney but the gurney had tipped and her face was now hidden in a storage compartment. He gently righted her, careful to keep her head still. Her nose was definitely broken and probably her right cheekbone as well. Her breath sounds were weak and he did what he could to stabilize her but before he was able to move her out of the vehicle, her eyes flickered, her body shuddered, and she stopped breathing.

After a few minutes of CPR, he heard someone yelling for help. Understanding he'd done what he could for the patient, he quickly checked on Marty before running to the other vehicle.

The pickup was in worse shape than the ambulance. The windshield was shattered and he could see two of the tires had popped. Carefully, he climbed the undercarriage and found a man dangling, strapped into his seatbelt, and a woman with her head settled against the pavement. The head wound looked bad, but he needed information before he alarmed anyone.

⌘⌘⌘

Jake heard footsteps and voices coming from somewhere, and he stretched his neck to find out where. The ambulance was smashed and lying on its side as well. It looked as though two people were able to escape the wreckage.

"Hey! Over here! Help us!"

Jake's shouting caught the attention of one of the paramedics and he raced over.

"You guys okay? Anyone hurt?"

"I'm fine but my girlfriend's pregnant. She's unconscious."

The paramedic climbed up so his head was at the driver's side window.

"Do me a favor, look at me. That's it. Follow the light. Do you know what day it is?"

"Wednesday."

"What's your name?"

"Jacob Morgan."

"Hi Jacob. I'm Dave. How old are you?"

"Please, just help my girlfriend. I'll answer whatever you want. Just help her first. Please."

"Alright. We called it in. Help should be coming any minute. Can you reach her?"

"Yeah."

"Feel her neck for a pulse."

"Okay."

Jake stretched over to Lily and was barely able to touch his fingertips to her neck. He was still and silent as he closed his eyes and waited to feel something. His eyes flashed open.

"Yeah. She's got a pulse."

"Okay. Let me see what I can do. I'm going over to her side of the car."

"All right. Hurry, please."

"What's her name?"

"Lily."

Within seconds the paramedic was lying on the road peering through the windshield.

"Looks like she banged her head pretty hard. She's got a gash on her forehead that'll definitely need stitches. How pregnant is she?"

"What?"

"How pregnant is she? Six weeks? Eight weeks?"

Frozen, Jake tried to figure out the answer. He hadn't even asked her.

"I don't know."

"You don't know?"

"I just found out today."

"Can you guess?"

"Probably what you said, six to eight weeks. But she was bleeding when we got in the car. I was taking her to the hospital."

"Okay. Hold tight. I hear the sirens. I'll call in the information you gave me. How old is she?"

"Twenty-five."

"Good. You sit tight. We'll have you out in a few."

"Hey!"

The paramedic's face came back into view. "Yeah?"

"Was anyone in the ambulance? Anyone sick, I mean."

"Yeah there was."

"Are they okay?"

"No, man. We lost her. Hang tight."

Jake shut his eyes tight and slammed his head back on the seat. Someone died because he wasn't paying attention. He was so focused on what was going on in his truck that he didn't notice the ambulance. And now someone was dead.

When he heard a small moan, he looked over at Lily. Her hand was pressed against her forehead, and she was struggling to open her eyes.

"Lily?"

"What happened?"

"We were in an accident. We hit an ambulance. Are you okay? How's your head? Does anything else hurt?"

She held up her hand to stop him from talking. It was bad enough she could barely open her eyes but she was sure her head would explode if he said another word.

"Just stop talking for a minute."

Jake started pulling on the buckle of his seat belt. Jamming his thumb on the button, he pushed as hard as he could but it wouldn't budge.

"I think I'm okay. My head feels like it was hit with a hammer."

"Does your stomach hurt?"

As if she'd momentarily forgotten, her hands flew to her stomach.

"No. It doesn't."

"That's good."

"What does it mean if it doesn't hurt?"

"I am sure it means the baby is fine. We'll get out of here and get you to a hospital. You'll see. Everything will be okay."

"What if it isn't?"

"Then we'll deal with it. For now, everything will be fine."

"I'm sorry."

"For what?"

"For not telling you sooner. I went to the doctor yesterday. I wanted to wait till I knew for sure."

Jake reached for her hand and gripped it tightly. "Don't be sorry. You had your reasons. We'll be fine. I promise."

She squeezed his hand and closed her eyes.

The sirens wailed as police and more paramedics approached the scene.

CHAPTER 45

Movement jostled Lily back into consciousness and the next thing she knew, she was being lifted into the back of an ambulance. Jake was stationed beside her, holding her hand talking to the paramedic. She was dizzy and barely had any recollection of the accident. The last thing she remembered before waking up was a slow motion feeling of falling.

Her head had stopped bleeding but it still felt like a knife was wedged between her eyes. She couldn't get comfortable as they hooked her up to an IV. An oxygen mask was strapped across her face. Something about blood pressure was discussed around her. A racing pulse had become an issue. All she wanted to know was if her baby was okay. The tiny little person growing in her belly was in trouble, and she'd gladly have given up everything just to know it was fine.

When she tried to speak, the mask muffled the sound. When she tried to move, she noticed her hands had tubes taped to them. She needed to tell them about the strange sensation she was getting in her stomach again. Not quite as painful as back at the house but uncomfortable nonetheless. No one seemed to be paying any attention to her. Her eyes flicked back and forth from Jake to the paramedic. They were so engrossed in conversation they seemed to forget she was even there. She wanted to scream for their attention, do something to make them look at her, to let her speak, but she couldn't think of anything.

Her head became foggy and she closed her eyes against the strange floating sensation that crept up on her. She heard a strange rushing beep. Her heart felt like it was going to beat out of her chest. She gasped for air and finally, when she was ready to sleep, Jake and the paramedic noticed her. The look in Jake's eyes was strange, like panic was dancing through them. She felt his hand squeeze hers, and she tried to squeeze back but couldn't muster the energy. Trying to smile softly to let him know she was okay, she couldn't make her mouth work right. She couldn't force her eyes open and the crazy beep grew faster and louder before distancing itself from her. Jake's eyes filled with tears, and he leaned down to rest his head on her stomach. His hands reached up to her face.

Lily couldn't understand why he was acting so strangely. She wanted to comfort him, hold him, and tell him everything was going to be okay. He was shouting, but she couldn't hear him. Everything was silent, nothing hurt, and she was filled with calm.

She watched as the paramedic pushed him out of the way and as he placed his hands on her chest, she watched her chest cave with each push. Jake was sitting back up against the wall of the ambulance with his hands on his head, his mouth was moving but she couldn't understand what he was saying. A jolt flew through her and her body jumped.

Looking down at herself, Lily realized her lips were tinged blue and her eyelashes were black against her pale skin. A red gash on her forehead stared back at her. Lifting her hands to her face, she came to a realization and took a step forward. The paramedic placed the paddles on her chest, and her body jumped again. Over and over again he tried, sweat beaded on his brow. He pumped her heart with electricity, filled her nonresponsive lungs with oxygen, and watched the monitor continue to flat line.

She laid a hand on the paramedics shoulder, whispered in his ear, and he stopped. Sitting back he stared at her lifeless body on the gurney. He turned to Jake, closed his eyes, and shook his head.

Jake's face fell as he squeezed his eyes shut. She felt the grief pour off of him as he collapsed onto her. Shutting her eyes, she forced herself to hear him. His voice ripped through her as if the volume had suddenly been turned on.

"Lily! No, Lily! Wake up. Wake up. I love you! Please, Lily. Please."

He screamed himself hoarse as he pleaded with her to come back to him. Sadness intruded upon her calm, and she knew she couldn't console him. He needed to let all the pain and anguish fill him up. If he was going to ever get past any of this, she knew he needed to feel it, all of it, and she held herself back from going to him.

On his knees, he continued to plead for the paramedic to do something more. He continued to beg Lily to come back to him. All she could do was watch and wait until it was time for her to go.

Suddenly, a small hand wedged itself into hers. A small child looked up, smiled, and tugged at her hand. Lily reluctantly allowed herself to be taken away from where she stood. As she passed Jake, he looked up, eyes filled with tears. She leaned down and kissed him softly on the cheek. Confused, he pressed his hand to the spot where her lips had touched. With one last small touch on his shoulder, she left him behind.

CHAPTER 46

The ambulance pulled in front of the emergency room doors but there was no longer any emergency. Jake hopped out of the back and watched as the two paramedics gently lifted Lily out. He stood rooted as they wheeled her through the doors. Billy came running up from the parking lot.

"Jake, what happened? Are you guys okay? Someone at the bar told me you two were in an accident. Where's Lily?"

Jake couldn't look him in the eye. Hands shoved in his pockets and shoulders slumped, the answer radiated from him. He could do nothing but stand there staring at the ground.

He heard Billy run into the hospital screaming for someone, anyone to bring him to his niece.

"Jake, what are you doing here?"

John Olsen walked up to him with Abby. Jake lifted his gaze and saw that they had been crying. He pointed to the emergency room.

"Are you here because of Madison?"

"Madison's here?"

"Yes. We found her on the floor and the ambulance brought her here."

A brick landed in Jake's stomach as he thought to the accident and the ambulance.

"The ambulance?"

"Yes. That's why we're here. Did you see her come in?"

Sitting on the bench, Jake tucked his head between his knees and covered his face with his hands. He hoped he was wrong.

"I didn't see her. Lily and I were in an, Lily was…Oh my God."

"What happened, Jake?"

"Lily's…Lily's dead. We got into an accident with an ambulance on the way here."

Abby clutched her chest and ran into the building looking for her daughter. John stared at Jake with sadness for a moment before following his wife inside.

Jake had no idea how long he'd been sitting on the bench when his father sat down next to him. Fresh tears began to fall just when he thought he had no more to shed.

"I'm sorry about Lily. She was an amazing girl."

Jake's head dropped farther down.

"I brought you some water."

Jake took the bottle and gripped it tightly.

"John and Abby wanted me to tell you that Madison is in the ICU. It wasn't her ambulance you hit. It was a ninety year-old woman who was on her way out. Madison should recover, though she's in very guarded condition. I didn't know she had a brain tumor."

Silence filled the night as Andy tried to pull some of the grief from his son. No one should feel what he was feeling. Though he saw relief blink for a moment when he told Jake about Madison, there was nothing he could do to ease the pain of losing Lily, of losing the baby.

"Come on."

Jake's eyes followed his father and he stood up. With his arm around his son, Andy led Jake into the building.

Danny was sitting in one of the chairs in the waiting room with Megan and Billy.

"Jake," Megan was the first to break the silence as she stood.

Fatigue threatened to overtake him and he grabbed his father's arm for support. Once he was seated, Andy walked over to talk to a nurse. Within a few minutes, a doctor came out into the waiting room and sat across from Jake. He nodded to Billy as he'd already had this conversation once before.

"Jake, I'm Dr. Maxwell. I'm sure you understand Lily passed away before you arrived at the hospital. Between the bleeding from the miscarriage, the head wound and the shock, her heart couldn't take it and stopped working. The paramedic did everything he could but in the end, there was nothing he could do. I am sorry. We've already called her parents. Is there anything we can answer for you?"

The truth rested heavy on Jake's shoulders, and he asked if he could see her. The doctor agreed and walked him back to the room where Lily's body was lying. She was covered with a sheet and the doctor explained they were going to bring her body to the morgue within the hour. Jake could take his time and say whatever goodbyes he needed to. He pulled the sheet down to her neck and Jake was surprised to notice how peaceful she looked. She didn't look dead, just sleeping. It didn't seem right that he wouldn't be able to stroke her hair until she woke up like he had only days before. I wasn't fair that he wouldn't be able to watch her eyes try to focus in those first few minutes after she woke.

The chair screeched across the floor as he pulled it up. Icy chills stung his hand as he placed it on top of hers and squeezed. She looked peaceful, but her skin was firmer than usual, not as bright. It was her but not the same. Resting his head on her stomach he closed his eyes and fell asleep.

It was an hour later when Andy walked into the room and woke his son.

"Jake, we need to go."

"Why?"

"They need to take her."

"Can I have five more minutes?"

"Five minutes, son. I'll let the doctor know."

Andy walked out of the room leaving Jake to say goodbye.

"I am so sorry this happened to you. There's so much I want to say, I just can't figure out the words.

"You are the best and brightest thing that ever happened to me. You showed me that I could live again without drowning in the past. I was so lost, so ordinary, and you helped me find my way. If it weren't for you, I'd probably still be stuck living with my ghosts."

A smile crept to his mouth and he laughed softly. "When I first met you I thought you were so pushy, always putting your foot in your mouth. God, I just wanted you to go away. And then I got to know you. I didn't want to ever be without you. And the baby. Why didn't you tell me? I know you wanted to be sure but you shouldn't have had to go through all that stress by yourself. I could've helped, taken some of the anxiety away. You were always so open. Why did you hide *this*?

"I can only assume you didn't think I'd take it well. You were probably right. But I swear to God I would've taken care of you and our baby. I would have moved to Atlanta, Connecticut, wherever you wanted to go. I'd have followed you anywhere. But where you are now, I can't follow. I can only hope that you'll watch over me and help me do what's right. I'm gonna love you forever Lily Burns. I know I couldn't promise you much, but I would have been all you needed to get by."

He touched his lips to hers for a moment before straightening up. Wiping the stray tears from his face, he kissed her walked out the door.

CHAPTER 47

Jake walked out of Lily's room and into the waiting room.

"Can I see Madison?"

Megan took him by the hand and led him to the elevator. They rode up in silence. She let him step onto the floor alone. He stood in the silence of the ICU floor not sure where to go or who to talk to. It wasn't until he saw Abby Olsen at the end of the hall talking to a doctor that he found a direction.

He waited patiently for the doctor to finish before he spoke. "How is she, Mrs. Olsen?"

She embraced him. "Oh, Jake. I heard about Lily. I am so sorry. If there is anything I can do…"

Her voice trailed off as she looked into her daughter's room.

"Thank you. I can't really talk about that right now. It's too much. I just came to check on Madison. See how she was doing."

"She's doing as well as can be expected. She had a small stroke and a seizure. Somehow she banged up her head, bit through her tongue, and tore out a few fingernails. Other than that, they are monitoring her. She should be fine. Most of the functionality of her one side has come back so they think none of the damage is permanent. She's just going to have to be looked after until, well, until the tumor takes over."

She began to weep softly, and Jake put his arms around her. Part of him was relieved Madison wasn't in the ambulance he'd hit earlier. The other part of him, the hidden part, wondered why Lily had died and Maddie was expected to make a full, if brief, recovery. Life had never been coy with him. It had always laid out its cards and begged to be called out on a bluff.

"Don't worry, Mrs. Olsen. We're all here for her. Let me know of anything I can do."

"Oh, sweetie. I can't ask any of that from you. Just you saying it makes all the difference. I appreciate it."

Jake gave her one last hug and started back toward the elevators.

"Lily brought you back, you know."

Turning and looking back at her, he smiled, punched the button, and stepped onto the elevator.

Andy was the last one waiting for him.

"Let's go home, Dad."

"You okay?"

"Not now, I'm not. But I will be. I have to be." New tears streamed down his face.

"For the first time, I believe you're right. That Lily had a way of making people better, didn't she?" Andy responded with fresh tears of his own. His son had been dealt a lousy hand in life and all he could hope for was healing.

"Yeah, Dad. She did."

Jake knew that even though Lily was gone, she'd remain with him. He knew that because of her, a new life, an eyes-wide-open life, waited for him on the other end of grief.

CHAPTER 48

Two months later.

Jake stepped off the boat at the end of the day. Cold and wet, he made his way to the locker room. He was alone. The feeling wasn't as uncomfortable as it once was. Gone were the days of ghosts and regret. Gone were the feelings of aimless wandering and the inability to let go of what drowned him. Lily had taught him to look for something more. Taught him to believe he was more than the sum of his past.

After showering and quickly getting dressed, he hopped into Lily's Jeep. Billy had made sure it was given to him. Jake hadn't asked for anything. Just the fact that Lily had been in his life was enough for him but Billy had convinced her parents to give him the Jeep and her camera. He'd taken pictures almost daily, trying to see the world, as Lily must have, through the perfection of a lens.

After a few quick stops, he pulled up to the front of the cemetery. Lily wasn't here. Her parents had her buried in Connecticut about a week after she died. Andy and Billy drove up with him. The ceremony was beautiful and her parents were gracious enough to allow them to stay at their house. While there, Jake took to sitting on the floor of Lily's room, soaking in everything that was her.

Photographs littered the walls. It was like being surrounded by everything she ever found beautiful, and he lost himself in it. It was that day her parents gave him the camera and expressed that they'd hoped he'd find the same beauty in the world that she did.

He hadn't been back to Connecticut since her funeral and wasn't sure if he'd ever be able to go back. Saying goodbye was the most difficult thing he'd ever had to do. He didn't want to look back and remember her in sadness. Instead, he took comfort in all the ways she'd made his life better in the short time they'd known each other. It was almost impossible for him to believe that in the span of less than three months, he found, fell in love with, and lost the most amazing person he'd ever met.

Pushing her from his mind momentarily, he stepped out of the Jeep and walked through the rows of headstones until he came to his son's grave. Kneeling beside it, he placed a bouquet of fresh flowers against the stone. Then he looked to his left, at the freshly dug grave with a layer of not yet rooted sod carpeted on top. A beautiful wreath and dozens of roses littered the ground. The headstone had not yet been placed but Jake's ultimate decision to allow Madison to be laid to rest next to their son was one he wouldn't regret.

In the end, Madison's past mistakes wouldn't define her. It was important to her in her last few months to right the wrongs, and that included forgiveness from Jake. He remembered one night, a few weeks before she died, they had their first actual conversation of substance. They'd spent years together but he couldn't remember one meaningful exchange until that night...

༺༻

Madison had called earlier that day and asked Jake to come over and talk. He'd been over to see her a number of times since she was in the hospital, but she was usually asleep or so knocked out on pain killers, he'd usually just sit in the chair next to her bed and watch television or play his guitar. But that day, when she called, she was unusually coherent.

Pulling up to the Olsen's house just after dinner, Jake walked up with his guitar strapped to his back. When Madison was awake, she enjoyed listening to him play. He barely knocked when the door flew open and Madison was standing there, freshly showered and dressed comfortably in old jeans and a sweatshirt. This was a far cry from the bed-ridden girl of the past month or so.

He fell back a few steps when she jumped out the door to hug him.

"Hey. You look great. Feeling better, I guess?"

"Yeah, I don't know. I woke up this morning, and I wasn't tired, my head didn't hurt, and I've taken like ten showers today, by myself, just because I could!"

Her laugh was infectious and Jake smiled at her exuberance. "That's awesome. So happy for you."

"Come in, come in. You brought your guitar? Good."

He walked into the house. John and Abby were sitting on the couch, watching television. Megan was cleaning up the dishes from dinner. They all had smiles on their faces.

"Hey Jake." Megan kissed his cheek while drying a dinner plate.

John stood and shook Jake's hand. "It's a good day today, Jake. Glad you could make it."

"I'm glad too Mr. Olsen. When she called earlier, she sounded so, normal I guess. Definitely different than the last time I was here."

"Are you hungry, dear? We have some leftover meatloaf. Megan made it."

"No thanks, Mrs. Olsen. I stopped at Billy's and had a burger after work."

"Well, if you get hungry, let me know and I'll heat something up for you."

"I will, thank you."

"Come on, Jake. Let's go to my room so we can talk." He stopped short when he saw her wiggle her eyebrows. "Oh my God! Look at your face!" she said, laughing. "I'm just kidding. I promise. We'll just talk."

Deliberately placing one foot in front of the other, Jake made his way to the back of the house and sat in the chair next to her bed while she sat cross-legged on her comforter. He'd grown comfortable with her since the accident. He was no longer repulsed by her, and he'd all but quit asking God why he took Lily instead of Madison.

"So what's all this about wanting to talk?"

"Well, since I have no idea how long I'll be lucid, I figured I'd take advantage of it. There's a lot I have to say to you, Jacob Morgan, and I need you to sit and listen.

Besides, what are you gonna do? Walk out on a sick girl? I think not." She joked like the fact she was dying completely escaped her.

Her eyes challenged him playfully, and he relaxed instantly. She was right, of course. He wasn't going to walk out on her.

"All right. So what's up?"

"First, I want to tell you how sorry I am for what happened to Lily."

His eyes shifted immediately to the floor and Madison moved so she was sitting directly in front of him, taking his hands in hers.

"I know it's hard. When I saw you two together the first time, I was out of my mind. The way you looked at her, the way you touched her—was never something you and I had. To be honest, I was so jealous. I couldn't understand. You two had known each other only moments it seemed and she had everything I wanted. Even though I knew why it wasn't like that with us, it would never be like that with us, I was jealous. And I was wrong. I am sorry."

"Maddie, you don't have to—"

She waved off his protests. "No. I do. I am so sorry for everything. For my behavior two years ago, hell ten years ago, and my behavior when I first came back. You don't deserve that. You never did. I could tell she was special. Hell, *I* was enamored. And I'm the most cynical person you'll ever meet."

"Yes, you definitely are. But, listen, you don't have to apologize."

"Dad told me Lily was pregnant."

"Yeah, she was."

"How can so much bad happen to someone so good?" Her voice was soft, full of regret.

He shrugged. "I haven't always been good. You know that. I could've been better to you. To everyone around me."

"You weren't like that until we started dating so I am taking responsibility for that, too."

"You can't take responsibility for someone else's actions."

"I can, too. I'm sick remember? Now shut up and let me get through this without crying." She squeezed his hands and was surprised when he squeezed back.

She watched as Jake finally relented, leaning back in his chair, and tossing his Yankees hat on the side table.

"Go ahead."

She brought her hands to her head and grimaced.

"Are you okay? Need me to get your parents?"

"No, no. I'm fine. Well, not fine since I have a tumor growing in my brain. But I just feel like I have so much to say. I had it all prepared and now everything's all jumbled. Just give me a minute."

She stood and shook out the tension as Jake watched with a new sense of familiarity. She looked the same, moved the same, but she wasn't the same Madison who left him with a dying baby.

"Okay. Look. I look back at who I was and I cringe. I mean, who the hell did I think I was? All those drugs, cheating on you—God I was so self-absorbed. I never cared about anyone or anything unless it had some use to me. And then I got pregnant. We got married, and little

Joey was born." For a moment, she was lost in the memories.

"The first time I held him, my whole life flashed before my eyes and I came to the conclusion that no kid should grow up with a mother like me. From that moment, I planned on leaving. I didn't know at the time he was sick. I didn't know he wouldn't leave the hospital. But that's why I never came to see him. I had already left. I didn't leave because I didn't love him or love you because I did. I swear to God, Jake, I loved the two of you like I'd never be able to love anything again. I left because I was ashamed that he'd grow up and figure out what a terrible person I was. And you were good. He needed to know you."

Finally Jake was given the reason for her departure. It didn't make it hurt any less but at least he knew. He'd never have to question himself again.

"We could have talked about it."

"Think about it. Do you honestly think that was something we could've talked about? Can you honestly tell me you can't see the logic in my thinking?"

"But he was your baby. He was sick. I can't see the logic in that."

"I know it's hard but I need you to try."

Jake's silent stare was the only response he gave.

"Dad took me to Joey's grave this morning. I'd never been there before. The headstone is beautiful. You picked a great location; right on the end, before the drop to the meadow. It's like he can see everything from where he is."

"Thank you."

"I need to ask you something. I will understand if you say no. But if I don't ask, I know I'll regret it."

"What is it?"

"I wanted to know if you'd be okay with me being buried next to him."

Color receded from his face as he was presented with a question he'd never thought would be asked.

"You don't have to answer now. Just tell me you'll think about it."

"I don't have to think about it."

"Please Jake, just listen. I know I don't—"

"Yes."

"What?"

"I think it would be perfect for you to be buried beside Joey. I think he'd like it." As the words came, he knew he was doing the right thing.

"Really?"

"Really."

"Oh my God, Jake. You have no idea how much this means to me. I know I don't deserve it."

"You're his mother. Regardless of anything that happened in the past, the fact remains that you're his mother and always will be."

He caught her mid-air as she leapt into his arms and kissed him on the cheek. In that moment, all the pain of the past washed away and they truly began the friendship they'd never had.

෴

That was the last conversation they'd had. Madison's health went downhill quickly after that. The next day, she was back in bed, barely able to move. The doctor's attributed it to random brain activity. Jake knew better. That day, in Madison's room, he could've sworn he'd seen Lily standing next to her. Even in death, Lily had a way of making things right, of presenting things in a new light.

He dusted off his jeans and walked back to his Jeep. Next to him on the passenger seat was his guitar. He'd finally finished the song he'd written for Lily and called Billy to ask if he could come in and play it. It'd been over two years since he'd played there. It had been a few months since Lily showed him the sadness in that. Tonight he'd play for her. He'd play for everything she ever taught him, everything he never saw until she opened his eyes. Today was her birthday. And tonight he'd play for her...

Three Days of Rain
By Jay Liberatore

Two days of sunshine
Three days of rain
Won't somebody give me a sign?
Is Hell frozen over,
Has God gone away,
Or am I just losing my mind?
I met me a girl by the railroad yard
On the way to my 9 to 5
She's sweet as a sip of southern tea
And cool as a country drive
Oh, but where I come from
A man don't become
A fool for love after only a kiss
But after some wine
On an evening this fine
I was singing her something like this.

I said, baby, baby
You sure look good in the summertime
Baby, baby
Won't you always be mine?

I would lay in the field
With her hair in my face
As the locks of it dangled and curled
And she'd talk about moving on down to Georgia
And her plans to take over the world
And I never would guess
If I tried my best
The truth I had known just then
I could live for a thousand years or more
I might never feel this good again

I'd say, baby, baby
You sure look good in the summertime
Baby, baby
Won't you always be mine?

There she goes again
Hair like a willow blowing in the wind
Falling softly on her summer skin
In my mind

Now who'd ever thought that a sinner like me'd
Have an angel know my name
I am evil, yes I'm evil
But she loves me just the same
She has given me light
When I'm lost at sea
And guided my troubled heart to land
She's given me shelter
'Til I'm able
To bury my ghosts in the sand

So I say, baby, baby
You sure look good in the summertime
Baby, baby
Won't you always be mine?

I'll be all that you need to get by
I'll be all that you need to get by

About the Author

Christine Hughes spent much of her childhood losing herself in books and creating stories about many of the people she'd met. Falling in love with literature was easy for her, and she majored in English while attending college in New Jersey.

Not sure where her love of reading and writing fit, she became a middle school English teacher. After nine years of teaching others to appreciate literature, she decided to take the plunge and write her first novel. Now at home focusing on making writing her new career, she spends her time creating characters and plot points instead of grading papers.

Made in the USA
Lexington, KY
14 January 2013